Natural
OBSESSION

Other Books by Anna Durand

Natural Passion (Au Naturel Trilogy, Book One)
Natural Impulse (Au Naturel Trilogy, Book Two)
Natural Satisfaction (Au Naturel Trilogy, Book Three)
Lachlan in a Kilt (The Ballachulish Trilogy, Book One)
Aidan in a Kilt (The Ballachulish Trilogy, Book Two)
Rory in a Kilt (The Ballachulish Trilogy, Book Three)
The American Wives Club (A Hot Brits/Hot Scots/Au Naturel Crossover Book)
Brit vs. Scot (A Hot Brits/Hot Scots/Au Naturel Crossover Book)
Dangerous in a Kilt (Hot Scots, Book One)
Wicked in a Kilt (Hot Scots, Book Two)
Scandalous in a Kilt (Hot Scots, Book Three)
The MacTaggart Brothers Trilogy (Hot Scots, Books 1-3)
Gift-Wrapped in a Kilt (Hot Scots, Book Four)
Notorious in a Kilt (Hot Scots, Book Five)
Insatiable in a Kilt (Hot Scots, Book Six)
Lethal in a Kilt (Hot Scots, Book Seven)
Irresistible in a Kilt (Hot Scots, Book Eight)
Devastating in a Kilt (Hot Scots, Book Nine)
Spellbound in a Kilt (Hot Scots, Book Ten)
Relentless in a Kilt (Hot Scots, Book Eleven)
Incendiary in a Kilt (Hot Scots, Book Twelve)
One Hot Chance (Hot Brits, Book One)
One Hot Roomie (Hot Brits, Book Two)
One Hot Crush (Hot Brits, Book Three)
The Dixon Brothers Trilogy (Hot Brits, Books 1-3)
One Hot Escape (Hot Brits, Book Four)
One Hot Rumor (Hot Brits, Book Five)
One Hot Christmas (Hot Brits, Book Six)
One Hot Scandal (Hot Brits, Book Seven)
One Hot Deal (Hot Brits, Book Eight)
Echo Power (Echo Power Trilogy, Book Two)
Echo Dominion (Echo Power Trilogy, Book Two)
Echo Unbound (Echo Power Trilogy, Book Three)
The Mortal Falls (Undercover Elementals, Book One)
The Mortal Fires (Undercover Elementals, Book Two)
The Mortal Tempest (Undercover Elementals, Book Three)
The Janusite Trilogy (Undercover Elementals, Books 1-3)
Obsidian Hunger (Undercover Elementals, Book Four)
Unbidden Hunger (Undercover Elementals, Book Five)
The Thirteenth Fae (Undercover Elementals, Book Six)

Natural OBSESSION

Au Naturel Nights, Book One

ANNA DURAND

JACOBSVILLE BOOKS  MARIETTA, OHIO

NATURAL OBSESSION

Copyright © 2023 by Lisa A. Shiel
All rights reserved.

ISBN: 978-1-958144-06-0 (paperback)
ISBN: 978-1-958144-05-3 (ebook)
ISBN: 978-1-958144-07-7 (audiobook)

Manufactured in the United States.

Jacobsville Books
www.JacobsvilleBooks.com

Publisher's Cataloging-in-Publication Data
provided by Five Rainbows Cataloging Services

Names: Durand, Anna, author.
Title: Natural obsession / Anna Durand.
Description: Marietta, OH : Jacobsville Books, 2023. | Series: Au naturel nights, bk. 1.
Identifiers: ISBN 978-1-958144-06-0 (paperback) | ISBN 978-1-958144-05-3 (ebook) | ISBN 978-1-958144-07-7 (audiobook)
Subjects: LCSH: Man-woman relationships--Fiction. | Vacations--Fiction. | Secrets--Fiction. | British--Fiction. | Americans--Fiction. | Romance fiction. | BISAC: FICTION / Romance / Contemporary. | FICTION / Romance / Later in Life. | GSAFD: Love stories. | Humorous fiction.
Classification: LCC PS3604.U724 N38 2023 (print) | LCC PS3604.U724 (ebook) | DDC 813/.6--dc23.

Chapter One

James

"*H*ere at Au Naturel Naturist Resort South Seas, we strive to do everything possible to ensure your stay is relaxing and pleasurable, so please don't hesitate to ask for anything you desire. We will do our best to satisfy you." I slump in my chair and resist the urge to groan and rub my eyes, because the two people watching me from thousands of miles away via teleconference hired me to do a job, not whinge about how awkward I feel. "How was that? I tried to do what you asked, Eve, and make it sound...sexier. That's not my strong suit, though."

"We know that, James." Eve glances at the man sitting beside her. Val Silva seems like a giant next to his wife, though she is of average size. "Do you have any notes for him, honey?"

"None at all," Val says in his Brazilian accent. "The opening remarks were for you and James to work out. I helped organize the athletic events."

"And you did a great job." Eve kisses her husband's cheek, then looks at me. "You're wrong, by the way. When you hit us with your concluding remarks, you sounded damn hot."

"Well, I'm glad you're happy with my work." But yes, I sound uncomfortable when I say that. "Do you have any other comments?"

"Keep leveraging your sexy British accent. It's your secret weapon."

Val smirks at his wife. "Only for women and gay men."

"I think even straight men can appreciate James's voice. But we've harassed the poor man enough for today." Eve raises her arms toward the screen. "You must be nervous about the grand opening, huh? Consider this a virtual hug."

"Ah, thank you, Eve." I shift uncomfortably in my chair. "And also, thank you for taking a chance on me. I know it's a big risk considering my background, and I want you both to know how grateful I am."

"We got to know you a few months ago when you visited our Oregon resort for your interview. That was all the info we needed about you. It was really brave to share your whole story with us."

"Don't worry," Val says. "We know you will succeed."

"Thank you." I reach for the mouse on my desk, about to click off the teleconference.

"One more thing," Eve says.

"What is it?"

"Smile, sweetie." She cranks her lips into that expression, using her fingers to stand in for an actual crank. "You have such a beautiful smile, and we all saw it when you were here. Let everybody see it now."

"I'll try. Goodbye, Eve. Goodbye, Val."

They wish me well yet again and finally end the teleconference. And I sink even deeper into my chair.

Someone knocks on the door to my office.

"Come in," I call out.

My assistant manager, Emilio, opens the door partway and leans his head through the gap. "Just wanted to update you on the American woman from Seattle whose connecting flight in San Francisco was delayed. Her plane finally landed on Fiji, and Rene radioed to say they just took off and should be here in an hour."

"She's the only one on that flight, correct? Other than Rene, but a pilot is rather critical." What a stupid thing to say. Maybe I'm more nervous about the grand opening than I realized.

"That's right, boss," Emilio says. "I'll gather all the guests once she arrives."

"Good. Let's give the other guests free cocktails while they wait."

"I'll take care of it."

Emilio leaves, shutting the door behind him.

I spend the next hour rehearsing my speech over and over, until the words finally stop making sense. I've practiced enough. Glancing at my watch, I see the American woman should arrive at any moment. Then I make sure my clothes still look all right. Although the rest of the staff will wear uniforms at all times, Eve and Val had insisted that I should dress like a general manager, whatever that means. They talked me into wearing a dress shirt, posh trousers, and leather shoes. Eve ordered me to "keep the top two buttons undone," though she didn't explain why. She meant my shirt, not my trousers.

Emilio pops in to tell me the last guest is here.

I hurry out to the reception desk and wait, leaning against the waist-high counter whilst I rest one arm on it. Pretending to be calm is bloody hard to do.

A woman breezes through the glass doors while lugging a wheeled suitcase with one hand. She grips a large purse that hangs over her shoulder and glances around whilst grinning. The closer she comes, the more of her I can see. Lush, dark hair cascades over her shoulders, though a floppy wide-brimmed hat sits atop her head, and her lips are painted bright red. Her hips sway, thanks to the moderately high heels of the sandals she wears. Spaghetti straps hold up her flower-print dress, which barely covers her arse and flounces with her movements. The dress also has a low neckline that gives me a spectacular view of her cleavage.

She removes her sunglasses as she reaches me. "Hi, you must be the man in charge. Rene told me you'd be waiting." She offers me her hand, and I notice her red nail polish, which matches her toes. "I'm Holly Temple. Sorry I delayed everything on day one."

"Not your fault." I see one of our bellboys carting the rest of her luggage down the hall past us. "I hope the remainder of your journey was less eventful."

She lets her purse fall to the floor at her feet as she moans with sarcastic exasperation. "Have you ever flown economy class on a thirty-four-hour flight? Holy moly. I was ready to crack open that emergency door and jump out."

"I'm glad you didn't."

"Rene was so nice to wait while I changed clothes at the airport on Fiji. I couldn't wear my sweats anymore. They were starting to smell bad." She steps up to the reception desk, sets her sunglasses down, and eyes the brochures and business cards that line one side of the desk. Snatching up one card, she squints at it, then lifts her brows at me. "Are you the general manager?"

"Yes."

She raises the card to study it more intently. "So, you are James By-the-sea?"

"It's pronounced Bith-see."

"Cool. I've never heard that name before." She holds up the card. "May I keep this? In case I have questions. Never been to a nudist resort before."

"Yes, keep the card. I will do whatever I can to make your stay enjoyable."

"Wow," she says with a sexy little smile as she bumps her shoulder into me. "I might never leave this place."

My cock jerks. *Fuck.* That's exactly what I need right now—to get an erection when I'm about to deliver my welcome speech. I cough into my fist and avoid looking at her. "I need to see your passport, please. It's company policy to make certain you are who you're meant to be."

"Oh, sure." She digs her passport out of her enormous purse and hands it to me. "Here you go."

I can't stop admiring her body. My God, she's beautiful. But I cannot—will not—get involved with a guest. My past prevents it. So I open the resort app on my phone and type in her name to bring up her photo, then check it against her passport. I need to check her age too, so I skim the information on the second page. My eyes refuse to blink as I stare at her birth date. *Bloody hell.* This woman is twenty-seven, which makes her eighteen years younger than I am. No, I absolutely will never act on the lust she inspires in me.

"The opening festivities will begin shortly, on the main patio," I tell her. I hand the child a folder. "This is your welcome packet, which includes a map of the resort and the island itself, as well as a list of our guest rules. But you can ask any employee if you need assistance, Miss Temple."

"Call me Holly."

"If you insist."

She bites her upper lip, releasing it slowly as she rakes her gaze over my body. "Mind if I call you James?"

"Not at all."

"Does anybody call you Jim or Jimmy?"

I feel my jaw tensing, but I force myself to relax. "No. I prefer James."

"Cool." She snags her sunglasses and purse. "I'll see you again in a few."

Ten minutes later, I stand on the large patio where all the guests have gathered. It's time to give my speech. Fortunately, the guests are all clothed right now. But in a matter of minutes, they will shed their garments. Holly Temple will shed her clothes. I'm about to see her nude body. *Don't think about that, you arse. She's young enough to be your daughter.*

I step onto the temporary dais and spread my arms. "Welcome to Au Naturel Naturist Resort. We are thrilled to have you as our guests for the next two weeks, on this privately owned island that offers the ultimate in privacy and luxury. I am James Bythesea, general manager. And these lovely people behind me"—I make a sweeping gesture to indicate them—"are my partners in bringing you the best holiday experience of your lives. Please don't hesitate to ask any of us whatever questions you might have. Your welcome packets include a list of our rules. Please abide by them."

A few groans erupt from the crowd of guests. One chap says, "Rules? I thought we came here to cut loose."

I raise a placating hand. "Rest assured, we don't have many restrictions. It's all common sense and common decency. But you will have many opportunities to explore the sensual side of life while here on Heirani Motu, which is the name of this island."

"Jeez, this is so boh-ring," a woman says while making a rather rude face. "When does the fun start?"

"In a moment." I take a breath and continue. "Remember, this is an adults-only, clothes-free naturist resort. The few exceptions to that rule are outlined in your packets. In consideration of our clothes-free mandate, we provide a few amenities other resorts don't." I gesture toward the far side of the patio. "The terracotta bowls located throughout the resort proper offer free access to sunscreen and insect repellent, while the white ceramic bowls contain condom packets. Our in-house pharmacy can also provide whatever medication refills you might need."

Everyone turns to glance at the bowls. Some guests giggle while others choose to smirk.

I finish up with the bit Eve and Val had convinced me to say, but this time, I don't feel as nervous about speaking the words. Not sure if I fulfilled Eve's request that I make that statement sound sexy, but she isn't here to critique me. No one laughs, at least. Holly Temple smiles at me and winks, then gives me the thumbs-up sign.

I raise my arms above my head. "And now, off with your clothes!"

Cheers erupt, and the guests begin to shed their garments. Soon everyone is naked, except for me and my employees. As I scan the crowd, careful not to stare at anyone's breasts or dangly bits, my attention stalls on one person.

Holly Temple. She waves at me and grins.

Christ, she is completely nude. *Of course she is, your moron.* I knew this would happen, but I hadn't counted on how desperately I would want this woman. I'd lusted for her when she still wore clothes, but now... I yank my sunglasses out of my pocket and slip them on. At least she won't see me leering at her. I'm too damn old to crave a woman as young as Holly Temple. So I will allow myself one minute to appreciate her naked body, then I will avoid the woman as much as is humanly possible, considering that I gave her my card and offered to make sure her stay is enjoyable. Suddenly, that word sounds filthy.

My breathing grows heavier as I watch Holly socializing with the other guests. She has the most perfect tits I've ever seen, full and round yet with the tips jutting up. The more I drink in the vision of her, the more my mouth waters and my cock thickens. I want to devour her nipples, then shove my head between her thighs to gorge myself on her cream. No woman has ever had this effect on me, and I don't know how to deal with it. I lick my lips and swear I can already taste her. I need to leave, now, before anyone notices the general manager is getting aroused. But then Holly turns away, and I can't stop staring at her perfect arse. I can barely breathe at all anymore.

How will I survive two weeks with Holly?

I rush into my office and shut the door. My cock throbs. Though I want to unzip my trousers and relieve the pressure, I refuse to succumb to my inappropriate hunger for Holly. The less I see of her, the less I'll fantasize about fucking her.

Yes, that's my plan. Self-control is my specialty, after all.

But so is self-destruction.

Chapter Two

Holly

James Bythesea intrigues me. I barely managed to restrain my curiosity so I wouldn't ask nosy questions about him.
He is gorgeous and sexy, yes, but I sense he's keeping secrets.
Any man who runs a nudist resort yet seems uncomfortable being
around naked people will pique my interest for sure. I've never met
a man like that before. Never visited a nudist resort either. But now
that I've met James, I need to know more about him.

What makes him tick? Does his uptight demeanor hide any
dark secrets? I bet he would be an incredible lover. I mean, with a
body like his—muscular but not overly ripped—he definitely has
the tools. Yeah, I noticed the bulge in his pants. That man wants
me, and I want him too. It's crazy, since I just met James. But I felt
drawn to him from the moment I saw him.

I found my way to my suite without any trouble, though the
bellboy offered to escort me there. He seemed kind of frazzled,
what with all the guests he has to deal with, so I assured him I
could get there on my own.

My suite is amazing.

The open plan lets me gaze out the windows as well as the sliding glass doors to the patio, all while still sitting on the bed. Or
lying in bed. But I haven't tried that yet. Even just perching on
the edge of the mattress, I can tell it has all the cushy goodness I

need. And the sheets… Damn, they feel as smooth as silk. Maybe they are silk. I spent most of my savings on this trip, so I'm hoping for all the amenities and luxuries. I love the way the bed has fabric draped over it like curtains, but pulled back to reveal the bed. The high ceilings are amazing too.

I tour the rest of my suite, from the bedroom to the living room, and I check out the bathroom too, of course. The living room has a desk that's outfitted with fancy writing paper plus a fancy pen. The entire suite features rich wood paneling, but the bathroom also offers a large tub and a multi-head shower. I'd love a bath, after my long, long, long airline trip in economy class. But first, I need to explore the outdoor section of my suite.

Pushing open the sliding glass doors, I step out onto the patio and inhale a deep, cleansing breath. Ahhh, no more stench of sweat and dirty diapers. *Goodbye, economy class. Hello, lap of luxury.* I'm so glad I endured a cramped airline ride so I could pay for this resort. The view alone makes it all worthwhile.

I settle onto a wooden chaise and let my body go boneless.

My thoughts keep circling back to James. Those beautiful blue eyes. That head of silky-looking brown hair. And what about those lips? They look ripe for the tasting.

In the distance, a jagged mountain rises from the azure sea, though the water turns a brighter shade of greenish blue closer to shore. Below my private patio, I see the swimming pool at the bottom of the hill that snakes around little peninsulas populated with chaises shielded by huge umbrellas or huts created with palm fronds and bamboo. Rather than detracting from the beauty of this island, the pool has been designed to complement the scenery. My patio includes a small hut too, in case I want a break from the sunshine.

After a few minutes of lounging, I head into the bathroom to rinse off the airline grime. Unpacking my stuff doesn't take long since I won't be wearing clothes for the next two weeks. After that, I read the entire welcome packet. It includes a map of the resort, inside and out. But it also includes a brief discussion of the weather, which includes frequent rains as well as the threat of tropical cyclones. Apparently, that's what they call hurricanes in this part of the world.

What should I do now? Watch TV? *Ugh.* I didn't fly halfway around the world to binge-watch my favorite shows. I came here for adventure, excitement, and romance. Right now, I'll settle for hot sex.

But the only man who has caught my eye is James Bythesea.

Well, he did say he would do whatever he could to make my stay enjoyable...

I slip on my sandals, grab my welcome packet and my smaller purse that has my room key inside it, and walk out of my suite. I'm on a mission. Adventure and excitement? Unlocking the secrets of General Manager James Bythesea sounds plenty adventurous, and I can already imagine how hot sex with him would be.

At the door to his office, I hesitate. My map got me here, but the rest is up to me. So I square my shoulders and knock.

"Come in." The sexy voice of James Bythesea sends a warm tingle chasing over my skin.

I push the door open and step inside, letting it swing shut on its own.

The click of the latch engaging catches his attention. He had been staring down at papers on his desk, but now he lifts his head to look at me over the rims of his reading glasses. His eyes widen for a second, two at most, then he reasserts his neutral expression. "What are you doing, Miss Temple?"

"Call me Holly, please." I approach the desk, which sits tucked against the wall, and perch my bottom on it. "You said you'd do whatever you could to make me happy."

"That was inappropriate, and I shouldn't have said it. You should speak to my staff if you need something."

"Are you reneging on your promise?"

"No. But I'm far too busy to cater to your whims." He goes back to staring at the papers on his desk.

This might be harder than I thought. "All your employees are so busy. Can't you please help me out, James?"

He sets down his pen, leans back in his chair, and clasps his hands over his belly. Then he sighs. "What do you want, Holly?"

I hold up my welcome packet. "I'm confused. The brochure says there will be a masquerade party tomorrow night, but we're all naked. This is a clothes-free resort. That means no clothes."

He tips his head down to look up at me over his reading glasses again. "I thought you read the brochure. It explains that guests will wear masks only."

"Oh, is that what it meant? I didn't understand." Of course I did, but I couldn't think of any other excuse to come to his office. "Where do we get the masks?"

"From the resort shop."

"Awesome. Thank you for the clarification." I bend one knee, my foot swinging. "I bet you rock your job, don't you? No uncrossed T's or undotted I's."

"I don't appreciate being mocked."

"But I'm not mocking you. I think it's adorable."

He waves a hand toward his papers. "I have work to do."

Okay, time to bring out the big guns. "In your speech, you said you'll strive to do everything possible to make sure our stay is pleasurable and that we're all satisfied."

His gaze flicks to my lower body. He winces and swallows hard, his Adam's apple jumping. Then he scratches under his collar and averts his gaze to the desktop.

What's his problem now? I glance down—and bite my lip. *Oops*. I'd been swinging my leg without thinking about it, and I accidentally flashed James a glimpse of my, um, lady parts.

I quickly close my thighs. "Please, James, I need your help."

"This is my job, not a babysitting agency."

"Babysitting? I'm only asking for your expertise."

He grunts. "You are hunting for a man, aren't you? I'm not interested."

"Of course you are." I've never been this brazen before, but I think the nudist lifestyle is making me bolder and wilder. Words tumble from my lips before I think about what I'm saying. "You want me, James, I can see it. I want you too. So let's have some fun together."

"You are a child. Go back to the playpen with the other toddlers."

"Child?" I say with a slight laugh. "I'm twenty-seven. Everywhere on earth, that qualifies as an adult."

"To me, you are a child."

Hmm, I'm getting the impression he's older than he looks. "You know my age. Shouldn't I get to know yours? Especially since you keep calling me a child."

James sits up straight and sets his elbows on the desk. But he doesn't look at me when he says, "I am forty-five years old. So now you understand."

"No, I don't." Does he think our eighteen-year age difference bothers me? I want to cut loose and be wild on my vacation, before I have to go home and go back to my crummy life. One steamy night with a much older man sounds like heaven. "I don't care about your age, James. You are the sexiest man I've ever met, and I know we could have incredible sex."

"That will never happen." He jumps up and stalks over to the door, flinging it open. "Please leave, Miss Temple."

I amble to the door, halting to face him.

His attention shifts to my tits. Then he coughs into his fist and veers his attention away.

That wild impulse inside me rears its ahead again, and I slant toward him to lay my palms on his pecs. "I know you were watching me out on the patio, after your little speech. You like seeing me naked. It turns you on. Devouring me with your eyes while hiding behind your sunglasses… Doesn't that seem like voyeurism?"

He stiffens and doesn't even blink.

I hoist myself onto my tiptoes to whisper into his ear, "I don't mind if you want to watch."

Then I walk out the door, glancing back to wave my fingers at him.

He slams the door.

What can I do now? I'm starting to feel tired from my long journey on a cramped airliner, so I head back to my suite to take a nap. Amazingly, I fall asleep as soon as I lie down. My mind conjures up dreams of James doing things to me that would make a porn star blush, and I wake up slick and tingly, almost on the verge of orgasm. I get out my vibrator to alleviate the aching need to come, making it a quickie instead of an extended session. Then I need to wait a while before I venture out of my room again.

I order a snack from room service, but the sweet young man who brings my food can't tell that I'm recovering from both the most erotic dream I've ever had and a self-administered happy ending. I make sure to hide behind the door when I open it for him, and I only peek my head out from behind it. Luckily, I don't need to pay right now. The resort will do that for me and add a tip based on the percentage I agreed to when I booked this trip. They really do think of everything here.

My snack takes just enough time that I'm no longer in danger of anyone noticing how horny I got from a dream about the general manager.

I make my way out to the public patio, where other guests mill around and chitchat. I've just sat down at a table, under the shade of a bamboo umbrella, when a blond man approaches me.

"Hey, I saw you at the orientation thing. Mind if I join you?"

No, I really want James to join me. But I guess I need to give him space. Might as well make a new friend in the meantime. "Sure. I'd love the company."

He sits down in the chair right beside me and offers me his hand. "I'm Kevin Benson from Carson City, Nevada."

I shake his hand. "Holly Temple from Seattle, Washington."

"Cool to meet you. It's wicked awesome here, isn't it?"

Oh, jeez. He's one of those guys. The kind who talk like they just stepped out of a stoner movie. James Bythesea speaks in complete, grammatical sentences. I never would've thought a man's grammar would make me hot, but damn, it does when James talks to me.

"You okay, Holly?"

"Huh?" I jerk myself out of my reverie and blink swiftly. "Yeah, I'm fine."

"Can I buy you a drink?"

"Uh, sure."

I spend the next half hour chatting with Kevin. He's a nice enough guy, and I do like the tropical drinks he orders for us. But the whole time I'm with Kevin, I keep glancing at the front desk, hoping to see James. I guess he's hiding in his office to keep my away, because I don't see him at all for the rest of the day. Not even at dinner. I go into the dining room, but no James there. I eat with Kevin and his two pals who all came here to meet women, I'm sure.

Well, I kind of came here to find a man. A fling, actually. So I can't fault these guys for wanting the same thing.

The bellboy catches me when I knock on the door to James's office. He informs me that the general manager has gone to his private bungalow for the night. I thank him and hurry back to my suite. Sleep does not come easily for me, not when I can't stop thinking about James. Am I slightly obsessed with that man? No, of course not. We clicked, I know we did, and none of the male guests I've met interest me at all.

I want a real man—like James Bythesea.

When I wake up in the morning, I feel blissfully refreshed. After grabbing some breakfast in the dining hall and finding no James in sight, I knock on his office door again. No response. Does he have a hidden security camera that shows him it's me standing out here? Oh, please. Even I'm not that paranoid. But since I've resolved to find James, I opt for sitting at a small table on the patio pretending to read, while I'm really watching for the general manager out of the corner of my eye. My sunglasses hide my intentions, the same way James had secretly watched me yesterday.

Still not stalking him. Nope. This is reconnaissance.

A familiar figure emerges from a door on the opposite side of the reception desk from where James's office lies. *Eureka*. I found my quarry.

James will talk to me today, whether he wants to or not.

Chapter Three

James

I hurry out of the building and down the main trail to a spot where I know I can find some solitude. The guests haven't done much exploring yet, according to my concierge, Malakai. They will soon, though, once they've settled into life on a South Pacific island. That means I have a day, two at most, to enjoy my favorite spot. I'd spent a good amount of time there during the ramp up to the grand opening, whenever I'd needed a break from the chaos.

Now I turn down the narrower path to my secret hideaway and settle onto one of the two rattan chaises positioned under a wide palm tree. My entire body relaxes as I lean back and open my magazine. I hear a cockatoo in the distance, and I hear the palm fronds rustling in the gentle breeze.

I lay my magazine on my lap and shut my eyes, exhaling a long breath.

"There you are," a cheerful voice announces.

Oh, bloody hell.

Groaning, I open my eyes. "What do you want, Miss Temple?"

Holly grins and sashays over to the chaise beside mine. She wags a finger at me. "James Bythesea, you naughty boy. You've been avoiding me, haven't you?"

"No. I simply have no interest in speaking to you."

"Baloney."

She sits down on the other chaise, fortunately with her legs together. If she flashes me another glimpse of her intimate regions... I grip my magazine so tightly that it makes a crinkling sound. Fuck, I want her. It's wrong, and I will never give in to this lust. But I can't stop her from harassing me. She is a guest, and it's my job to ensure everyone who stays here has everything they need.

You like seeing me naked. It turns you on.

Holly's words from yesterday, when she had cornered me in my office, echo in my mind as I jerk my head to stare at the trees instead of her. "I'm on a break. That means I'm off duty for the next thirty minutes, and I don't need to cater to your whims."

"Okay." She stretches out on her chaise, bending one knee, and shuts her eyes. "I'll enjoy the sunshine while you read."

I grunt.

She pulls in a deep breath, lifting her tits, and lets it out slowly as her lips curl into a satisfied smile.

Though I try to ignore her, my cock twitches. She didn't see that, thankfully. I grab my magazine and try to read it, but my vision blurs, and I'm assailed by thoughts of what I could do to Holly's body, how good it would feel to push inside her and—

"Are you okay, James?"

I blow out a sharp breath. "Stop talking to me. I'm reading."

"Really? You've got amazing skills."

"What are you on about now?"

She stretches out one hand to tap my magazine. "It's upside down. Never met anybody who can read an entire magazine that way."

I flip the magazine over and wind up tearing a page.

"Kind of wired today, aren't you?" the blasted woman says. "Maybe you need a massage."

"No, I do not," I snarl. "Go play with the other children and leave me alone."

She swings her legs off her chaise and faces me. "Not until you apologize for calling me a child again. Why are you so rude to me?"

"Because you insist on harassing me." I hurl the magazine into the bushes, and a flock of small birds erupts from it. "I do not want to fuck you, Holly. I'm not attracted to you at all."

She lifts her brows. "Oh, really. Then why are you staring at my boobs?"

My gaze has landed on her left nipple, not her entire breast. That hardly excuses my behavior. I want her so badly that the need scrambles my brain, and my cock twitches again. I need to fuck her, right now, and get this inappropriate lust out of my system. But I can't do that. Why does Holly have this effect on me?

As my gaze drifts down to her groin, where I glimpse curly dark hairs and glistening drops of her dew, Holly laughs softly. It's a sweet sound that awakens something deep inside me that I've kept buried for such a long time. And it makes me want her even more.

To kiss her just once...

No, I cannot do that.

Holly leans toward me and lays a hand on my arm. "Desire isn't a crime, James. I'm not asking for a lifetime commitment. In two weeks, I'll go home and you'll never see me again. Let's have some fun in the meantime. I'm a grown woman, and I love sex."

She has left me only one option—to leg it and escape.

I peel her hand off my arm. "You might not be a literal child, but you are far too young for me. I don't shag women who are young enough to be my daughter." I rise and turn toward the trail. "Believe me when I say I'm sparing you from making a terrible mistake."

"James—"

I stalk back down the trail without glancing back. Whether I can keep to my vow and stay away from her, I have no bloody idea. Holly Temple tests my willpower, tests it so often that I don't know how much longer I can stop myself from doing the worst thing possible for both of us.

Holly seems to have made seducing me her mission.

Desire isn't a crime, James.

I hope she never realizes how wrong she is.

Halfway down the trail, I stop to compose myself. If that's even possible. I feel as if someone has inserted an electric wire into my spine and turned on the power. This is ridiculous. I never react this way to anyone. But the sexiest woman I've ever met has unleashed something inside me, something I can't control. My entire body feels shaky. I approach the nearest tree and set my clenched fists on the trunk, then rest my forehead on them. The breath gusts out of my lungs, and my shoulders sag.

No, I will not have an attack. I refuse to allow it.

What is wrong with me? I haven't been with a woman in such a long time that I can't remember what I'm meant to do. That's my only excuse for my behavior with Holly. Even if she only wants sex, I can't do that. I'm in no condition to get involved with any woman. But I shouldn't have treated Holly the way I did. If she knew what I've been through, what I'd survived, she wouldn't want me anymore.

But I will never tell her. It's too dangerous.

Eve and Val know my story, though not the worst parts of it. They took a chance and gave me a job for which I had no qualifications. They did that simply because they believe in me. I will not abuse their trust by cocking it up on day two.

"James? Are you okay?"

I stifle a groan. Why can't she leave me alone? I have no choice now, so I turn to face Holly. "I'm fine."

"Are you sure? You don't seem fine."

Marshaling all my self-control, I stop short of growling at her again. And I do the right thing, for once. "I apologize for my behavior earlier and in my office yesterday. It was uncalled for."

"Thank you, James. But you didn't need to apologize."

"I behaved abominably."

She walks up to me, halting an arm's length away. "You are not abominable. You were very sweet to me when we first met."

Holly thinks I was sweet? She must be barmy. But the way she's smiling at me makes me feel something I can't tolerate, not anymore. It's too much like affection.

"I need to get back to the resort. Good day, Miss Temple."

"May I walk back with you?"

"Yes, if you must."

I stride down the path with Holly beside me, and try to stop my eyes from glancing sideways at her. Even a glimpse of her face feels like more than I can handle.

"Where did you work before this?" she asks. "At another resort?"

She's making small talk, but I cannot answer her question. The truth would make her run back to Seattle as fast as possible, so perhaps I should tell her about me. It might be the only way to prevent her from trying to get to know me.

But no, I can't expose my past to this girl.

"I've switched careers several times," I say. "My past is entirely uninteresting."

Now I'm a liar.

"Uh-huh." She bumps her shoulder into me. "You're not very good at fibbing, are you? But I get it. You aren't comfortable talking about yourself."

"No, I am not."

"That's okay. And FYI, I'm an emergency dispatcher."

I halt and turn to look at her. "That must be a very stressful line of work."

She shrugs. "I wanted to help people, and emergency dispatch is one way to do that."

What can I say to her that won't sound moronic? I never would've guessed that the woman who seems determined to seduce me would turn out to have a serious and noble career. It makes my new job seem trivial.

"You are quite a woman, Holly."

"Why? Because I answer 9-1-1 calls all day long? Lots of people have jobs where they help others. I don't even risk my life, the way cops and firefighters do."

My mobile chimes, and I instinctively read the new text. "It's my assistant manager, Emilio. I need to check in with him."

"Sure, go ahead." She bites her lower lip. "Could we, um, have a drink later or something?"

Cold rushes through me like an ice dam splintering. I go rigid, unable to stop myself from fisting my hands. She wants to have a date with me. But even I am not enough of an arse to take her up on that offer. I know what she wants, and it is not polite conversation.

"No, Holly. You are still far too young, and I am far too old. Find a bloke your own age."

At least I didn't call her a child this time, but maybe I should have.

I stalk down the path and straight across the patio to the reception desk. Emilio is waiting there for me.

"Hey, boss," he says. "Mariel needs your help in the shop. All the masks are still in the storage room, but she accidentally left her key in there. Guests are getting restless. They're all very excited about the masquerade party."

"Can't you handle that?"

Emilio shrugs. "You're the only other person with a key to the storage room."

Val and Eve hadn't wanted all the employees to have a universal key card, for security reasons. I understand their reasoning, but it complicates my job since each employee has a key that's limited to their sphere—departments such as housekeeping, the gift shop, and reception.

"I'll take care of it," I tell Emilio.

Then I march down the hallway that ends at the entrance to the gift shop. When I walk inside, Mariel is standing in front of the checkout counter, wringing her hands and biting her lip.

I touch her arm. "It's all right, Mariel. You are not in trouble. We're all under stress with the grand opening and our first round of guests. I'll get your key card out of the storage room, so there's nothing to worry about."

"Thank you, Mr. Bythesea."

"We're a family here, so please call me James like the other employees do."

"Thank you, James."

I pat her arm, then head for the storage room at the back of the shop. My key card grants me access, and I find Mariel's key lying on the floor where she must have dropped it. Now that a catastrophe has been averted, I help Mariel retrieve the masks from the storage room. While she arranges them on a table at the front of the shop, I make my way to Emilio's office to discuss what preparations are still needed for the masquerade party. After that, I start back toward my office. The journey takes me past the gift shop.

And I instinctively glance into the shop, where I spot a familiar face browsing the selection of masks. Holly picks up one that has feathers attached to it, then she grins and says something to Mariel. Both women laugh. The sound of Holly's laughter drifts through the open doorway.

I can't stop myself from skimming my gaze over every inch of Holly. Fuck, that body. I feel all the blood evacuating my brain and rushing down to my cock. Just a glimpse of her does this to me.

Holly removes the feather mask and picks up one that seems to be made of black lace. She slides it down over her eyes and smiles with sensual satisfaction.

I race back to my office—to hide from Holly. What a ruddy coward I've become. Once I'm slumped in my desk chair once again, I allow myself a few minutes to consider my options. Avoiding Holly is impossible. I can't risk shagging her. Even if we did have a fling, how could I look her in the eye afterward?

Suddenly, the solution to my problem occurs to me.

Yes, it's perfect—or perfectly insane. Either way, it's the only safe method for eradicating my lust. One good shag with Holly and I'll be back to normal. But I can't let her know I'm the man fucking her. She seems like the sort who wants an adventurous holiday, which means my plan is the best solution.

I hurry back to the shop to prepare for tonight. Thankfully, Holly is gone. While Mariel is helping customers, I select a mask and ring up the purchase myself.

Tonight, I am going to seduce Holly Temple without her ever knowing who I am.

Chapter Four

Holly

I return to the patio with a small white bag in my hand, the one that holds the mask I will wear tonight for the big masquerade party. I felt sexier the moment I put the mask on, which is dumb. But it's the truth. While I was browsing the selections Mariel had arranged on a table, I kept thinking about James. He's clearly damaged in ways I can't even guess. As much as I like him and want to sleep with him, I can't keep chasing after the man. I'm beginning to stink of desperation.

Just as I sit down at a table, I reach a decision. If James won't screw me, I'll find another lover for the night. Honestly, one-nighters have never been my style. This will be my first foray into casual sex.

A shiver of excitement ripples through me. Adventure? Hot sex? Oh yeah, I will make it happen tonight. I mean, this resort is chock-full of attractive, sexy men. How hard could it be to find a one-night lover? If things go really well, it might turn into a full-on fling for the rest of my stay here.

Kevin approaches my table. "Hey, Holly. Want to come play a game of miniten with me and my friends?"

"Mini-what?"

He grins. "Miniten is short for mini tennis. It's a game invented by naturists, and it's totally crazy. You'll love it."

I push my chair back and hop to my feet. "I'd love to try that."

Kevin escorts me to an area behind the resort building where a small tennis court seems to have been set up. There's a net, and I see quite a few guests gathered alongside the grass court. Kevin leads me over to the others and explains how the game works.

First, he picks up a wedge-shaped wooden box and shoves his hand inside it. "This is the thug. You hit the ball with it instead of with a racket. Naturists like this game because it's more laid-back than tennis and it doesn't hurt your private parts. Guys don't need jockstraps, and girls can go without a sports bra."

"I see. Well, I'm definitely intrigued by this game."

Kevin gives me a crash course in miniten, leading me to a spot a little ways from the court so I can practice hitting a tennis ball with the thug while the other guests begin the first match. I learn a lot just by watching those two couples play. I learn more than the rules of miniten, though. I also discover that Kevin is not only a sweet guy, but a gentleman too. He doesn't seize the opportunity to feel me up when I stumble and almost fall down. He grasps my arms only to help me up. No ass grab.

Should I ask him to be my lover tonight? No, I think I'll wait until this evening and find a partner at the party.

After we observe three miniten matches, Kevin announces that I'm ready to participate in a real game. He's my partner, and we play against two of his buddies—Mason and his girlfriend, Taylor. Kevin and I whup them good, then opt to play against another couple. In the midst of the match, I catch sight of someone standing at the periphery of the grassy area, under the eaves of the main resort building.

James is watching me from behind his sunglasses.

A tingle sweeps over my skin.

No, I will not think about him anymore. I vowed to find a less-damaged man, and I will stick to that decision. But he seems more confident somehow, standing there observing, his posture relaxed, with a slight smile on his lips. That man is gorgeous. Hotter than anyone I've ever met. I can't help that I crave him and that I long to know more about him, like what makes him so skittish about being with me. I don't buy that it's just my age that bothers him.

Damn. I really need to stop thinking about James. Stick to my plan. Find a normal guy. Have some fun.

James walks away.

And I go back to playing miniten with my new friends. But my phone chimes, alerting me to a text, and I check it without thinking.

How are you? asks my former coworker, Andrea. *Please come back to work. We miss you.*

That part of my life is over. I can't go back there.

Maybe you'll change your mind sometime. You were the best of us.

My throat tightens. I hesitate, then type one word: *Maybe.* And I stuff my phone back in my little purse.

After that, I go to the dining hall for lunch. No crummy cafeteria food here. Like everything else at Au Naturel, the meals are excellent and in fact better than anything I ate at home. An all-inclusive resort gives me the chance to sample dishes I would never have experienced if I hadn't come here. I could live on Heirani Motu forever.

But I'll be leaving in a couple of weeks. Better squeeze in all the adventure and hot sex I can until the day I fly home.

I spend the afternoon on the beach, enjoying the sunshine. The toasty warmth lulls me into a semi-trance, but I manage to rouse before I turn into a cinnamon stick. I take a walk, alone, just to waste time until the party. Back home, I avoided big get-togethers because I didn't feel comfortable in those situations. But here, all of the stress from my old life has melted away, and I can finally be the real me.

Apparently, the real me likes to proposition older men. Who knew?

Don't think about James anymore. Get ready to party all night.

Well, maybe not all night. I need sleep, after all.

As I exit the dirt path onto the patio, I catch sight of James, who's talking to the concierge, Adrian. While I watch, James actually sort of smiles. Wow, he knows how to do that after all.

I stick to my resolution and walk right past James as I head down the hall to my suite. The info about the masquerade party had said there will be appetizers and sweet treats but no formal meal. So I order room service and eat in my suite. Why did I fly to a far away island just so I could spend most of my time alone? I think I'm nervous about my fling plan, and that's why I've kept to myself today, except for my experiment with miniten.

That changes now. It's nine o'clock. Party time.

I slip on my black lace mask and adjust it until it feels comfortable, then step into my sandals. I reach for the door knob, preparing to head out, but I freeze there. *Suck it up, woman, and live up to your self-created hype. Go for it now.*

I pull the door open and march into the hall, veering left toward the lobby and the patio beyond. But I halt at the edge of the lobby, near the glass doors. The scene before me oozes steamy romance, from the subdued lighting provided by plum- and rose-colored mini-bulbs scattered around the patio, to the soft, sensual music that emanates from speakers I can't see. A bar has been set up on one side of the patio, and a buffet table stands at the opposite end. When I approach the buffet, I examine the snack options but decide against eating right now. Instead, I go to the bar and order a martini.

While I sip my drink, I amble around the periphery of the patio, which has become a makeshift dance floor. Couples maintain a discreet distance between their partners, ensuring that other guests won't feel uncomfortable. After a while, a few couples split off to sneak down one of the trails. I finish my drink and set down my glass, then start my search for a hot prospect.

A man whose body I recognize comes over to me. Even when he's wearing a mask, I can tell it's Kevin. He has a tattoo on his chest, but I would've recognized him even without that. I spent a good chunk of the morning playing miniten with him, after all.

Kevin offers me his hand. "May I have this dance, Holly?"

"You know it's me?"

"Yeah. I'd know those tits anywhere."

Maybe I should be offended by that statement, but I realize he isn't being lewd. He's stating a fact. So I take his hand. "I'd love to dance with you."

Kevin turns out to be a respectful partner who never drags me around the patio or tries to cop a feel of parts of my body that he shouldn't try to grope. We chat the whole time, and I do enjoy being with him. He's cheerful and fun, sweet too, but he doesn't stir my desire. Even his sexy body can't arouse me. Kevin seems to get the picture, because he eventually excuses himself to go hang out with his friends.

And I wander to the far side of the patio, at the edge of the trees. I wind up standing near one of those terracotta bowls full of condoms, but it doesn't look like I'll need protection tonight. So far, my plan has fizzled out. Most of the other guests seem to have already found partners, and even Kevin is guiding a blonde girl away from the patio. He snatches a condom packet along the way.

Maybe I should go back to my room and watch dirty movies on TV. That seems like the only way I'll get any action tonight. I run my finger around the edge of the terracotta bowl, gazing down at the foil packets, and sigh. Then I force myself to lift my head and face the party again.

A man has just entered the patio. He saunters this way, his attention solely on me and his face shielded by a black mask that reveals only his eyes, mouth, and chin.

My pulse revs up. Is he coming for me? *Please, please, make it be true.* He has the kind of muscular body that I have no doubts could drive me wild. And that dick… *Whoa, mama.* I swear it's thickening more with every stride he takes toward me. Even when he halts a few feet away, I can't make out his eyes. The subdued lighting combined with that mask leaves them in shadow, though they glint when he tips his head to the side briefly. His tongue darts out between his lips, moistening them.

"Hi," I say, like a fucking moron. What a fabulous pickup line. I smile and try again. "My name is—"

The god standing before me seals my lips with two fingers and shakes his head. Then he drags those fingers down to my chin, only to pull them away.

Can't catch my breath, not with my pulse racing. Can't tear my gaze away from his shadowed eyes either. "Who are you?"

He wags a finger at me.

No names. Okay, I can work with that. He's so damn hot that I'll do anything he wants. I think I just found my naughty adventure.

The stranger holds out his hand, palm up.

Dance with him? Oh, hell yeah. But it had better lead to something so steamy that my throat will be sore from screaming in ecstasy.

I place my hand in his palm.

He settles his other hand on my back, barely grazing my skin. The delicacy of his touch intensifies my desire, and I feel myself growing slick and tingly. Never before have I gotten turned on so quickly or so intensely. Maybe it's the anonymity that gets me hot, or the man who's dancing with me. Probably both. I don't care how or why this is happening. I pray he'll fuck me soon.

Though we dance, we stay in one place, right beside that bowl of rubbers. He doesn't glance at the bowl, though. My sexy stranger keeps his focus on me the whole time, and little by little, he presses his hand into my back more firmly, then slides it down until he's grazing my ass cheek.

He lowers his head to nuzzle my neck. His warm breaths tantalize my skin.

I lose all my self-control, thrusting my fingers into his hair, plastering my body to his muscles, rocking my hips into his erection. *Hoh-lee shit.* I've never done anything like this in my life, but I will not stop now. I catch his earlobe between my teeth and release it gradually, loving the way he groans and grips my ass with one big, strong hand.

I'm almost panting now.

My clit throbs twice when he begins to massage my bottom, and I can't stop myself from closing my fingers around his cock.

He jerks upright.

"Please," I whisper. "Please don't stop."

Can't believe I'm begging. But I need him inside me right now, need it so badly that I feel like I might explode if he doesn't take me. Don't care who sees us. Don't care how much noise we make.

He cups my face in his hands. My nipples brush against his chest, and I shudder from that exquisite contact. When he rubs his thumb over the corner of my mouth, I lick the pad. A deep groan resonates in his chest, and he tips my head back.

Then he presses his mouth to mine.

Chapter Five

James

The second my lips meet Holly's, the last remnants of my self-control fly away. Not that I had much willpower. When I saw Holly standing there on the patio with the sensual lighting bathing her in the aura of a golden angel and that lace mask concealing part of her face, I knew I couldn't turn away and skulk back to my bungalow. Now I'm kissing her, tasting her soft lips as I crush my mouth to hers and lash an arm around her waist to drag her more snugly against me.

Holly moans and opens for me.

I can't hold back anymore, and there's no reason I should. She wants me, though she doesn't know it's me, and I want her so powerfully that I can't think about anything else. When she flicks her tongue out to taste my lips, I ravish her mouth, teasing and exploring, relishing every contour and the silky texture of her tongue. She wriggles against me, and my cock throbs for her. I know I won't last long if I don't take her body right now.

I step away from her, but the loss of her body plastered to mine feels like torture.

She bites her bottom lip, letting it slide free with aching slowness.

Holly Temple is the most luscious woman I've ever known. I let myself take a moment to simply appreciate the beauty of her body, of every curve and swell, from her breasts that would fit in my palms and their taut nipples that I need to devour. Her shapely thighs look strong too, and she'll need that strength for what I mean to do to her.

Am I honestly going to do this? Seduce her anonymously? Ravish her body like a ravenous beast? I suck in a breath and release it in a rush. Yes, I will do that. I need to do it, and there's no turning back now.

I snatch a foil packet from the terracotta bowl and raise it between us.

Her lips curve into a lustful smile. "Oh, yes, please."

Last night, while I lay in bed trying to talk myself out of doing this, I'd realized my plan has a serious flaw. If I speak to Holly, she will know who I am. Only three other British men are in residence here, and none of them sound like me. I'm hardly a master of voice acting, so I can't trick her with a different accent or tone of voice. That leaves me one option.

I will not speak. I'll fuck Holly in silence.

Claiming her hand, I guide Holly off the patio and down the trail that eventually leads to the beach. But I won't take her there. I mapped out this encounter in my mind multiple times today, and I know exactly what to do.

I stop us in the trees, but where we can still see the main building and the lights on the patio. Then I back her up to a palm tree and kneel at her feet.

She bites her lip again, gazing down at me while I inhale the scent of her cream. She traces her fingertips over my lips. I push her thighs apart and comb my fingers through the hairs on her mound, delicately, slowly, until she slaps her hands on the tree trunk, digging her nails into the bark.

"Yes," she breathes. "Oh, yes, yes, do whatever you want to me."

Holly would give a stranger blanket permission to use her body? I can't believe it, but that fact turns me on even more.

I move closer, grasp her ankle, and lift her leg until I can set her knee on my shoulder. She manages to wriggle her toes and tickle my spine. How flexible is Holly? I'll find out soon enough. While she follows my every movement, I spread her folds with two fingers, then trace another one down her slick flesh as delicately as I had combed her hairs. She gasps and stiffens. I toy with her clit until she whimpers, then drag my tongue up her inner thigh. When my nose brushes against her mound, I hear the rough sound of her nails scraping the tree's bark.

"Keep teasing me. Do it until I can't take it anymore."

Her brazen statement drives me to go further. I reach up to pinch her nipple, then glide my fingers down her belly, barely touching her skin, as I lift my head to witness the look on her face. Her eyes have drifted half-closed, and she arches her back like a sexy serpent, the movement hoisting her tits. Though I want to go on teasing her, I know I can't make this last as long as I'd like. My hunger for her is too strong, and I haven't done this in such a bloody long time.

I push my head between her thighs and latch on to her clit, devouring her with abandon, licking and sucking and scraping my tongue down her folds and back up again.

Holly's face pinches into an expression of sheer pleasure and blissful pain. "Oh God, make me come, please."

I plunge two fingers inside her, pumping them while I consume her flesh. Holly hooks her leg behind my neck, as if she's begging me to push my fingers deeper and fuck her with my mouth until she can't take it anymore. I press the heel of my hand into her cleft while I keep thrusting my fingers into her, and I suckle her nub so fiercely that it must cause her pain, but she grips my head with one hand as if she never wants me to stop.

Her inner muscles pulsate around my fingers. I shove two more inside her and stroke her inner wall while her breaths shorten and quicken.

"Oh God!'

All her muscles go rigid as her body milks my fingers and she curls inward, clutching my head with both hands until the last spasm subsides.

My cock feels like it's about to burst.

I surge to my feet and pin her to the tree with my whole body, ruthlessly rubbing my erection into her belly.

She seems mildly dazed. Her cheeks are pink, and the same color dapples her chest. Her lips are swollen too, from the way I kissed her earlier and from what I've just done to the girl. But I've rocketed past the point of no return, reeling through outer space with nowhere to go but onward.

I bend sideways to snatch the foil packet off the ground and rip it open. Once I've covered myself, I grasp her wrists in one hand and pin them to the tree above her head. My heart is pounding, I can't catch my breath, and I know this won't be a slow and sensual shag. No, all I can do right now is fuck her like mad.

"Hurry. Do it now, please, take me hard."

The husky tone of her voice pushes me over the edge. I crush my body to hers with my cheek pressed against her face and the bark of the tree scraping my nose and chin. I don't care about that or anything. As I grasp the back of her thigh and lift it with my free hand, she bends her knee and tries to hook it around my hip. I won't let her do that, can't let her do that. Control of this moment belongs to me, and that fact fires a white-hot bolt of need through me.

I lift her thigh a bit higher, so she can't clutch me that way, and thrust into her. She cries out. I hold still for a moment, relishing the feel of her body molding to my cock, the heat and velvety smoothness of her flesh more intoxicating than wine. I pump into her in a steady rhythm, groaning while she gasps and arches her back, rubbing her nipples over my chest.

"Let me touch you. Let me see you, please."

No, I can't do that. I thrust faster, faster, diving deeper with every lunge, while her cream dribbles onto my balls. To be inside her at last feels better than anything in the universe and more addictive than any drug. I punch into her hard enough to make her cry out and keep up the brutal pace while she begs me once again to let her see me. She can't move much or touch me with any part of her body unless I make that happen. The way she pleads…It means I'm in control of her body right now.

I fucking love that. I shouldn't, but I do.

Her desperate, wordless pleas fill the air.

She's on the edge, I can tell. Pressure bears down on me, and I know I'll come soon too. But I don't want that, not yet. I pull out and flip her around so she's pinned to the tree with her arse brushing against my cock. I want to keep fucking her until we both come, but I need to torment her with pleasure. When she wriggles her arse against me, I lay my palms on her back and slide them down to her cheeks, then up again to her shoulder blades, keeping my touch feather light and repeating the motion until she begins to writhe and gasp.

"Oh God, yes, more, please, more."

I drag my tongue down her spine, my lips grazing her skin, until I reach her arse cheeks. Then I pull my mouth away.

She moans and wriggles again. "That felt so damn good. Do it again."

I shove a hand between her thighs to push two fingers inside her while rubbing her clit, leisurely, deliberately, tormenting her until she's gasping again and begging me to make her come. When I sense she's on the edge, teetering toward climax, I pull my hand away.

"Don't stop, I need to come. Please, please, do it. My heart is pounding, and I can't take it for much longer."

I'm on the edge too, solely from listening to her beg for me to end the exquisite agony of thwarted pleasure. I grasp her hips and plunge inside her. No slow build-up this time. I need to brand her body with my cock so she will never want anyone else. Mindlessly, I pound into her again and again, not stopping even when she comes and screams from the ecstasy of her release, because I need to finish this. Holly's climax goes on and on with her body gripping me fiercely even as wildfire scorches down my spine, straight into my cock. Rapid spasms force me to spend myself deep inside her, and I throw my head back to shout. After a few more thrusts, I'm done.

For a moment, I stand here frozen with my cock still surrounded by her flesh. Holly sags against the tree, her eyes closed, struggling to calm her breathing. The way I took her, it robbed me of my breath and my sanity too. I didn't just do that, did I? But it happened. I took her with ruthless determination, and it felt bloody incredible.

I want to take her again, but I won't. Holly might be sore after this, and besides, I vowed to myself that I would only shag her once. She's out of my system now.

Yes, she definitely is.

Holly turns around, still sagging against the tree. The leaves of the palm branches that sway above us rustle in a breeze that kisses our skin.

I take two steps backward and hold out my hand to her.

She accepts it without hesitation.

We wander back to the patio and into the resort building. Though I see our night clerk at his post, he simply gives us a quick nod, seeming not to recognize either of us. How any man could fail to remember Holly, even when she's wearing a mask, seems impossible to me. I would recognize her if I saw only her sexy little toes.

I haven't felt this good in years. Maybe never.

We stop at the door to her suite. I lift her hand to kiss it, then walk away, resisting my every impulse to glance back. If I do that, I know I will end up in her bed. At least now I won't be gagging for it anymore. I've sated my lust for Holly Temple.

I follow the hallway to its end and veer left to head for the rear exit. Moments later, I enter my private bungalow. Shedding the mask, I drop onto the bed and fall asleep within a matter of minutes. When I wake in the morning, I can't believe I slept the whole night through, because that hasn't happened in longer than I can remember. Sex with Holly relaxed me in ways I'd forgotten were possible.

But I will never touch her again.

Chapter Six

Holly

I yawn and stretch my entire body, writhing under the sheets just to feel the silky fabric on my skin. Everything seems brighter and softer and sweeter and better, all because I had the most amazing sexual experience of my life last night. With a stranger. Whose face I couldn't see. Never heard his voice either. But wow, that body. He knew exactly how to use it to drive me crazy. I've never let a man boss me around like that, but I loved every second of it.

Another round of steamy goodness sounds fantastic. But I don't know who that man was. I'd peeked out the door to watch him sauntering off down the corridor until he rounded a corner and moved out of my sight. Who was that masked man? Not a super-hero. But definitely a sex god.

If I saw that body again, I'd recognize it for sure. So, I'll keep my eye out. I mean, everybody here is naked, except for the staff. Shouldn't be that hard to find my sex god.

After a long and luxurious shower, I blow dry my hair and skip down the corridors to the dining hall. Then I eat the most decadent foods I can find until I feel completely satisfied. Well, not completely. Only my mystery man can give me that kind of pleasure. A quick survey of the guests in the dining hall tells me the god is not here. I go outside and check out the men there, but I still don't see the one I want.

Damn. What should I do now?

Since I have no other ideas, I knock on the door to James's office. No answer. I knock again. Still nothing.

"James isn't in there."

I turn to find the assistant manager, Emilio, standing a few feet away. "Where did he go?"

"To Fiji. He'll be back this afternoon."

"Could I go to Fiji too? I'd love to do some shopping." No idea if they have good shops there, but I want to spend more time with the general manager. To make friends with him, that's all. Probably.

Emilio makes a pained face. "Not sure if the boss would allow that."

"Why should he mind? We're friends."

"You are? I didn't know the boss had any mates."

James probably wouldn't agree that I'm his friend, but that man desperately needs someone to hang out with, even if it's a platonic thing. I give Emilio my sweetest smile. "Please can I go to Fiji too? A field trip would be so much fun."

"Uh…" He hunches his shoulders and aims a sheepish smile at me. "All right. I guess James wouldn't sack me for that."

"Of course not. He's a good man."

Emilio waves toward my body without breaking eye contact. "You might want to get dressed. Fiji isn't a naturist resort."

"Oh, right. Just give me a few minutes to get ready."

Emilio trots off to the reception desk while I rush back to my room. I opt to wear the outfit I'd had on when I arrived at the resort, including the floppy sun hat. After grabbing my big purse, I hurry to the lobby where Emilio is waiting for me.

"I talked to Rene," he says. "He remembers you, and he's happy to fly you to Fiji for shopping."

"Did you tell James about that?"

"No, but I sent him a text. If he remembers to check those. The boss is sort of allergic to texting."

I can't help laughing. "Allergic? Oh, I will cure him of that. Don't worry."

"You'd have to be a miracle worker to make that happen."

I wink. "Just leave it with me."

Am I arrogant to assume I can convince James Bythesea to unclench his body and his mind? Well, it doesn't really matter if I fail. I want to have a good time, period. If James is too uptight to even be friends with me, I have plenty of other options. Coming to this island has awakened me in so many wonderful ways. I suspect I'll never be the same after this vacation.

I jog most of the way to the airstrip, which is nothing more than a long grassy field. James stands beside the plane, but Rene has just climbed into the pilot's seat when I get there. I'm breathing so hard from running that I'm half gasping.

James whirls around to see who else has arrived. His brows shoot up, and his eyes bulge. "Holly, what are you doing?"

"Didn't check your texts, hey? Emilio said you probably wouldn't."

"Text?" His brows squish together as he pulls out his phone and starts swiping one finger over the screen. Then he looks up at me with his head still bowed. "You want to come with us? It's a supply run, Holly, not a tourist excursion."

"But it could be both. You did say you'd do anything you can to make my stay pleasurable."

Sighing, he bows his head even more and scratches the back of it. "Yes, I did say that."

I'm guessing he wishes he had never spoken those words. So I'll let him off the hook if he wants. "I can go shopping by myself. You and Rene can do your thing, and I'll do mine."

James lifts his head, those beautiful eyes aimed straight into mine. "I cannot leave a guest unattended outside of the resort. You know nothing about Fiji, or the South Pacific."

"Are you offering to be my shopping buddy?"

"Yes, I suppose I am." And he sounds none too happy about that, though less grumpy than yesterday or the day before. He opens the rear door of the plane. "I'll ride in the backseat. You should sit up front with Rene, where you'll have a much better view."

"Really?" I kiss his cheek and grin. "Thank you, James. You're a sweetie-pie."

His lips tick up the tiniest bit. "Follow me."

James leads me around to the other side of the plane and opens the door for me. He also offers me his hand as I climb in, and he gives my bottom a push when I need a little extra help. Once I've settled into my seat beside Rene, James shuts the door. A moment later, he climbs into the backseat.

"This is such a cute plane," I tell Rene. "The blue and gray stripes are slick. And wow, this seat is cushy."

Rene chuckles, and his smile tightens the wrinkles around his eyes. "No one has ever called this plane cute before. James is probably groaning silently. Time for headsets, or we'll never be able to talk over the engine noise."

I pull on my headset. When I twist around to see James, he already wears his headset. The poor man looks to be stuffed into the back like the proverbial sardine. "Are you sure you're okay back there? You'd have more room up here. Wanna switch?"

"No. I'm reasonably comfortable where I am."

"Okay, if you're sure." I face forward and do up my seatbelt. Then I glance back at him over my shoulder. "Where are you going to fit those supplies? Doesn't seem to be any room."

"The cargo will be small. I shall manage."

Leaning around my seat as much as I can, I shake my head. "I don't get it. What kind of tiny cargo are you picking up?"

James fidgets and screws up his mouth. "We, ah, underestimated the popularity of one of our gratis items."

While Rene starts up the plane's engine, I study James. "Nothing you just said makes any sense. Are you a drug mule?"

"Don't be ridiculous."

"Are you going to explain? Or is this a top secret mission?"

He stares at the back of Rene's seat. "We are running out of condoms."

"Ohhh, I see. The other guests are having more fun than you expected, huh?"

"Yes." He waves toward the windshield. "You might miss something exciting if you keep harassing me."

I face forward and gaze out the front. I'd ridden in this plane a few days ago, in this very seat, when I arrived for my vacation. But I didn't do any sightseeing. I'd been too tired to enjoy the scenery, but today will be different.

Since James doesn't want to talk, I'll chat with our gray-haired pilot. "I'm curious, Rene. How do you transport all the guests to the island with this little plane?"

"I don't. We have a larger plane for that. But this one is faster and cheaper to operate, so I fly the Cessna whenever possible."

"What's a Cessna?"

"The type of airplane. This is a Cessna TTx."

Whatever. The details about the resort's planes doesn't matter, anyway. I was just making conversation. "Are you from Australia, Rene?"

"Yeah, I am." He smirks at me. "What gave me away? Must've been my Aussie charm."

Rene and I chat for a while, and he tells me jokes that make me laugh so hard that my abdominal muscles hurt. Every time I glance back at James, he's watching me with a slight smile on his lips. James does seem a lot more relaxed today, and I can't help wondering what changed. Maybe he got a massage.

"Look at that," Rene says, pointing out the windshield. "It's your first taste of South Pacific wildlife."

I lean forward to peer out the windshield. "Where is it? What is it? I can't see anything."

"Right there." He points again. "See those dark shapes in the water? Those are humpback whales."

"Seriously?" I crane my neck but still can't make out anything down there.

"I think you need a closer look, eh?"

The plane abruptly plummets toward the ocean. I yelp and grip the chest strap on my seatbelt. "Rene, what are you doing? We'll crash."

"Nah." The plane levels off, and he waves toward the water again. "Now you can see the whales."

My pulse is racing, but I slant forward anyway and at last see what he does. Whales. Two of them. The gigantic beasts gracefully emerge from the water, and their massive tails rise up, only to slap back down again.

"Oh, my God," I say, as I watch the whales, riveted to their movements and their beauty. "This is incredible. I live in Seattle, but I never saw any whales or dolphins or anything there." I plant a firm kiss on Rene's cheek. "Thank you for showing me the whales. They're amazing."

"That's all I get?" he says, huffing. "A peck on the cheek?"

"Yes," James tells him. "That is all you get, Rene. You are meant to fly the plane, not snog with the guests."

I'm guessing that "snog" means kissing or maybe making out. James does sound annoyed now. Well, he didn't want to date me or screw me, so he lost the right to be jealous. But I do kind of like that he's jealous. It makes me feel...horny. That's weird, but I never second guess my sexual urges. Besides, James is the hottest man alive.

How can I still want him? I had sex with someone else last night.

I don't have time to think about that because I can see an island in the distance, and we are rushing toward it. "Is that Fiji?"

"Yes and no. The nation of Fiji is an archipelago made up of more than three hundred islands. You arrived here at Suva-Nausori International Airport, and that's where we'll land today. Suva is the capital city of Fiji." Rene turns the plane toward the island that grows bigger every moment. He smirks and winks. "James can show you around while I get those desperately needed supplies."

Condoms are desperately needed? Well, I wouldn't want anybody to run out of protection, and I'm still hoping for another steamy encounter of my own. With James? Or with my mystery man?

I'm so confused right now.

But I forget all about that once we land at the airport and James calls for a taxi to pick us up. We spend a good part of the day shopping, though I don't buy that much. Just a few trinkets. My favorite acquisition is a cowrie shell necklace that's long enough I can drape it around my neck twice. James doesn't say much during our excursion, but he watches me the whole time—especially when I dance to the rhythm of three street musicians who play guitar and ukulele. Despite the fact James wears his sunglasses the entire time, even indoors, I know he has his gaze nailed to me. I can feel it.

On our last stop before heading back to the airport, James takes me to a park in a forest, where we walk down wood-plank walkways to see the sights. It's beautiful here, and I love listening to the birds. We wind up standing across from a small waterfall that cascades down a steeply sloped rocky area. I hover near the edge, but James takes a position behind me. He wears his sunglasses, of course.

I turn toward him, absently running my fingers over the cowrie shell beads on my necklace. "Why don't you come over here, James?"

He seems relaxed, except for the way his fingers curl toward his palms. "I prefer to stay where I am."

Of course he does. But I walk over to him, halting inches away, and coil my necklace around my middle finger. "I know you've been watching me through those sunglasses. Do you like what you see?"

He swallows hard, making his Adam's apple jump.

I lay my other hand on his chest and toy with the unhooked top button of his shirt. My fingers graze his skin. When he sucks in a breath, I raise my hand to lift the sunglasses off his nose just enough that I can see his eyes. "Why not show off those gorgeous baby blues? You'll have a better view of me if you ditch the shades."

He stares directly into my eyes for a moment, and my nipples tighten from the heat of his gaze. Then he clears his throat and steps back. "We should go back to the airport. Rene will be waiting."

Sighing, I shake my head.

Chapter Seven

James

*I*n the car on our way back to the airport, Holly wriggles in her seat to turn mostly toward me. *Bloody hell.* I want to go back to the resort and hide in my office, not get another lecture from Holly about how uptight I am. Being a coward seems like the better option. But the woman is unstoppable, which only makes me want to shag her again. She enjoys tormenting me, especially with her body, and she clearly wants me to ravish her.

Holly has no idea I've already had my way with her. And the memory of last night both arouses me and makes me hate myself.

"Sooo," she begins, "Emilio told me you don't like texting. I promised him I'd disabuse you of that."

"Of what?"

"Being allergic to texting. Do you ever check your messages? Or do you let them pile up on your phone?"

"That's none of your concern." I'm gripping the steering wheel like it might fly away as well as gritting my teeth. Only Holly turns me into an ogre. "I don't need to text anyone. I can simply ring them on my office phone or my mobile."

"But the younger staff members prefer text. Especially if they need to tell you something they don't want the guests to hear."

"Naturists are not known for being prudish."

She clucks her tongue and shakes her head. "You are the general manager, James. Do your bosses know you ignore all your text messages?"

I squirm, though only a little.

Holly pokes me in the side. "Just give in and embrace texting. You'll feel much better if you do."

"No, I won't. Besides, I don't have time to keep glancing at my mobile to check for messages."

She falls silent, and peripherally I can see her studying me. When I glance at her, she's puckering her lips and squinting at me. "Do you have your text alerts turned off?"

"My what?"

"Does your phone go bloopety-bloop sometimes?"

"No."

She pokes me in the side again. "Let me guess. The only sound your phone makes is when it rings."

"Why else would it make noise? It's a mobile phone, not a child's toy."

"James, James, James." She pats my thigh. "It's time to leave the twentieth century behind and finally embrace the new millennium. Your phone can let you know when you have a text. Give it to me, and I'll turn on those alerts. Didn't anybody ever show you how to do that?"

"My da—" I freeze with both hands on the wheel, suddenly paralyzed because I almost spoke a word I haven't said aloud in years. I've thought it often, but never spoke the word.

The car begins to swerve toward the other lane.

I can't move. Though I see another vehicle coming toward us in the opposite lane, I cannot do anything to stop us from crashing into that car. With my hands locked on the wheel, I can only watch as the disaster draws nearer. A chill engulfs me. My heart pounds so fast that I begin to feel weak, as if I might pass out.

"James!" Holly shrieks.

Then she grabs the wheel and jerks it to steer us back into our lane.

I snap out of my trance, blinking rapidly.

"What the hell was that?" she asks. "You almost killed us and the other driver."

"I didn't—" My hands are shaking, and a cold sweat has broken out on my brow. "I didn't mean to do that. I'm sorry for frightening you."

"You'd better explain to me what just happened. Maybe I should drive the rest of the way."

"No, I'm fine. It was…nothing."

Her mouth has fallen open, though she seems unable to speak.

I focus on the road. The airport is just ahead of us, coming into view now. My hands are still shaking slightly, but not enough that Holly would notice. The rest of my symptoms have abated.

Holly sighs and faces forward.

What *did* just happen? I've never had an incident like this while driving. But I've never almost blurted out that one forbidden word either. Does my reaction have anything to do with the woman seated beside me? She is eighteen years younger than I am.

And I almost told her that my daughter tried to teach me how to text, but she didn't finish the task. *My daughter.* The one who is no longer in my life. The one whose name I will never speak. Our lives blew apart because of me. I destroyed myself and my family.

Holly doesn't speak to me as we park on the tarmac and get out of our vehicle. But halfway to the plane, she stops me with a hand on my arm. "Are you ever going to tell me what happened in the car?"

"No." I dig my mobile out of my pocket. "But I'd like for you to show me how to text."

Her lips curl up a touch, creating the sweetest dimples in her cheeks. "I'd better sit in back with you, then. We'll have the whole ride to the resort to get you up to speed."

I barely squelch a miserable groan.

Holly climbs in first, and her tiny dress rides up just enough that I can see she is not wearing any knickers. She walked around all day with a bare arse? A slight breeze could have lifted her dress.

Once we're both strapped in, Rene starts the engine. Within moments, we're in the air, heading back to Heirani Motu. The backseat is a tight space, which means Holly keeps brushing against me while she gives me the tutoring session I apparently need. Every time she leans over to point at something on my mobile's screen, the neckline of her dress sags outward enough that I can't help noticing her tits.

Did she dress that way on purpose? To torture me?

I'm being paranoid. But Holly does love to show off her body and try to goad me into fucking her. She thinks her efforts have failed. But I woke up this morning feeling more relaxed than I ever have before, all because I shagged her last night. I'd hoped once would be all it would take to rid me of this lust for her. No such luck. Spending the day with Holly inflamed that hunger even more.

At least now I know how to use the ruddy texting feature on my mobile. No one can harass me about that anymore. Not even Holly.

The second our plane lands on Heirani Motu, Holly leaps out and strips off her clothes. She waves her dress in the air and spins around. Her cowrie shell necklace flaps about. "Yes, yes, yes. That feels so much better."

All the blood in my brain seems to be flooding down to my cock. Any moment, I will develop a raging erection. I have only one option to prevent Holly from realizing my dilemma.

I hurry away, walking so fast that I'm almost running. I do not look back. Getting away from Holly has become my only goal, and I reach my office so swiftly that I collapse into my chair and need a few minutes to recover my breath. Now I'm a coward who hides from a woman, on top of my sin of seducing her in secret. I know I should tell Holly to bugger off, but instead, I let her rope me into spending time with her.

No more. For her good as well as my sanity, I will treat her as only another guest.

I have two hours left until my shift officially ends. Rene shows up shortly after I sequestered myself in my office and knocks on my door to let me know he has the "supplies" we'd gone to Fiji to retrieve. I walked away from the plane without bothering to collect the boxes of condoms. Christ, I'm losing my mind. I apologize to Rene, but he simply shrugs and smiles.

"Don't blame you, mate. Holly would scramble any man's brain."

But not his brain. Only mine.

Since all my other employees are busy, I take on the task of re-filling the terracotta bowls. When I reach the side of the patio that overlooks the miniten court, I see Holly playing a match with three other guests. She leaps up to bat the ball with her thug, sending it flying past her opponents. They scramble to retrieve the ball while Holly high-fives her partner. It's the bloke I'd seen dancing with her last night at the masquerade party.

My fingernails scrape the cardboard box that I hold under my arm, and my jaw tenses.

Holly leans in to whisper something to her new friend.

And I start to grind my teeth. That man touched her. I want to punch the bastard, but I get distracted by admiring the beauty of Holly's body, though I know I should tear my gaze away from her. When her breasts sideswipe that other bloke's chest, I suddenly have trouble breathing.

A memory bursts into my mind—Holly's body pressed against me, both of us naked, her nipples rubbing on my chest. My groin tightens.

Holly notices me. She smiles and waves.

I turn away, pretending I haven't seen her. As I fill the last terra-cotta bowl, I sneak one condom pocket into my trouser pocket. Why did I do that?

The woman I fucked last night seems as if she's about to trot over here to torment me with that body and her erotic innuendo.

I spin around and rush back into the building. A sideways glance assures me Holly is not following. I finally met a woman who wants me and who I want too, and she turns out to be too damn young. I need to rid myself of this obsession, somehow, once and for all.

By the time I slam the door to my office shut, I have a full-on erection. Christ, I need to stop craving Holly's body. How hard can that be? I'll simply wish her to disappear, and it will happen.

My hand wanders down to my groin, seemingly of its own volition. My mind torments me with images of Holly playing miniten, every inch of her on full display, and I suddenly realize I'm stroking my cock through my trousers. No, I will not wank off. That would be giving in. I must reassert my self-control, though I have no clue how to accomplish that feat.

I let my head fall back against the chair and shut my eyes. But I can't banish the visions of Holly playing miniten, Holly lounging on a chaise, Holly whipping off her clothes the moment she stepped out of the plane.

Bugger me.

This morning I had felt much more relaxed and able to confront another day with Holly on the island. Even when she inserted herself into my supply mission, I had been all right. Only when she stripped her clothes off did my obsession reassert itself. That gives me an idea. It's the only option, and it helped last night. Another injection should inoculate me against Holly's appeal. Yes, I know exactly what to do.

I need to secretly shag Holly one last time.

But there's no masquerade party tonight. How can I seduce her without revealing my identity? Well, I could slip a note under her door. Yes, that's brilliant. I pull out a desk drawer and hunt about until I find a package of blank note cards. Perfect.

After writing my note, I realize my shift has ended. I head for my bungalow, but on the way, I stop off at the door to Holly's room and push my note under it. Then I wait at the end of the hall, just round the corner, to watch and make sure Holly finds the note. A few minutes later, she walks up to the door to her suite and opens it with her key card.

She takes half a step, then stops. Kneeling, she picks up the envelope into which I had tucked my note. Her brows furrow. But they smooth out again as a seductive smile curves her lips. She enters her suite and shuts the door.

Holly approves of my note. She must do. Why else would she smile that way when she read it? Of course, she has no idea who wrote that invitation, except that it's the same man who seduced her last night.

As I rush to my bungalow, the words I'd written to Holly replay in my mind. *You were incredible last night when we made love under the palm tree. May I see you again? If you want that, leave your door unlocked and wait for me in your bed. I will come to you at midnight.*

I have dinner alone in my private quarters, then lie on my bed imagining all the things I want to do with Holly, to banish this obsession for good. Glancing at the clock repeatedly does not make the time go by faster. But at last, it's time to go to the woman who has possessed my mind and my body since the moment I first saw her. I strip off my clothes, slip my mask on, and sneak out of the bungalow.

All the guests seem to have settled in for the night, and I don't bump into anyone. Once I reach Holly's door, I discover she's left it unlatched for me, though I doubt a casual passerby would notice that. I push the door open and steal inside the room. Holly has left the light in the entryway on, but I flick the switch to turn it off. As I step into the room itself, I realize only a single lamp on the nightstand illuminates the space, casting a warm, soft glow.

The vision before me steals my breath.

Holly lies nude on the bed, stretched out on her back with her head on the pillow. The lamp's glow seems to burnish her skin, lending her the appearance of a goddess awaiting her lover.

When she sees me, she smiles. "There you are. I was afraid you might chicken out."

I shake my head, sauntering up to the bed, and toss a condom packet onto the nightstand. She has pulled the covers back. I stand here immobilized by her beauty, drinking in the vision of her sensual body while my cock stiffens.

Her gaze flicks to my left hand. Her brows lift briefly, then that smile returns. "Whatever you want, I want. Don't be shy."

I climb onto the bed, straddling her thighs, and set down one of the two silk scarves I'd been holding. I'd sneaked into the resort shop after hours, using my master key to go inside and buy the items I needed for tonight. I left a note for Mariel, so she won't wonder why money appeared in the till overnight. But now, it's time to focus on Holly—on banishing my need for her body.

One more night, and I'll be free.

Chapter Eight

Holly

My mystery man has come back. I'd hoped that maybe he might ditch the mask tonight, and I left the entryway light on to encourage him to reveal his identity. He didn't take the hint. I wanted to see him again, to feel him inside me again, but I also have a slight ulterior motive. I want to know who he is.

"Who are you? I promise not to tell anybody what we've been doing together. Please won't you show me your face?"

He shakes his head.

Damn. Maybe I should tell him to show me his face or leave, but I need to experience his body one more time. Then, I'll say adios to the best lover I've ever had, because I know I won't be able to take the secrecy anymore after tonight.

"Okay, you can keep your mask on."

He relaxes visibly. Then he grasps one of the scarves in both hands, stretching it taut, and tips his head to the side as if he's waiting for my permission. To tie me up? Or blindfold me? Maybe he wants to do both, since he brought two scarves. Just thinking about that makes me so wet that it's almost embarrassing. I'd been slick and ready before he walked into the room, strictly from imagining what we might do together. But now...I could almost come just from watching his dick getting hard right before my eyes. It makes my mouth water.

I flirted with James today, and tonight I invited a stranger into my suite. Maybe I've gone crazy. The way I've been vacillating between wanting James and wanting my anonymous lover doesn't bother me as much as it should, which is weird. I'll think about that in the morning.

"Let me taste you, please. I fantasized about doing that while I was waiting for you."

He shakes his head again and leans in to hold the scarf an inch away from my eyes.

"Yes. Anything you want."

My mystery man ties the scarf around my head, blindfolding me. Now that I can't see, I grow more excited, and a delicious little shiver rushes through me, accompanied by a tingling sensation that sweeps over my skin. My breaths quicken, and so does my pulse. He pulls my wrists together and binds them with the other scarf. The silky texture feels so good on my skin that I arch my back and let out a soft moan.

The man who has me at his mercy groans deeply.

I bet he has a sexy voice. I'd love to hear it, just once, but I doubt he'll go for that.

He raises my bound wrists above my head and secures them to the headboard with the same scarf. I can tell that's what he did because the cool wood of the headboard rails grazed my skin. I can't move my arms now, which is also a clue. Now I can't see or touch him unless I use my legs. I lick my lips and wriggle, but I'm not trying to get free. I've never experienced this level of excitement for any other man. Maybe it's the thrill of not knowing who he is or what he wants to do to me that intensifies my arousal until it almost hurts.

"Oh God," I breathe, as he drags one finger down my chest from the base of my throat straight down to my hips. "Please, more, don't stop."

He twirls that finger in the hairs on my mound, over and over, teasing me until my heart begins to pound. Then he palms me down there, his hand encompassing my flesh from the top of my mound to the skin just below my entrance. He holds his hand there, not moving even a millimeter. His other hand cups my breast, and he rasps his thumbnail over my nipple.

I cry out.

His tongue rasps over my taut peak, then he pulls my nipple into his mouth and suckles it.

Another cry bursts out of me as I writhe beneath him. The movement makes his palm rub against my slick flesh, and I instinctively buck my hips, pleading for more. His fingers dip inside my opening, spurring me to buck my hips again. I'm so desperate for him to fuck me, even with only his fingers, that I can't control myself.

He pulls both his hands away.

A frustrated noise erupts out of me.

My mystery man chuckles.

I was right. This man must have a hot voice, because his throaty chuckle alone makes my clit throb. But when I raise one leg, trying to hook it around his hip, he lays his hands on my knees and gently pushes them down until I'm pinned to the bed by those big, rough palms. Does he do manual labor for a living? Maybe he just doesn't care about moisturizing.

God, I love the way it feels to have him holding me down.

The bed jostles as he adjusts his position and pushes his knees between my legs to spread them wide. I grip the headboard rails hard. He slips one finger between my folds and strokes my clit, moving his fingertip in leisurely, deliberate circles, using only the gentlest pressure to torture me with pleasure.

I jerk and gasp.

He slides his fingertip down my cleft, oh-so-slowly, making me writhe and gasp and repeat the word please until I can't breathe anymore. I never knew being blindfolded could make me desperately aroused. This man understands my body so well that it's almost scary, but I never want him to stop teasing me. When he thrusts his finger inside me, I jerk again. He pumps that finger with the same deliberate slowness he'd employed with my clit, waiting until my chest is heaving and I'm whimpering again before he thrusts a second finger inside. My back bows up as my mouth falls open, but I have no breath left to express my need.

When he adds a third finger, a half-strangled scream is torn from my throat.

His fingers stop moving.

"Keep going, I'm begging you, make me come."

Those fingers curl inside me until he's touching my inner wall, petting me with maddening leisure. Every millimeter of my skin has grown sensitized to the slightest touch, so much that the barest draft might set me off.

He yanks his fingers free.

"Whuh…" I can't even finish that word. My ears are ringing, my heart feels like it might explode out of my chest, and I'm so on fire for him that I know I'll go insane if he doesn't fuck me soon.

The bed jostles again. Soft, warm lips brush against mine.

He leans in, and his cock grazes my belly. When he breathes into my mouth, even that turns me on. I try to kiss him, but he shies away. A second later, his lips land on my earlobe. He catches it between his teeth and suckles, only to abandon my lobe a moment later. I can feel him moving around again, though I can't decide what he's trying to do now.

Until his cock settles onto my belly.

What is he up to? This guy has ideas for things I've never experienced before, and I love it.

He rubs his length up and down my skin.

When I try to bend my knees, he carefully pushes them down onto the mattress, then lies down between my legs. I know he's doing that because I can feel his body wedged there—and his hair brushing across my hips, not to mention his nose and lips. He eases my thighs further apart to seal his mouth over my clitoris.

The second he licks my nub, I go off. My body goes rigid and curls in on itself, lifting my feet off the bed and bending my head forward. If I weren't blindfolded, I'd be watching him devour me. But I swear the blindfold makes me come even more powerfully as I grip the headboard rails so hard that my fingers ache and my nails scrape the wood. I have no breath to scream, and the only sounds I can produce are strangled gasps.

Just as my orgasm seems about to fade, he moans against my clit, the sound vibrating into me. One last pulse does me in.

I go limp, breathing so hard and fast that I can't move or speak.

The bed jostles yet again. I think he sat up, since I no longer feel his body heat or his hair tickling me. He pushes his fingers under my head to release the blindfold, then whisks the fabric away.

I blink rapidly, struggling to adjust to the lighting. It's muted, but I still need a moment to get used to the change.

My mystery lover still kneels between my legs, but now he squats and shoves his arms under my thighs to lift them. Once has them hooked over his shoulders, he leans toward me and sets his palms on either side of my pillow. Then he rocks his hips forward just enough that the head of his cock grazes my cleft. I want him inside me so badly that I'm thrashing my head and unleashing sharp cries.

"Fuck me now, please, I can't wait anymore."

I swear his lips curve into a wicked smirk, but I can't be sure about that. The mask he wears casts shadows over the only parts of his face that are exposed—his chin, mouth, and eyes.

He rolls his hips in a circular motion, rubbing the head of his erection round and round my nub at a measured pace, as if he wants to spend forever doing nothing else. Though I can see he's breathing harder, and I can hear it too, he doesn't speed up the movements, not even when he switches to gliding his entire length up and down my cleft. When I get used to that, he changes it up again, pulling his hips back so he can plunge them forward again and bump his crown into my rigid clit.

I'm throbbing for him again and on the verge of another climax.

"Untie my hands, please. I need to touch you."

He shakes his head slowly. The man who drives me wild slips one of my legs off his shoulder and sets it on the mattress. When I try to bend my knee, he gently pushes it down again, encouraging me to keep that leg straight. So I simply watch while he shifts one of his legs to cradle my raised thigh between his knees. His dick rubs against my inner thigh.

My sex god reaches over to the nightstand to retrieve the condom he'd brought with him and rips the packet open, rolling the latex over his length. With a guttural groan, he slaps his palms down to frame my head between them and thrusts inside me at last.

"Oh, yes. Fuck me like crazy. Don't hold back."

The fullness of him feels so damn good. His face hovers inches above mine, but I still can't make out his features, thanks to the smoky lighting. I don't care if I'll never see his face, because all I can concentrate on right now is the sensation of his cock gliding in and out, in and out, rubbing against my clit with every thrust. His movements grow faster and rougher with every passing moment, and the liquid sounds of our bodies merging mingle with the slapping of flesh on flesh. I can smell how turned on I am, and I love the way his breaths gust over my face. His lips have peeled back from his gritted teeth, like he's struggling not to take me too hard.

"Don't hold back. Fuck me as hard as you want."

He pauses for a couple of seconds, gazing down at me. Then he pulls his hips back and slams into me so forcefully that my body jerks. Meaningless cries spill out of me, one after another, and my ears start to ring because I can't suck in a complete breath. The bed thumps and creaks. He grunts and shouts. The climax builds like an electrical storm, sizzling through my sex and sensitizing every nerve while he pounds into me so fiercely that I can't hold back anymore.

A lightning bolt of pleasure slams through me.

I throw my head back and scream until my throat goes hoarse. He pummels me a few more times before he roars and collapses on top of me.

My voice refuses to work, and I'd bet he couldn't speak either even if he wanted to say something. The power of our orgasms has stolen our breath. My heart thrashes like it wants to bust out of my chest. He lies on top of me with his head on my shoulder, the plastic of his mask rasping against my neck.

Finally, he flips over to lie on his back beside me.

When I regain the ability to speak, I can't come up with any eloquent words. "Holy shit. I mean, you are—That was even more amazing than last night."

He doesn't speak.

I tug on my bindings. "Mind setting me free?"

The man who drove me out of my mind a moment ago sits up and leans over to untie the scarf that had restrained my wrists. But when I reach for him, he jumps off the bed.

"I love being with you. But if we're ever going to do this again, I need to know who you are. I need to see your face. Can you do that?"

He shakes his head.

I push up into a sitting position. "Can't say I'm surprised, but I am disappointed. If you don't want anyone to know about us, that's okay. But I need to know who you are, or else we can't do this again. The choice is yours."

For a moment, he doesn't move, his attention locked on me. Then he snatches the other scarf off the bed and slants toward me to kiss my forehead.

I let out a long sigh. "That was goodbye, right?"

He nods.

And my mystery lover walks out the door.

Chapter Nine

James

I collapse onto the bed in my bungalow and stare up at the ceiling. Only the moonlight from outside the window illuminates the space. What have I done? Used a woman for my own pleasure and abandoned her, that's what. I swore to myself this would be the last time, and I would have banished my lust for Holly after this final encounter. Being with her obliterates my self-control. That's my only excuse for how feverishly I took her body, and how badly I want to do it again.

No, that was the last time.

Holly accepted my decision. Though I hadn't vocalized it, she asked if this was goodbye, and I nodded my agreement. It's over. I will treat Holly Temple as a guest only, avoiding her as much as possible from this moment forward.

Although I try to sleep, memories of my two liaisons with Holly plague me. She let me do whatever I wanted to her. Why? She is not a moron. Holly knew what she was doing and consented to all of it. She clearly enjoyed our encounters. She even seemed to…love it. Maybe I should confess what I've done, but I can't bring myself to do that. She might want more from me. A relationship.

I will never go down that road again.

Eventually, I fall into a restless slumber. I wake in the morning feeling less than refreshed. My only task from now on is to do my job and ensure everything runs smoothly at the resort. I can handle that. I have no choice but to forget about Holly and move on.

Forget about her? Is that even possible? I vowed one more shag would cure me of my obsession with her, yet I can't stop thinking about Holly for one full hour.

And I haven't even left my bungalow yet.

I take a cold shower, though the myth about that easing a man's lust is sheer bollocks. But I do manage not to get a painfully hard erection this morning, so perhaps that myth has a sliver of merit. Focusing on work will be my salvation. If I told Holly about my past and what I'd done, things I can never take back or forget, she wouldn't want me anymore. Maybe she already doesn't. Holly let an anonymous stranger fuck her, so I imagine she will find another lover.

Though I go to the dining hall to grab some breakfast, I take it back to my office to eat. The relative peace and quiet I find there lasts for about an hour. I've buried myself in statistics, analyzing all the data about our first few days in operation since the official launch. Everything looks as well as I could've hoped, though I want to make it much better.

Will turning this resort into a rollicking success erase my worst mistakes? It's doubtful. But I'll take not cocking it up. Asking for a miracle seems pointless.

Peripherally, I notice a figure has stepped onto the threshold of my office. I'd left the door partway open, because I suddenly needed to not be locked in my office like a criminal in a prison cell. I might have felt like a prisoner for years before I came here, but this job was meant to take me away from all that rubbish.

Keeping my head down, still focused on my statistics, I speak without knowing who is standing there. And I make the wrong assumption. "Emilio, is that you? I'm rather busy at the moment."

"I've never been mistaken for a man before. Not sure if I should be offended."

My head snaps up, and I stop blinking. Why? Because Holly is standing there in the nude, leaning against the doorjamb. She has a pink flower tucked behind her ear.

She tips her head to the side. "Do I look like Emilio to you?"

"No, ah...of course not." I sit up straighter and attempt to give her a disinterested look. "What do you want, Miss Temple? I'm quite busy."

"May I come in? I promise not to seduce you."

How does she make everything, even a naughty comment, sound sweet and almost innocent? "Not now. If you need something, you can ask Emilio or another member of the staff."

"Only you can help me out this time. Please, may I talk to you? It'll just take a minute, promise."

I shouldn't give in, but I suspect the most expedient way to get rid of her is to let her tell me whatever it is. I slump in my chair and sigh. "Come in, if you must."

She sashays over to my desk and sets her bum on the edge furthest from me. "I'm sorry for the way I keep upsetting you. I don't know how that happens, but I'm hoping we can clear the air and be friends."

"You are a guest. I am the general manager. That doesn't leave any room for friendship."

"Sure it does." She smiles and slants toward me to tap my nose with one finger. "If you loosen up a little."

Her breasts are dangling in front of me. I try not to glance at them, but it's hard to avoid that when she's leaning over to harass me. Fortunately, she pulls away. But she's still naked, and my mind insists on tormenting me with replays of last night, when Holly lay spread out on that bed with her wrists bound and her eyes blindfolded, ready for me to do whatever I wanted to her.

She slides off the desk. "At least have breakfast with me."

"I've already eaten. And as I said, our relationship will remain guest and manager only."

"You just admitted we have a relationship. Why not go a little further and make it a friendship?"

"No, Miss Temple."

She folds her arms over her chest, an action that luckily conceals most of her breasts. "You need a friend, James. I've talked to several members of your staff, and they all agree with me."

"You've been interrogating my staff to get information about me? That's unacceptable."

"Relax. I chatted with them to be nice, and because I like talking to people. They happened to mention that you rarely hang out with them, and you never talk about yourself."

My knuckles have begun to ache. When I glance down at them, I realize I've been clenching my chair's arms. With more effort than it should take, I release the tension in most of my body. The desk conceals the one stiff part of me that I can't control.

"Come on, James," Holly says. "I'd like to be your friend, that's all. Having a conversation with me won't actually kill you."

"I'm afraid I can't do that."

"Won't do it. That's what you mean."

"Think what you like." I rest my elbows on the desk and stare down at papers that no longer make sense to me. "If you need a friend so desperately, go find a boy your own age."

"You're implying I'm a child again." She moves to stand right beside my chair and leans over until her face is millimeters from mine. "I'm going to be totally honest with you. I do want us to be friends, but I can't deny I'd rather we were lovers too. For the past two nights, I got naked with a man who wouldn't show his face or speak to me. I have no idea who he is, and honestly, I don't want to know anymore. I'm done with him, done with anonymous flings. Sex with a mystery man was incredible, but I know being with you would be even better."

I refuse to look at her, but I can't prevent myself from asking a question. "Why would you fuck a stranger who wanted to remain anonymous?"

"Thought it would be an adventure. It was, but anonymity doesn't turn me on anymore. Besides, I felt weird about the whole thing once it was done. I'm not the casual sex kind of girl."

Despite my every effort not to swerve my head toward her, it happens anyway. Her hair tickles my cheek. I swallow hard. "Listen to me, Holly, and heed my advice. You do not want to get involved with me. You're a sweet, if strange, woman who could have any man you want. Go back to that miniten bloke. Forget about me."

She gazes at me without blinking for a long moment. I can't resist gazing right back at her, allowing myself to drown in those mesmerizing eyes. Holly has crawled under my skin so deeply that I doubt I will ever her get out of my system. But I will not drag her into my world either. If I did, it would erase all the light and sweetness that makes her so irresistible. How can I convince Holly to give up her quest to worm her way into my life?

"I don't want to forget about you," she says. "I'd much rather get to know you, James."

She has left me no choice, and so I summon all the darkness inside me to snarl at her. "But I don't care to know you, Miss Temple. Why would I? You are a silly, fickle child who will fuck any man, even a bastard who won't show his face. Return to the playground with the other children, where you belong."

Her lips pucker. Her eyes narrow.

She wants to argue, I'm sure. That means I need to get even nastier, though the very thought of doing that turns my stomach. "I do not sleep with little girls. And I certainly have no interest in becoming your next conquest. Slags like you appeal to me slightly more than a desiccated corpse."

"Did you just call me a slut? That's what Brits mean when they say 'slag,' right?"

Why doesn't she sound angry? She should have already slapped me and stormed out of my office, but she hasn't done that.

Holly takes hold of my chin with her thumb and forefinger, forcing me to keep gazing at her. "I'm not a slut. Before I came here, I'd never done anything like what I did for the past two nights, and I won't go there again. But I know what you're trying to do, and it won't work. Your snarling and your asshole attitude aren't convincing."

"Get out of my office. Now."

"No, not yet."

She mashes her lips to mine. For several seconds, I stare into her eyes, which remain open, and struggle against a nearly overpowering impulse to thrust my tongue into her mouth, drag her onto my lap, and take her right here in my chair. My pulse beats like a drum, hard and fast, stealing my breath and my good sense. Not that I have an abundance of sense. I'm teetering on the verge of giving her exactly what she wants.

Holly peels her lips away from mine and straightens. "Think about what I've said. The only way you're getting rid of me is if you have me deported back to America."

She whirls around and marches out the door.

For precisely nineteen minutes and fifty-three seconds, a span I count on my desktop clock, I remain frozen in this chair. Holly is not as frivolous as I'd convinced myself she was. The woman refuses to give up. Why she wants me, I can't fathom. But I must never let her have her way. Perhaps I should confess all my secrets to her, so she might finally realize I'm not the sort she or any woman should get tangled up with, not even for a night of wanton sex.

I've already given Holly that. Twice.

At last, I shake off my paralysis and return to my work tasks. I can't focus, though. Holly's words keep echoing in my mind, and I seem incapable of eradicating the memory of her face hovering so close to mine, a hair's breadth from my lips—until she kissed me. Christ, those warm, soft lips, the way they molded to mine. How can I concentrate on work now? Holly has gotten her way, after a fashion. She has eliminated my brain's ability to function.

I need fresh air. To clear my mind. And to erase those moments with Holly.

After finishing up a few things, I leave my office and inform Emilio that I will be down at the beach getting a bit of exercise in the sunshine. He comments that I "could use a tan" so I don't become "as pale as Count Dracula." I casually exit the building so that Emilio won't think I'm in a hurry. I have no reason to rush, anyway. This is meant to be a soothing respite from my duties and, yes, an escape from Holly too.

As I stroll down the wooded path that leads to the beach, I take time to appreciate the scenery. A breeze rustles the leaves of the palm trees as I admire the orchids, gardenias, and other flowers that add color to the surroundings. The island also has bamboo, pine, and mangrove trees. When I accepted a job here, I had bought a book about the natural environment in this region of the Pacific, so I have no trouble identifying the species. I pass two chaps, both guests, who smile and nod to me, but I don't see anyone else in the vicinity. I've gone beyond the view of the patio, forging deeper into the forest where the only sound is the chirping of birds. The further I travel, the more I hear the hints of surf lapping onto the shore.

The tension has sifted out of me more quickly with every step I take away from the resort proper. Maybe I'll lounge on the sand for a bit and let the warmth of the sun melt away the last vestiges of my anxiety.

As I approach the periphery of the beach, I halt. A figure sits on the sand. A figure I would recognize in the pitch dark, because I have explored it thoroughly with my hands and mouth. I know that body better than I know my own. Holly Temple is the woman on the beach. She has her knees bent and her arms folded over them. I can't see much else. Though I should turn around and leave, I find myself instead skulking closer, halting near the sand but keeping myself hidden in the shadows.

Holly lies back, reclining on the sand with her body stretched out and one knee slightly bent. She combs her fingers through her hair, then skims her hands down her throat, over her luscious breasts, and lower until her fingertips graze her mound.

My breathing grows shallower. My fingers curl into my palms, and heat rushes through me. I should walk away. I mean to do that. But I can't move a muscle.

Holly arches her back, stretching her arms above her head.
And I know I'm doomed.

Chapter Ten

Holly

James must assume I don't know he's there, spying on me while I sunbathe. Considering how nasty he was to me earlier, I should yell at him to go away and quit acting like a peeping tom. But I don't want to do that. Maybe I like that he can't stop gawking at me, and maybe I even like that he's hiding behind a palm tree. Unfortunately for his snooping plans, he didn't move quite far enough away from the edge of the beach to conceal himself in the shadows.

Is it wrong that I'm getting turned on because I know he's watching me? Oh, who cares. Right, wrong, none of that matters to me when James is spying from behind a tree with his sunglasses shielding his eyes. I already knew he liked to watch me from behind those glasses, and I told him I don't mind if he does that. Today, I've realized I want him to see me.

My two nights with a mystery man had been hot. I don't want some other guy, though, anonymous or not. I want James. Something about him intrigues and arouses me. This island has affected me in the strangest ways, but I like it. Now, if I can just seduce James...

Since I know he's still watching, I decide to have some fun with him. I crawl on my hands and knees toward the water until I'm close enough that wavelets lap around me. Then I lie down again, on my back, facing the ocean. The waves tickle my skin at first, but they gradually grow larger until small breakers crash over me. I rise to my knees and turn around to give James a good view as the water sprays up around me.

He must be so horny by now.

I skim my hands over my body, then spread my thighs and slip one finger between my legs to massage my clit. Throwing my head back, I moan and rub harder, and I can still glimpse James over there. The sunlight flashes off his sunglasses. If he wants to spy, I'll give him a sizzling show. Shamelessly, I push my whole hand between my thighs and rub it up and down my cleft, pushing my fingers into my opening with every movement. The heel of my hand grinds into my nub, and my breathing grows heavier.

Laughter erupts from deeper into the woods.

Aw, shit. Guests are coming this way—unlike me. I won't be coming on this beach. Reluctantly, I trudge across the sand and follow the trail that leads back to the resort. I don't see James. The other guests nod and smile or say hello as they pass by me, and I reciprocate.

A shadow shifts among the palm fronds alongside the trail. Light glints off a reflective surface.

James. It has to be. Maybe my fun isn't over yet.

I turn down a different trail that dead-ends at a waterfall. Though I haven't visited that spot yet, I saw it listed on the map of the island that was included in my welcome packet. The resort's website features pictures of that waterfall, so I know it's a gorgeous spot. I'd rather visit that place with a friend, but in a way, I will do that. Yes, I'm hoping James will follow me there.

Maybe I should wonder about my new attitude toward a man who seems to be stalking me, but I don't believe that's his intent. James wants me as much as I want him, yet he's terrified to admit that. His nastiness earlier proved less than convincing, if he'd really been trying to chase me away. First he called me "sweet, if strange," then he turned around called me a "slag" and compared me to a dessicated corpse. Most women would probably walk away from a man like that without a backward glance. Some would slap him in the face. But me? I encourage him to spy on me.

This isn't a silly lark. I honestly want to dig deep into his psyche and figure out what makes him tick. I sense something in him that I've felt in myself too, a kind of darkness no one else would notice and that I used to try to ignore. Well, maybe darkness isn't the right word. It's a secret desire for more than plain vanilla sex.

When I reach the waterfall, I halt alongside the pool that the water cascades into and take a moment to appreciate the exotic beauty of this place. The wooden railing around the site has a rustic, natural feel that perfectly suits the setting. A towering sheer cliff rises so far above me that I think it must be at least eighty feet high. The narrow cascade pours over the edge and straight down to the pool below, pummeling the water. The turbulence generates a low curtain of mist, but lush greenery covers the rocky periphery of this hidden spot in the forest. Gorgeous flowers of types I've never seen before create bright flashes of color.

The crack of a twig snapping echoes off the rock walls that surround the waterfall.

I turn toward the trees behind me—and smile when I notice a dark shape there. James, of course. Who else would it be? Though I had intended to tease him a bit more, the way I had on the beach, now I have a better idea. Since the moment I met James, I've wanted to learn more about him, but he always wriggles out of talking to me. Or snarls his way out of it. No more. I've got him alone in the forest, and I will have my way this time.

Pretending I don't see him, I amble past the end of the prepared trail and continue a little ways into the wild woods.

"Where are you going?"

That baffled voice is familiar. I spin around. "Finally came out of the shadows, huh, James? I meant it when I said I don't mind if you watch me, but I had no idea you would take it this far."

"What? I haven't—You shouldn't be out here alone, especially off the trails. You might slip and fall into the water."

"It's really sweet of you to worry about me, but I didn't intend to go any further into the woods."

He sighs, and his entire posture sags. "Please come back to the resort with me."

"Not yet." I walk past him and glance back over my shoulder. "Come on, James. Let's admire the scenery."

"I can't convince you to leave this place."

"Nope. Might as well give in." I wait for him to catch up, then lead him to the edge of the rock-strewn river that the waterfall plummets into, which gives us a nice view of the cascade. I inhale a deep breath of fresh island air. "Isn't it gorgeous here? The air smells better, sweeter, and the water is so clear and shimmery it's almost unreal."

"Shimmery is not a word."

"Of course it is. Look it up in the dictionary, and you'll see."

"I shall take your word for it." James inches closer to the path's edge, stopping right beside me. He stares down at the water far below us. "We shouldn't stand this close to the edge."

"There's a railing. We won't fall in."

His expression turns pinched. He scratches under his shirt collar while he studies the deep, clear water.

The man really will not unclench, will he? I have more ideas about how to help him loosen up, though. "Okay, I get it. You aren't comfortable standing here. Let's find a safe spot and sit down to talk."

He jerks his head up and squints at me. "You're trying to trick me into exposing my secrets to you."

"Did I say anything about that? No. I want us to have a friendly conversation, that's all."

"We cannot be friends."

"You know I won't give up until you agree." I cross my heart with two fingers. "Promise I won't push you to talk about things you don't want to discuss. Okay?"

"I will agree on one condition." He starts unbuttoning his shirt. "You must wear this."

He shrugs out of his shirt and hands it to me, but he's still wearing a T-shirt. Am I disappointed? Yes. Surprised? Nope.

"But I'm not allowed to wear clothes," I say. "Resort rules. It's a clothes-free island."

"As general manager, I'm granting you special permission to ignore the rules."

Wow, he's uptight to the extreme. But if I want to know more about him, I need to make this one concession. I take the shirt and button it up halfway. Then I spread my arms. "Am I conversation-ready now?"

"Yes."

I let him decide where we should sit, and he guides me back down the path to a side trail that takes us across a rope bridge and onto the opposite bank of the river. We're far enough away from the waterfall that its rumble has become softer. But we've stayed close enough that we can still see the water tumbling over the edge into the pool. The fronds of a large palm tree create a canopy above us as we sit down on a grassy area alongside the trail.

I tuck my legs under me and lean against the tree. "I'll go first. Ask me anything."

James wriggles around while wincing, like he can't get comfortable. Finally, he opts for leaning back against the wide trunk of the tree. He doesn't look at me when he at last stops fidgeting. "Why did you really want to holiday on this island? All the other guests came as couples or groups of friends. But you arrived alone."

"I came alone because I wanted to escape from my life for a while. Two months ago, I found out my boyfriend of three years had been sleeping with one of my co-workers for the past six months. Randy dumped me for her." I gaze down at my lap, fingering the hem of the shirt James loaned me. "He said I wasn't adventurous enough in bed. That's bullshit. I wanted to get playful and try sex games or just a new position, but he didn't want to do it. Missionary only, that was his style."

"It was an excuse, I imagine. He wanted out."

"Yeah, obviously. Any excuse to get away from Holly." I lean my head against the tree, turning toward James. "I had another reason too."

"For escaping from your life?"

I nod. "Six weeks ago, I had a traumatic experience at work. A woman called 9-1-1 because her ex had broken in and was threatening to kill her. I let the cops know, then stayed on the line with her until the end."

James watches me in a different way now, not like he wants to spy on me as he had been doing. No, he seems interested in whatever I might tell him.

"Something happened," he says. "During that emergency call."

"Yeah." I bend my knees and wrap my arms around them. "The woman died. I sat there helplessly listening while her husband beat her to death. The cops got there thirty seconds too late. Nobody's fault, just one of those horrible things that happen way too often these days. But it wrecked me."

I bite my lip and wince from the first sting of tears that want to flow. Sniffling, I swipe at my eyes. But I can't stop the two lonely tears that slide down my cheeks.

James clasps my hand. His patience and tenderness at this moment surprises me. I sniffle again, and he digs a handkerchief out of his pocket, offering it to me.

Wiping my nose with it, I try for a smile. "Thanks. But I'm getting your pristine handkerchief all dirty."

"I don't care about that."

Since I got weepy in front of him, I feel like I should explain. "The incident with the woman caller upset me even more deeply than I wanted to admit at the time. I had nightmares for a month after that."

"You are a good woman, Holly. That's why the experience traumatized you."

"Can I ask you one question?"

He pulls his hand away and stares at the bridge. "I did agree to this. Go on and ask, but I won't tell you everything you want to know."

"Understood." I consider which question to ask first, while James avoids looking at me. Then I dive in. "Why are you so afraid to be with me? It can't be only because of my age."

He sighs and rubs his eyes. "I knew you would ask me that."

"You said you'd tell me."

"I know." He folds his arms over his chest. "Your age does bother me, Holly. You are young enough to be my daughter, and I am too old to change."

"Never asked you to change."

"But if we became involved, romantically, you would try to change me, eventually. I'm not the sort any woman should want."

"I don't understand why you're so down on yourself. Any woman would want an attractive, intelligent, professional man like you."

His mouth tightens. "You have no idea who I really am or what I've done."

"You said almost the same thing earlier. It's time to tell me. What have you done, James?"

For a moment, he sits there as still as a statue. Finally, he turns his face to me. "I destroyed myself, my family, everything that mattered to me. That's what I did. I became a pariah, hated by everyone who had ever known me."

His voice is imbued with a depth of pain and self-loathing I can't comprehend. What on earth happened to him? I want to throw my arms around him and murmur soothing words, but I doubt he would accept that.

"Will you tell me more?" I ask. "Please, I'd like to understand."

His expression has turned hard, and his body seems to be strung as taut as a tightrope. His voice becomes even snarlier when he speaks through gritted teeth. "I am a destroyer. Getting entangled with me will ruin you. I've been stalking you, Holly. You are not a potential lover or girlfriend, but only an obsession that has taken hold of me, one I can't shake off."

"I don't understand."

"And you never will." James scrambles to his feet and glares down at me. "Your stunt on the beach proves how irresponsible you are. You will never understand me, and I will not tell you anything more about my past. Stay away from me for your own good, before my obsession destroys us both."

He jogs across the bridge, disappearing from sight before I can even stop my mind from reeling. What the fuck was that? He switched from nice guy to snarling bastard in a heartbeat, all because I asked why he's afraid to be with me.

I know only one thing for certain. I've become as obsessed with James as he is with me.

Chapter Eleven

James

I break into a sprint as I leap off the bridge and pelt down the trail, heading back to the resort. I've left Holly alone in the forest. Part of me wants to go back there and make sure she's all right, but the fear overrides common sense. Why did I share anything of myself with her? Holly knows exactly which buttons to push to set me off, but I won't blame her for my behavior moments ago.

She seems determined to burrow inside me, so perhaps I should confess what I've done. Once Holly knows I'm the anonymous arse who seduced her twice, she won't want me anymore.

I turn onto the main path and start toward the resort proper, almost sprinting, breathing so hard that my ears begin to ring. Black spots appear in my vision too. I stumble into a tree, on the verge of hyperventilating, and sink down to the ground, shutting my eyes. Slow breaths, that's what I need. Relax, breathe, let my heart rate gradually decrease.

"James, what's wrong?"

Holly's worried tone makes my pulse spike again. I open my eyes and find her kneeling beside me, looking as concerned as she sounded. "I'm fine. Just needed a rest."

"Baloney." She lays a palm on my face. "You're pale and clammy."

"Go away, Holly."

"Can't do that." She picks up my trembling hand, then feels my wrist. "Your pulse is through the roof. Are you having any chest pain?"

I do not respond—mostly because I can't think, and I feel like I'm dying.

Holly clasps my face in both her hands. "I'm an emergency dispatcher, James. That means I'm trained to deal with a medical crisis until the EMTs arrive on scene. Let me help you."

I try to sit up but slide back down again. "Yes, I have chest pain. Feel like I'm dying, but I doubt I am."

"Have you had any heart problems before?"

"No."

"Any other medical issues?"

I shake my head. "I'm dizzy and nauseous too."

"You're shivering."

"It's a slight chill."

"Hmm." She's still wearing my shirt, but now she takes it off and drapes the garment over my shoulders and torso. "Before the physical symptoms hit, did you have any weird emotional reactions? A sense of impending doom or loss of control?" She checks my pulse again. "Your heart rate is coming down, and that's the only reason I'm not calling for help. I think you might've had a panic attack. But I need to know the answers to my questions before I can help you properly."

Though my first impulse is to lie to Holly, I realize that in this situation, I need to tell her the truth even if it makes me feel like a ruddy moron. "You may be right. I've had panic attacks before, though not often."

"When was the last one? Before this time, I mean."

"A few months ago." I wince. "Or possibly yesterday."

"That happened when you were driving, right? You almost crashed us into another car."

I nod, because my throat has suddenly grown tight.

She keeps hold of my wrist as she combs her fingers through my hair in a soothing gesture. It does reassure me, more than I would have expected. I close my eyes again and relax against the tree, letting her fingers ease my anxiety.

"Feeling better?" she asks. "Your pulse is almost normal now."

"Yes, I do feel better." I open my eyes to gaze straight into hers. "Thank you, Holly. You are a remarkable woman."

"Anyone with basic medical training would have done the same thing. It's not remarkable."

She keeps brushing her fingers through my hair, and her entire demeanor has transformed from wildly sensual to serious and mature, exactly what I would expect from someone who deals with people in distress every day. I might have underestimated Holly.

She sits down beside me, resting her cheek on my shoulder.

"What are you doing?" I ask.

"I figured you'd need a few minutes to compose yourself after that panic attack. How often do you have those?"

"Until a few months ago, it hadn't happened for years. I thought I'd gotten over that, but clearly I haven't."

She's naked again, but I'd barely noticed that while she triaged me or whatever medical types call it. Oddly, her lack of clothing doesn't bother me even now that I've recognized her state of undress.

"You have no reason to feel embarrassed," she says. "Experiencing panic attacks doesn't mean you've done anything wrong or that you're mentally unstable. But it can be stressful worrying about when another one might strike."

"You don't need to coddle me anymore. I'm fine now. Just exhausted."

She clasps my hand. "You need rest. Think you can walk back to the resort?"

"Yes."

Holly helps me up, and though my legs are a bit shaky, I manage to walk. I succeed in buttoning up my shirt on my own. She lays my arm across her shoulders for support. I can't believe I had another attack while Holly was with me, and maybe I do feel a touch embarrassed. But mostly, I'm grateful that Holly was here.

Did trying to forge a friendship with her trigger my panic attack?

If it did, then I have even more reason to keep her at a distance.

By the time we reach the main patio, I no longer need Holly to support me physically. She suggests, and I agree, that I shouldn't go back to work today. When we step up to the reception desk, I tell the clerk that I will be taking the afternoon off. Then I ring Emilio on my mobile and inform him too. He asks if I need to see our in-house physician, but I assure him Holly has already assessed my condition.

"Holly Temple?" he says slowly, sounding confused. "A guest treated you?"

"Miss Temple is an emergency dispatcher with medical training. I'm exhausted, that's all. Must be the stress of the grand opening. I'll be fine, Emilio. Just need a good rest."

"You do work too hard, boss. Glad Holly could be there for you."

Holly hadn't been comfortable with the idea that I would lie to my staff about my condition. But she understands why I prefer that they don't know. The grand opening causes enough stress for all of us.

Seconds after I say goodbye to Holly, Emilio enters the lobby. He stares at me as if I've grown a second head.

"What is it?" I ask.

Emilio lifts his brows. "Your shirt. It's…"

"It's what?"

Holly nudges me with her elbow. "He's shocked that your shirt is untucked."

"Yeah, boss," Emilio says. "Didn't think you knew a shirt could be worn that that way."

I'm too exhausted to complain, so I shake my head and leave the lobby. I return to my office strictly to turn off the lights and lock the door behind me. Holly insists on walking me to my bungalow, against my objections. Honestly, I didn't object that strenuously. I'm too bloody knackered to do anything but sleep. Though I try to talk Holly out of coming inside, she insists on doing that as well. The stubborn woman ushers me into the bedroom and pulls the covers back for me too.

When I collapse onto the bed, she sits on the edge near my feet and begins untying my shoelaces. "Panic attacks can happen for no reason at all, but I have a feeling yours are triggered by something terrible in your past."

"Even if that is the reason, I don't want to talk about it."

"I know." She pulls off one shoe and starts on the other, focused on her task, not even glancing at me while she speaks. "I've seen you at your worst, and I'm not running away. When will you accept that I can handle whatever it is you're struggling with?"

"You have not seen me at my worst. Not even close."

She tosses my other shoe onto the floor and shimmies closer, now sitting near my hip. "You should know by now that I can deal with just about anything."

"We will never be a couple, Holly. Give up on me."

"Can't do that." She reaches for my belt, and though I should stop her from unbuckling it, all my muscles have gone limp. "We're kindred spirits, James."

"Bollocks."

She frees my belt and tosses it onto the floor. When she reaches for the button on my trousers, I grasp her wrist to stay her hand. She pulls it away.

"Go, Holly. Enjoy your holiday in the sun."

"I will leave when you fall asleep. Then I'll come back to check on you later." She rises but leans over to kiss my forehead. "If you don't answer when I knock on the door, I'll get Emilio to let me in."

She is relentless.

Though her tits are dangling over my face, I can't muster any lust.

Holly pulls the covers over me. "Have a good nap."

Then she leaves.

I fall asleep quickly, and for once, I don't dream of Holly naked and writhing while I fuck her. I do dream of her, but this time, my subconscious haunts me with visions of us holding hands, kissing, feeding each other, laughing and talking and doing everything normal couples do. None of that can ever become reality.

When I rouse, I do feel more rested and fully recovered from my attack. But I also seem to have developed a strange ache inside me. Not another panic attack, but a longing for something that can never be.

I yearn for more than sex. I want a relationship with Holly Temple.

She will never accept that I can't give her what we both want. To watch while my darkness consumes her...that would be the worst torment of all.

I've just sat up when Holly knocks on my door. I know it's her, though I can't see through the walls. No one else would come to my bungalow unless a cyclone was about to make landfall. Since I know ignoring her will not deter the bloody-minded woman, I shuffle to the door and crack it open a few inches.

"Your patient is fully recovered," I say. "No need for a checkup."

"Let me in so I can see for myself."

"That is unnecessary. You can see I'm fine because I'm standing right here."

She chews on the inside of her cheek, which causes her lips to pucker on one side. Then she sighs. "Okay, I'll accept that. But you are under strict orders not to do anything except rest. Got it?"

"Yes, yes, I understood your command."

She smiles with sexy sweetness. "Don't order room service. I'll bring your food to you."

"Holly, that's not—"

"Don't bother telling me it's not necessary." She ruffles my hair. "I will bring you dinner. No arguments."

"Please wear clothing when you come back here. I might have a genuine heart attack if you're au naturel."

"But we're all supposed to be au naturel. That's the name of the resort, after all."

"I will beg if that would convince you to wear clothes."

She laughs in the loveliest way. "You're adorable, James."

"And you are insane."

Holly kisses my cheek and walks out the door.

I turn on the telly and try to find something to watch, to take my mind off what happened today and the fact that Holly insists on caring for me. Somehow, I must convince her to stay away. If she doesn't find another man to torment, she will keep trying to dig down through the many layers of my invisible scars until she excavates my secrets.

My gaze wanders to the windows and the pink and gold rays of the sunset that illuminate the treetops and the sky. I've never seen anything as beautiful—except for Holly.

A knock rattles my door, as if she has the psychic ability to know when I'm thinking of her. I shuffle to the door and swing it wide open.

Holly pushes a cart laden with food into the room. It's the sort of cart we use for delivering meals to guests in their suites. She is technically wearing clothes, though her outfit consists of only that dress she'd worn on the day she arrived and wore again when we took our trip to Fiji. I wave my hand to get her to release the cart, then push it over to the table in the corner by the window.

"Where did you find a cart?" I ask. "Room service is closed for the night."

"Sure, but I asked the desk clerk to please-please-please get me one of those thingies."

"You can charm the trousers off anyone, can't you?"

Holly moves closer until her body grazes mine. "There is one man who hasn't fallen under my spell."

"Please go now, Holly. I can feed myself."

"I brought food for two."

"Take your meal and leave."

"Uh-uh." She settles her lovely arse on one of the two chairs that flank the table. "We're eating together."

She believes I haven't fallen under her spell, but I have done. I've let her commandeer my life too many times, helpless to resist her smile and her sex appeal and her sweetness. But I cannot allow her to do it this time.

So I grab my portion of the meal and set it on the table, then push the cart to the door. "Take your food and go, Miss Temple."

"James, we need to talk."

"No, we do not."

I stride up to Holly and sweep her into my arms to carry her to the door. She links her hands at my nape, but I ignore that, despite my cock deciding it should wake up right now. I open the door with one hand. Holly wraps her arms around my neck more snugly. I ignore that too, setting her down just past the threshold. Then I shove the cart outside.

"Good night, Miss Temple."

I slam the door.

Chapter Twelve

Holly

James, James, James, what will I do with you? That thought had kept me awake until midnight. When I finally fell asleep, I dreamed about—what else—James Bythesea. Yeah, okay, those were dirty dreams that left me wet and achy when I woke up this morning. Despite that, I'm still kind of annoyed by the way he dismissed me last night. If he thinks I'll give up because he slammed the door in my face, that man had better find an underground bunker to hide in because yesterday only served to enhance my resolve.

I'll get under his skin, eventually. I suspect his panic attacks have an emotional trigger, since he seemed okay until I got him to talk about his past. Of course, all he told me was that he's bad news and a puny little girl like me can't handle a big, bad beast like him. Oh, come on. Does he seriously believe nonsense like that will scare me?

James isn't as beastly as he thinks.

No clothes today, no matter what the general manager thinks. This is my vacation, and honestly, that man will have to get used to seeing me naked because I will not hide in my room just so he can feel safe.

As I leave my room, I'm still mulling over how I can help him release all that pain he's hiding. Once I reach the dining hall, though, I forget about that and focus on which sweet, gooey, fattening foods I want for breakfast. *Hello, vacation.* Nobody should diet at a resort. That means I consume pancakes and bacon plus hash browns, waffles, and of course plenty of syrup. Whipped cream too. Once I'm done stuffing my face, I amble out to the patio and drop onto a chair at one of the tables. The big umbrella provides shade, and a palm tree partially conceals this corner of the patio.

Maybe that's why James doesn't notice me as he hurries across the patio, heading down the main path.

I notice him, though. And I abandon my table to follow him. He's been sort of stalking me, so I decide to do the same to him. What business could he have in the woods? Or on the beach? I doubt Mr. Uptight would go skinny dipping. Maybe he's fleeing to that spot hidden deep among the trees where I'd found him reclining on a chaise on my second day at the resort.

Keeping a discreet distance, I trail him down the offshoot path. Yep, he's returning to the scene of the crime. It absolutely is a criminal offense to let a sexy man like James hide out in the woods alone.

As I stroll into his secret hideaway, James glances up and groans. "Miss Temple—"

"My name is Holly." I drop onto the chaise beside his. "Come on, James, quit acting like we're nothing more than guest and general manager. We've shared intimate things with each other."

"Intimate? That's rubbish." He leans his head back and shuts his eyes. "I'm having a lie-down. There will be no conversation."

"No problem." I rise and swing one leg over his chaise, then settle my rump onto his thighs. "We can have sex instead."

His eyes fly open. "No, Holly."

I scoot forward until the bulge of his cock grazes my groin. "You want me. Quit pretending you don't and just fuck me, James."

He doesn't move or speak, but he's breathing harder, and he traces his tongue over his lips while staring at my tits. "Nothing has changed. You are still a child, and I am still not interested."

"You're a bad liar." I palm the bulge in his pants, which has gotten bigger since I settled onto his lap. "What's the harm in having a little fun? You are the only man I want."

"Except for that anonymous wanker who enjoyed you twice."

"Are you jealous?" I unhook the button on his pants and grasp the zipper. "I regret what I did with that man. It's always been you I want inside me."

I start to drag his zipper down.

He slaps a hand over mine to peel my fingers away. "Enough."

I slant forward, mashing my breasts to his torso, and the fabric of his shirt rasps over my nipples. The sensation feels so good that I want to beg him to take me. Instead, I bend my head so I can drag my tongue over his bottom lip. "Give in, James. You know you want to."

His hand is trapped between my groin and his jeans. I can't resist rocking my hips forward.

And he sucks in a sharp breath.

I slide a hand down to push his palm deeper into my cleft. "I need you inside me. Can't stand to go another minute without you filling me up. But you can start by petting me."

"No." His voice has grown rough, imbued with a deep hunger. "That will never happen."

I writhe against him, and his fingers dip inside my opening. "You're getting hard. Why waste a perfectly good erection? Ravish me, James."

His cheeks have turned ruddy while he seems to have trouble catching his breath.

I push all of his fingers inside me, moaning and rocking my hips, desperate for him to screw me in any way I can get him to do it.

James leaps off the chaise.

I get dumped on the ground. The back of my head smacks into the adjacent chaise.

He hoists me to my feet. "Are you injured?"

"No. My pride is a little bruised, though."

"I've told you time and again that I will never shag you. Perhaps now you'll finally believe me."

He stalks off down the trail.

Why would the fact we almost did the deed convince me that James doesn't want to "shag" me? He's floundering for any lame excuse not to give in.

I follow him back to the resort, arriving just as he slams his office door shut. The desk clerk gives me a strange look, but he has the courtesy not to ask what's going on. I'm sick and tired of James refusing to admit he likes me. We are both adults, which means we can get it on whenever we want and have no reason to feel ashamed of that.

James harbors a lot shame, I'm sure of that. But I can't think of any other way to break through his shell. Once I've done that, I hope he will finally open up to me, for real this time.

What if I've pushed him too far? James is worth the risk.

I barge into his office and kick the door shut.

He sits slumped in his chair. His hair is messy, like he might've been repeatedly shoving his hands into it. The lump in his pants is visibly bigger—and stiffer, for sure. Should I do this? He won't hurt me. I feel that in my soul, but maybe I should lure him to my room instead of doing this in his office.

Lure him? Yeah, I'm sure he'll go along with that.

No choice. It's here or nowhere.

He shoots me a dark look. "Leave, Holly. I can't protect you from me right now."

"You will never hurt me." I consider moving closer to him but decide against it. "You want me, James. Torturing yourself will only make the need worse, but I think you already know that."

He absently strokes himself through his pants and still struggles to catch his breath. His gaze flicks to my groin. He shuts his eyes and groans with a depth of need that makes my clitoris throb. "Leave now, I'm begging you."

My pulse has revved up, and I'm so slick down there that I want to rub myself to orgasm. "Stop torturing yourself, James. Just give in and do it."

For a moment, he holds perfectly still, not even blinking.

I lick my lips.

He surges out of his chair, rushing toward me, pinning me to the wall with his entire body. "You will regret this."

"No, never."

He crushes his mouth to mine in a punishing kiss, devouring me with his tongue and nipping at my lips. I hear the metallic sound as he yanks his zipper down, and I feel the smoothness of his cock rubbing against my belly. Holy shit, this is really happening. I've pushed him over the edge, and now I will experience James unleashed at last.

He fumbles to get something out of his pants pocket, then uses his teeth to open the condom packet. His chest heaves as he manages to sheath himself before claiming my mouth again. With one hand, he hoists my left leg, then hoists the right one with his other hand, all while still ravishing my mouth.

I strap my arms around his neck.

He thrusts into me so powerfully that I cry out, but his mouth muffles it. James begins carefully, seeming to employ every last shred of his self-control to keep the pace slow and steady while his cock penetrates me deeply. The feel of him inside me, gliding in and out, consuming my body in the most erotic way, it makes me struggle for breath and claw at his back. He hisses in a breath while still kissing me, and suddenly, his thrusts become wilder and faster as if that last thread of control has snapped. His hips piston like a crazed machine, pounding relentlessly while my body bounces up and down.

My orgasm thunders through me so suddenly that I don't have time to tense up in anticipation of it. I scream into his mouth and dig my nails into his back while my inner muscles grip him, and the slapping of our bodies turns almost manic. If my eyes were open, I know they would roll back in my head. The pleasure ripping through me like a tornado steals my breath and makes me feel like I'm spinning around and around inside that whirlwind.

James groans like he's never felt anything so good before. With one last brutal thrust, he blows apart inside me. Neither of us moves. We stare into each other's eyes, and his are wide like he can't believe what just happened. I probably look the same way. *Hoh-lee shit.* When James cuts that cord and unleashes all his passion, it's mind-blowing.

Eventually, he pulls out of my body and sets me down on my feet. I sag against the wall with one hand on my chest, waiting for my heart to stop hammering and my ears to stop ringing. My face feels warm, and my cream trickles down my inner thighs.

James staggers backward two steps, almost bumping into his desk in the process. His cheeks are flushed. "Holly, I—That was—"

He gapes at me.

I try to smile, but that probably makes me look drunk or dazed. "Yeah, it was incredible. We should do that again, after I've got control of my body again."

His eyes widen so much they're almost bulging. "Again? No, no, this was… I took you like a wild, rutting beast."

Of course he's panicking. I should have anticipated this reaction. But once I'd set my sights on shattering his tightly held sense of control, I hadn't thought about anything except convincing him to fuck me. James looks almost forlorn while he gazes at me, and I can't let him stand there until he topples over from the shock of what we did.

I approach him and settle my palms on his chest. "Relax, James. We had sex, it was amazing, and the world did not end because of what we did."

But I swear the earth tilted on its axis when we both came.

He rubs his jaw. "I shouldn't have let this happen."

"You didn't do anything wrong."

James peels my hands away from his chest. "Why did you push me to do this? It's wrong. You are too fucking young, and I'm too bloody damaged. Why did you do it?"

Repeating things doesn't seem like a good sign, but I believe I can help him come to terms with his own passion. "Listen to me, James."

He shuffles backward but loses his balance and crashes into his chair, falling onto the seat. "You have been pushing me toward this ever since the day we met. Why won't you leave me alone? I cannot give you whatever it is you think you want."

I kneel beside his chair. "It felt good, didn't it?"

"Shagging you like a demon? It was inexcusable."

"But you liked it." I carefully lay one hand on his, where he's gripping the chair's arm tightly. "There's no shame in admitting to the truth. I loved it. And I bet you did too."

"Why did you push me to do that?"

That's the third time he's asked, so it's time I explain. "You've been so pent up that it was driving you crazy. I mean, you had a panic attack because of one intimate conversation. Since I've seen you watching me, I know you want me as much as I want you. But I didn't make you do anything. Holding in all your passion like that, you were bound to blow your top sooner or later. I gave you more incentive to let go, that's all."

"But why? I've given you no reason to give a toss if I'm pent up."

"I care what happens to you, James. If you'll let me, I can help you."

He wrenches his hand free. "I don't need a nurse or a therapist. I need you to leave my office. Please."

"Okay. Let me know when you're ready to talk. And please call me if you feel like you're going to have another panic attack."

I kiss the top of his head and leave.

Chapter Thirteen

James

I stay slumped in my chair for fifteen minutes, gazing at the wall without actually seeing it. Holly shattered my willpower in a matter of minutes—less than that, actually. She all but begged me to fuck her, and I gave in. Maybe that had been the world's most unbelievable shag, but that doesn't make the situation any less dangerous. Not because of my panic attacks. Not because I hunger for Holly so fiercely that I've resorted to spying on her.

No, the danger comes from my past. I lost everything once, and I can't go through that again.

Someone knocks on the door, yanking me out of my semi-catatonic state. "Who is it?"

"It's me, boss."

Emilio? Perfect, that's just what I need. I glance down at my lap and realize I haven't zipped up my trousers. Worse, I forgot to remove the condom and I can still smell Holly's cream on me. I shed the condom, zip up, and hook the button on my trousers, then stand and try to compose myself. I push my fingers through my hair in an attempt to smooth it out, but my clothes still seem disheveled.

Emilio knocks again. "Everything all right, boss?"

"Yes, fine." I pull the door open. "What is it?"

He eyes me up and down, his brows rising. "Finally going semi-casual, eh? This is the second time you've left your shirt untucked."

I glance down. *Bloody hell.* I quickly tuck in my shirt and clear my throat. "Was there a reason for this interruption?"

He grimaces and clears his throat. "Well, ah, a few guests heard strange noises coming from inside your office, and they were concerned you might have, uh, had an accident."

Guests heard me fucking Holly like a maniac? *Bugger me.* I should resign immediately and fly home to... Where? I have no home anymore, except here at the resort.

"I'm fine, Emilio. Whatever they thought they heard, it was nothing."

"You sure, boss? I've never seen you, uh, looking so casual."

He's being diplomatic. I look like hell, I'm sure.

"Well, all right," Emilio says. "Glad it was nothing. But remember, we have the big outdoor luncheon today."

"Of course. I'll be there."

But I had completely forgotten about that. It's one of the biggest events we have planned for these two weeks of the grand opening, yet it slipped my mind. Why? Because I've let Holly drive me out of my head, knowing she was doing it on purpose and knowing that she believes she can save me by harassing me. It's bollocks. I need to keep my distance from her.

How many times have I told myself that?

I finish up some administrative tasks in my office, then head out to oversee the setup for the luncheon. It's more than a meal, though. We've planned an outdoor event with music, games, and prizes as well as a gourmet selection of foods from around the world. Val Silva had suggested including Brazilian offerings, since he was born and raised in that country, and the luncheon idea had blossomed from there.

As I exit the building, a terrible thought haunts me. Will this event crash and burn because of me? I trust my staff and know they can handle anything. But if I suffer another panic attack... No, I can't worry about that right now. Focus on the event. Make sure everything is just right. Those should be my only thoughts right now.

Once I reach the lawn, where guests have been playing miniten for the past few days, I realize my people have already set up the banners and decorations, and they've brought out the tables too. I halt at the periphery, and for a few minutes, I simply watch my staff getting those tables ready, both the ones that will hold the buffet and the ones where guests will eat. I insisted on padded wooden chairs, not plastic ones that will make everyone's arses hurt. My edict applies to the entire resort.

Clearly, I don't need to worry about this event. Just as I turn to walk away, my mobile rings. I don't recognize the number, but as the general manager, I can't refuse to answer. I swipe to accept the call. "James Bythesea speaking. How may I help you?"

"Wow, you sound so hot on the phone."

My fingers tighten around my mobile. "Holly? How did you get this number?"

"It's on your card. Duh."

"Oh. Yes, of course it is." I resist the urge to smack my palm on my forehead. "What do you want, Miss Temple?"

"I can practically hear you tensing up. First, you say Holly. Then you go back to Miss Temple, all in the space of eight seconds. I counted."

"What do you want?" I try not to grit my teeth, but she does not make it easy for me. "If this is a harassment call, I don't have time to play your games. We're preparing for a major event."

"Yeah, I know. I'm looking forward to the jamboree."

"It's a luncheon, not a jamboree."

"Mm-hm." She pauses, and I can hear rustling sounds in the background. "Your employees are handling everything, right? And I need some assistance, James. You're the only one who isn't busy right now. Please assist me."

Why does she keep saying the words assist and assistance? In a sultry tone, no less. "This is sheer harassment, isn't it?"

"No. It's called flirting, James."

I grunt.

She laughs. "Come on, you need a break."

From doing five minutes of work? The most meaningful thing I've accomplished today was getting a leg over with Holly. Not that it meant anything. It didn't, not at all.

"I need you, James," she says, employing that sultry tone again. "You're free right now, and I need advice."

"About what?"

"Come to me, James. I'm at your favorite reading spot."

She ends the call.

That bloody woman. What is she plotting? I should ignore her, but instead of doing that, my feet decide to take me down the main path into the forest. Before I realize what I've done, I find myself stepping into the little clearing where I have oc-casionally tried to enjoy a few moments of silence. Every time,

Holly has found me here. Today, I've come to her like an obedient puppy.

I freeze at the entrance to the clearing.

Holly lies nude on a chaise with a ray of sunlight shimmering across her body, highlighting her breasts. She looks so beautiful that for a moment I can't breathe.

Then she stretches her arms above her head and smiles. "You came."

"Attending to guests is my job."

She slides off the chaise, sashaying up to me. "You are very attentive, James, and you always know what your guests need."

"You said you required advice. About what?"

Holly spreads her palms over my chest, leaning into me. "You, of course. Advise me on how to seduce you."

"You've already done that, but it will never happen again." I pry her hands away from my chest. "I've had enough of these games."

I pivot on my heels and stomp away from her. Just as I reach the main trail, Holly trots up beside me and places her body directly in my path. I stifle a groan. "Holly—"

She lifts her heels off the ground to meet my gaze head-on. "Walk with me to the beach. Please."

"Why?"

"Relaxation."

"No thank you."

I push past her and jog up the path to the resort.

Holly catches me up as I step onto the patio. "If you won't walk with me, then let's talk."

"Piss off."

"You're being unreasonable."

I flash her a scowl. "No, that is your forte. You unreasonably expect me to do whatever you want simply because you demand it. You're behaving like a spoiled child."

"And you are acting like a pigheaded jackass."

"Go away, Holly."

She steps in front of me and folds her arms over her chest. "Not until you answer one question."

"No more games. I've tolerated your behavior for too long."

I bend over to pick her up by the waist and throw her over my shoulder. She doesn't fight or speak while I march across the patio and through the lobby in full view of three guests and the desk clerk, who gawps at me. I swiftly make my way down the corridor to Holly's suite and unlock it with my master key. Then I kick the door open and carry her to the bed where I dump her like a sack of rubbish.

Breathing hard, I glare down at her. "The games are over. For good."

She grins. "Damn, you are so hot when you go all alpha male. You really should do that more often."

I stalk out of the room, slamming the door.

Though I want to rush back to my office and hide, I refuse to do that anymore. Holly would find me there, and she would love to see me frazzled. Oddly, I don't feel frazzled. Maybe it's adrenaline, but I feel more invigorated than I have in years.

Which has nothing whatever to do with Holly.

As I pass through the lobby, the clerk at the reception desk calls out to me. I pause to glance back. "Yes, George?"

"Emilio asked me to let you know there's a problem with the big dish."

"What sort of problem? Is it burnt? Can't someone cook more of it?"

George makes a pained face. "No, sir, it's the big satellite dish. Emilio tried to explain the problem, but I don't understand that technical stuff."

Neither do I. But I try to sound reassuring for George's sake. "I'll find out what's going on. Do you know where Emilio is?"

"In his office. He just came back from the mountain."

"Leave it with me."

We have only one mountain on this island, and a bloody enormous satellite dish squats atop to provide all our internet and cellular services. My mobile still works, which suggests the problem isn't system-wide.

As if I know what the blazes I'm talking about.

I find Emilio in his office, and he explains that we have reduced internet coverage due to some sort of chip or switch malfunctioning. Most of what he says flies so far over my head that it must be in outer space. We need new whatsits, that's all I glean from our conversation. Emilio needs to help with the final setup for the luncheon, but before he leaves, we agree that I will fly to Fiji after the big event to retrieve replacements whatsits. I ring Rene to arrange for the flight.

Once I've made all the arrangements, it's time for the luncheon. Music echoes across the patio as I head for the main lawn, the sounds growing louder as I draw closer. Like the food, the music is international too, and right now the band is playing Caribbean reggae. The guests are all seated at various tables, chatting and laughing and shoving food into their mouths the way they should when they're on holiday.

I scan the vicinity for an open seat but can't find one.

Emilio approaches me. "Need a place to sit, boss? I've saved one for you."

"That was kind of you. I appreciate it."

"Sure thing. Just follow me."

I trail after Emilio as he leads me to what seems like the only table that has a chair available. When I survey the guests, my stomach drops—into the center of the earth, I think. Holly sits in the chair beside mine.

"Here you go, boss," Emilio says, pulling out the chair for me.

I thank him and gingerly take my seat.

"What a nice surprise," Holly says. "The big boss is joining the peons for a meal."

"There are no peons here. Only employees and guests."

"I know. It was a dumb joke."

While everyone around us engages in conversation and laughter, Holly insists on trying to do the same with me. I resist, naturally. Sitting beside her is temptation enough, but speaking to her is a recipe for disaster. Eventually, she gives up and talks to the woman seated on her other side. They have a boisterous conversation about the naturist lifestyle, but I can't focus on what they're saying. I'm too busy worrying about everything I've done wrong this week.

I can't go on like this. My job must take precedence over everything else, which means I cannot waste any more time on whatever Holly means to do to loosen me up. The chatter around me oddly helps clarify my thoughts, and I at last come up with a plan to save my job. I make a mental list of the steps involved.

No more shagging Holly.

No more following Holly.

No more spying on Holly.

No more spending time with Holly.

No more speaking to Holly.

No more jealousy when another man speaks to Holly.

Perhaps my list is a bit anal and somewhat disturbing, but I know the rules I've set for myself will allow me to move on from whatever I've been doing with that woman. I'm grateful to Eve and

Val for taking a chance on me, and I will not ram a wrecking ball through the opportunity I've been granted.

Holly Temple is nothing more to me than another guest.

After everyone has eaten, the games begin. I take that as my cue to politely exit the festivities. I need to meet Rene at the airstrip soon, anyway, so I can't stay even if I wanted to do that. The guests have been gracious so far about the internet being spotty today, but they will grow restless soon. We need to fix the satellite dish.

After returning to my office to check my email, I make my way to the airstrip. Rene is waiting for me. I climb into the back-seat, though he offers to let me sit in front. I prefer to ride in the back, alone, with only my thoughts to occupy my time. After ten minutes of sitting here, I realize Rene still hasn't started up the engine.

"Is something wrong?" I ask. "We should be taking off, shouldn't we?"

He twists around in his seat to look at me. "No worries, mate. We're waiting for the other passenger, that's all."

"What other passenger? This flight is strictly a supply run to get the whatsits we need to fix the big dish."

"Emilio called while I was waiting for you. A guest begged to be let onto this flight."

The door is thrown open, and Holly climbs into the plane.

Bloody hell.

Chapter Fourteen

Holly

I smile brightly as I take a seat beside James. "Hey there, stranger. Hope you don't mind sharing the backseat with me. I was in the mood for another plane ride, so I can see the whales again, hopefully. Aren't they the most beautiful creatures you've ever seen?"

James squints his eyes but doesn't grumble or tell me to "piss off," like he did earlier. "We have individual seats. You make it sound as if we're sharing a bench. And you might not see whales at all. But you will certainly miss out on the festivities here."

"Don't care. I'd like to come along, but if you really don't want me to, I'll go back to the resort."

He studies me for a moment while Rene starts up the engine. Even while we pull on our headsets, he keeps watching me.

I settle into my seat and glance out the windows.

James points at my body. "Is that dress the only clothing you brought with you to the resort?"

"No. I also have my grimy sweats I wore during the whole, incredibly long, cramped and stuffy airline flight."

"I see." He puckers his lips briefly, then sighs. "I could drop you off at a clothing store so you can shop, while I go to the electronics shop to get those whatsits that we need for the satellite dish."

"Whatsits?"

"The computer rubbish. I don't claim to understand it, but we need chips or circuits or some such thing to get our internet service working at full capacity again."

I can't help smiling. He is unbelievably adorable when he's confused by technology. "If you don't understand it, how will you know which whatsits you need?"

"Emilio gave me a detailed list. And he rang the electronics shop to make sure they would have all the bits and bobs."

"Technology really isn't your thing, is it?"

He sags against his seat. "No. I can manage my mobile phone, but I'm useless with most other technology."

"You've had forty-five years to get used to it."

"When I was born, there were no smart phones and the internet did not exist."

"Good point." I nudge him with my elbow. "I think you're doing remarkably well considering how ancient you are."

One side of his mouth ticks up into a slight smirk. "Thank you, Miss Temple, for that ringing endorsement."

I lay a hand on his thigh. "I like it when you tease me. It means you aren't as uptight as you think."

His gaze lowers to his leg, where I still have my hand resting on it. His face crimps just enough to accentuate the lines around his eyes.

I pull my hand away. "Sorry. I didn't mean to get overly tactile with you."

"Overly tactile? You don't speak the way most people your age do."

"My parents raised me to be a lady, not a social media whore. I don't even like social media."

"You don't?"

"That's a sinkhole I don't want to get sucked into."

He stares at me like I've said something shocking.

Rene twists his head around to look at us and grin. "You two are a great couple."

James rolls his eyes and focuses on the view outside his window.

I try to change the subject. "Do you think we'll see whales today?"

"Never can tell," Rene says. "You might get lucky."

Oh, I got lucky this morning for sure. But I won't mention that to Rene.

I don't pester James for the rest of the flight, instead focusing on the view and searching for a sign of humpback whales. We don't see any, though. Once we land at Suva-Nausori International Airport, James commands me to "stay right there" and jumps out before I can ask him why I should do that. I find out seconds later when he pulls my door open and offers me his hand, helping me exit the plane.

And he keeps a hand on my back as we walk to the car that's waiting for us. James is a gentleman at heart, whether he believes that or not.

He takes the driver's seat. I slide in on the passenger side, leaning over to kiss his cheek.

"What was that for?" he asks.

"Behaving like a gentleman. It's rare these days." I remember the last time he drove a car, and I need to ask a question he probably won't like. "Are you sure you're okay to drive? Things went sideways the last time."

"Today is different."

"How?"

"Because it is."

I give up and admire the scenery while we drive through the town of Suva. "Let's go to the electronics store first."

"The plan was to drop you at the clothing shop."

"Plans change. I want to stay with you."

He compresses his lips. "You won't have any fun at a shop full of technical rubbish."

"I can have fun anywhere, anytime."

"Yes, I have noticed that."

We lapse into silence, and I go back to examining the buildings and the landscape. The South Pacific is nothing like what I'd expected when I signed on for a naturist vacation. Fiji reminds me of Southern California in some ways, not that I've ever spent much time there. I suppose it's the green mountains and palm trees that make me feel that way.

Our visit to the electronics store doesn't take much time. James buys all the doohickeys he needs, and we leave the store ten minutes later. He wants to head back to the airport, of course. The man is allergic to taking time off.

"We need to fix the satellite dish," he tells me when I suggest a slight detour. "You said you don't want to visit the clothing shop, so it's time to leave."

"And then you'll go back to work."

"This is my job, Holly. I can't play silly buggers with you every day."

I barely manage to stifle a laugh. "When did you ever do that?"

We've just parked the car, about to traipse across the tarmac to the plane in which Rene waits for us. I settle a hand on James's thigh and massage it. "Play with me, please. Just for a little while."

"Can't. The resort needs me."

"We had so much fun this morning in your office. I wish you could be like that all the time."

He turns his head toward me, but his sunglasses conceal his eyes. "No, Holly, you do not want me to behave that way again. I have…darkness inside me that would taint you."

James thrusts his door open and stalks toward the plane without even waiting for me to get out. By the time I catch up, he's already buckled into his seat. I get buckled up just as Rene starts the engine.

For the entire trip back to Heirani Motu, he stares out the window and refuses to look at or speak to me.

I hit a nerve, but I have no idea how I did that. All I said was that I wish he could always be like he had been this morning in his office. When James let go of his inhibitions, it had been amazing. He hides all that passion deep inside himself, but I still can't figure out why. Here in the plane with Rene is not the time to discuss James's hang-ups.

He leaps out of the plane the second we've landed and the engine has shut down.

I race to catch up to him. "Slow down, James."

Naturally, he ignores me. Are all British men this pigheaded? He's the only one I've ever met, so I can't answer that question. I decide to let him ignore me for a while and strip off my clothes as I head for the miniten court. The games have all ended. I take a walk, then get a cupcake in the dining hall. None of that distracts me for long. My thoughts keep returning to James Bythesea.

But I'm not thinking only about sex. The more time I spend with him, the more I need to understand him. Will he let me? Not voluntarily, that's for sure. I've had minimal success in getting him to open up.

Time to try again.

I knock on his office door.

"Come," he says in that sexy voice.

Does he realize how much I want to screw him when he speaks the word come? He could say "sauerkraut," and even that would make me hot for him.

I open the door and slip inside, shutting it behind me.

James exhales a long sigh, slouching in his chair. "What now, Miss Temple?"

"Let's talk."

"Unless it's related to my job, I don't have time for a chat."

I park my rump on his desk. "You really need to unload all that darkness you think you have inside you. Let me be the vessel that carries it all away."

"That's a ruddy awful metaphor. Darkness can't be whisked away like a package in the mail."

"Okay, maybe I'm not the best at metaphors, but you know what I'm saying." I slant forward, laying a hand on his cheek. "Let me help you. Share your darkness with me."

"It's darker and deeper than you could possibly imagine."

Jeez, he is outrageously stubborn. I slide onto his lap and link my hands at his nape. "Tell me anyway. I want to know you. And don't insult my intelligence by claiming I couldn't possibly understand. I've dealt with people at their absolute worst. I've talked them through the most horrific situations, but I didn't let that ruin my life. I'm uniquely qualified to be your counselor."

He sits perfectly still, his gaze locked on mine.

I sink deeper into his lap and rest my cheek on his shoulder.

Every muscle in his body seems to relax instantaneously, as if he flipped a switch inside himself. He rests one hand on my hip. "You are an unusual woman."

"Thank you. I wouldn't want to be boring or normal." I nuzzle his neck. "You aren't boring or normal either. That's why we're good for each other."

"Perhaps we are." He lifts his free hand to comb his fingers through my hair. "I've done things I wish I could forget. Did them for the right reasons, I thought. But I wound up destroying everything and everyone I loved."

Is he actually about to share some of his secrets with me? I won't mess it up by speaking. He needs to do this in his own time.

James rubs his eyes and grimaces. "I had a wife and two children. Now, they're all gone."

"Oh God. What happened to them?"

"They are not dead." He wraps his arms around my waist, tugging me a smidge closer. "They left me. Couldn't stand to live with me anymore. My wife divorced me and left England, taking our children with her. They hate me as much as she does."

I hadn't meant to speak up a minute ago. Should I keep talking? Not sure what the best tactic is right now. So I go with my gut instinct. "When was the last time you saw your family?"

"Five years ago. I have no idea where they are these days. But my children would be adults now." He squeezes his eyes shut. "Shannon would be twenty, and Adrian would be twenty-three. Sometimes I wonder what they're doing, what they studied at university, but I will never know."

"Why not? Can't you contact them?"

He lets his head fall back against the chair but keeps his eyes shut. "No, I can't. For reasons I would rather not discuss right now, I will never be able to find them even if I wanted to do that."

I ask my next question carefully. "What did you do that was so horrible your family left you?"

Are his lips trembling? I think they might be. Whatever went down all those years ago must have been truly horrific.

James opens his eyes and pulls in a sharp breath. "I thought I could do this, but I'm not ready yet. I'm sorry."

"Don't apologize. I can wait." I clamber off his lap. "Thank you for telling me about your family."

He gazes at me with a question in his eyes. "You honestly don't mind that I stopped short of telling you everything?"

"Of course not. It's your story, and you should share it in your own time. I'll see you later."

I walk out the door.

But it swings open again.

When I turn around, James is looking at me with so much pain in his eyes that I long to pull him into my arms and just hold him.

He clears his throat. "I, ah, wondered if you might…have dinner with me."

"I'd love to."

The man looks so adorably relieved that I can't stop myself from smiling.

He scratches his cheek while avoiding my gaze. "We could have dinner in your suite. I'll bring the food."

"Sure. Can't wait for our first date." I wince. "Sorry. I shouldn't assume that's what you meant."

"It is what I meant. I'll be there at eight."

He closes the door slowly, as if he's having trouble letting me go. That too is completely adorable. James is a much sweeter man than I ever realized until today.

Only after I've returned to my suite do I remember I should have asked a question. Does James want me to dress for dinner? Or should I stay nude, according to the resort's rules? Since he didn't urge me to wear clothes, I'll assume I don't need to do that. I know he likes me naked.

When will I get to see him in the buff? I've barely even gotten a glimpse of his dick. Something about our encounter this morning felt familiar, though I can't figure out in what way. But that's crazy. I'd never been with James before.

I do yoga in my suite, trying to chill out despite the excitement that rushes through me every time I think about my dinner with James. I take a shower after that, then blow-dry and style my hair. For my last bit of coiffing, I slap on a bit of makeup and some vanilla-scented body lotion. Women's magazines often claim vanilla is a scent that will drive a man wild. Tonight, I'll find out if that's a myth.

Not that I plan on seducing James tonight. After our conversation earlier, I think we should stick to eating and talking.

Three crisp knocks rattle my door at exactly eight o'clock.

I swing the door open a second later, since I might have been sort of waiting there for James to show up.

He offers me a bouquet of gorgeous purple flowers. "Dendrobium orchids, just for you."

"Wow, thank you." I take the bouquet and lift the flowers to my face so I can inhale their scent. "Mm, they smell like honey."

"Nothing could smell as good as you do."

Warmth flushes my skin from head to toe.

Maybe I will seduce him tonight after all.

Chapter Fifteen

James

Holly steps aside to make way for the cart of food I'm pushing across the threshold. I halt just inside the room and glance around. "Where shall we dine?"

Her cheeks dimple as a smile lights up her face. "Dine? I can honestly say no one has ever asked me that question before. I've been asked where I want to eat, but never where I shall dine."

"You're mocking me."

"No. I think you are the absolute cutest." She waves toward the patio. "We shall dine on the terrace, my lord."

She is mocking me, but in an affectionate way. I can't believe I asked her to have dinner with me. I shouldn't be doing this, not with Holly, not when I am the wrong man for her. But I couldn't stop myself. When Holly climbed onto my lap, I forgot all the reasons why she belongs with anyone else but me.

I will not shag her tonight. This is a friendly meal, nothing more.

As I push the cart out onto the patio and set about moving the plates and bowls and all the other accouterments onto the table, I try my damnedest not to look at her nude body. I've seen her naked every day since the moment she arrived on the island, but somehow, I feel even more uncomfortable with her lack of clothing tonight. I've fucked Holly three times, yet that hasn't made me any less awkward around her the rest of the time.

Perhaps I should confess. Not tonight. I need a little more time with her before she realizes I'm a bastard.

I pull a chair out for Holly.

She smiles again as she settles onto the seat. "Thank you, James. You're very thoughtful."

"My mum drilled it into my brain that a man should always treat a lady with respect and deference."

"Are your parents still alive?"

I drop onto my chair, on the opposite side of the table, and scoot it forward while I conspicuously avoid answering her question. Perhaps I am hoping she won't notice, or at least won't press me for an answer.

"Well?" she says. "Are your parents living? Mine are. They live in Florida."

"I assume that means they're retired."

"Oh no, they still work. Dad is a sheriff's deputy, and Mom works for a local fashion designer."

Now I must tell her the truth. She volunteered information about her family, and only an arse would refuse to reciprocate. I focus on removing the lids from the containers of food as an excuse not to look at her. "My parents are living as well, but they want nothing to do with me."

"Because of whatever that horrible thing was that you did?"

I mumble something that isn't quite a response to her question.

"Relax, James, I'm not interrogating you. We're having a conversation. If you aren't comfortable answering my question, that's fine."

I grab the bottle of wine I'd brought and struggle to remove the cork, wincing and grunting from the effort. "Bloody stupid bottle."

Holly snatches it away and easily uncorks the bottle. She hands it back to me. "There."

"Ah, thank you. I'm not usually so inept."

She laughs, and the light, sweet sound makes my throat go thick. Holly seems not to notice my reaction. "You aren't inept. You're nervous. It's been a long time since you had a date, huh?"

"I think the dinosaurs were still alive the last time I had dinner with a woman."

"Oh please. You aren't that old." She holds out her glass while I pour wine into it. "Would you feel more comfortable if I put on some clothes?"

"That won't help. I've memorized your body, and whenever I shut my eyes, I can't stop myself from visualizing every inch of you."

She pauses with her glass hovering millimeters from her lips. "For a guy who hasn't dated since the Jurassic period, you sure know how to sweet-talk a girl."

"Was that sweet-talking? I thought I was babbling rubbish that would make you want to slap me."

She sips her wine and slowly licks her lips. "You honestly have no idea how hot you are, do you?"

"I'm a bumbling idiot."

She stretches her hand out to grasp mine. "James, you are the sexiest man I've ever seen. And when we got it on in your office this morning, I came so hard I think I actually left my body for a minute. You did that. Stop denying your passion and set yourself free."

"What happened this morning was…an aberration."

"No, it was the real you." She strokes the back of my hand with one finger, teasing my skin and awakening my cock. "The next time we have sex, I'd love to take your dick in my mouth to lick and suck and devour the flavor of you."

I cough into my fist, then grab my wine glass and down the entire contents in one long gulp.

"Take a breather," she says, "before you choke on that delicious pinot grigio. Wouldn't you rather die during sex than while guzzling wine?"

"There is no good way to die. It's oblivion either way."

She studies me for a moment while still stroking the back of my hand. "I want to ask you more questions, but I'd bet every penny I have that you aren't ready to tell me the rest yet."

"You would be correct."

"I can't help wondering what happened to you." She retracts her hand. "But I won't push."

"You only push when you want me to fuck you."

Holly takes a bite of her food and chews it slowly while keeping her gaze on me. "Mm, this food tastes like heaven. But I bet you taste even better."

She tastes better than any dish ever crafted by any chef in the world. But I can't tell her that. She has no idea I've devoured her and made her come while I had her pinned to a palm tree and the stars glittered overhead. If I confessed what I've done, would she forgive me?

You are a one-man wrecking ball, James, and you will always destroy what you claim to love. No woman will ever want you again, including me.

The words my ex-wife had spoken to me once, years ago, reverberate through my mind in a never-ending cacophony I cannot block out. Yes, Holly will come to despise me. My wife had been my age, and we had children to keep us together. But it didn't work out that way. A young, vibrant woman like Holly deserves far better than to tie herself to a human wrecking ball.

I've already set that ball in motion. It's too late to stop the inevitable.

"Are you okay?" she asks. "You look a little green around the gills."

"Let's eat."

I dive into my meal to avoid any further conversation, but Holly won't let me off that easily. She insists on trying to engage me in chitchat by talking about the other guests and all their supposedly humorous antics. I might find her stories entertaining if I weren't consumed by the realization that I cannot have her in any meaningful sense. For sex? Yes, I can have her that way. But in a relationship? No, I won't do that. Holly deserves better.

Once we finish our meal, I clear the table and push the cart over to the door. As I reach for the knob, though, Holly grasps my hand.

"Don't go yet, please. Stay for a little longer."

"That's a bad idea."

"Why?"

I gaze into her eyes, wanting desperately to pull her into my arms and kiss her. "I'm toxic, Holly. That's all you need to know."

"Then what was dinner about? If you have no intention of letting me get to know you, why ask me out on a date?"

"I shouldn't have used that word. We are not dating."

She plants her hands on her hips. "You're panicking because we got a little closer tonight, and that scares you. But I won't give up on you, James. You're worth fighting for."

Holly opens the door for me.

I push the cart out into the hallway, then pause to glance back at her.

She lunges forward to take my face in her hands and touch her lips to mine. "You *are* worth fighting for."

Holly shuts the door.

A strange tingling sensation sweeps over me from head to toe, raising the hairs on my arms and my scalp. I've never experienced anything like this before. It isn't unpleasant. In fact, it feels…good. Holly swore I am worth fighting for, and said it twice, with even more conviction the second time.

Holly believes in me.

I return the cart and dishes to the kitchen and go back to my bungalow. Though I expect to have trouble sleeping, after what Holly said to me tonight, I instead fall asleep almost as soon as my head meets the pillow. For once, I don't suffer from nightmares of past mistakes and how those actions might affect my future. No, I dream of Holly. Sweet, kind, determined Holly who wants to save me.

Despite my epiphany last night, I know that becoming a better man won't happen instantly. It will take time. I will cock it up on occasion, but with Holly there to guide me, perhaps I can change.

Should I admit to Holly that I tricked her?

A lump forms in my throat when I consider the implications of confessing. My mind insists on forcing me to envision the worst possible outcomes, but for once, I ignore that and choose optimism. I will explain to Holly why I deceived her and apologize for it. She'll understand. Holly forgave me for acting like an arse, growling and insulting her repeatedly, so I doubt she will tell me to piss off.

For the first time since the grand opening, I spend most of the day outside of my office, helping my employees and taking care of any guest complaints that require a general manager's expertise to resolve. I catch glimpses of Holly throughout the day, and she seems to be having fun. She always finds a way to enjoy life, no matter what.

She is wonderful.

When I seek her out to ask if she will have lunch with me, I find her sitting at a table on the patio chatting to the bloke I've seen her with before. I think his name is Kevin. Though I experience a twinge of jealousy—because she's leaning over to touch Kevin's arm while speaking to him—I manage to overcome the envy. Holly wants me, not him.

She glances up when I reach their table. Then she smiles with such joy that I can't resist the urge to return that expression. Her smile broadens. "James, you're in a good mood today. It suits you."

I'm not in a good mood. I feel bloody fantastic. But I won't admit that in front of what's his name. "Holly, do you have plans for lunch? I imagine you two want to dine together."

Kevin rises and walks past me, giving my arm a light slap. "I've got a lunch date with Sophie, so Holly's all yours."

The woman herself approaches me, hooking her arm around mine. "I am all yours, James. How do you want me?"

Naked. Writhing. Slick with sweat and begging me to—

She pokes me with her elbow. "I can tell what you're thinking, but I was talking about lunch. Where would you like to eat? The dining hall, the patio, my room, your bungalow…"

"I was thinking of a picnic on the beach."

"What a great idea." She wraps her arm more tightly around mine. "Now, the big question. Do we swim before we eat?"

"Well, ah…I don't swim."

"Don't or can't?"

"I dislike swimming."

"Maybe the problem is that you've never gone swimming in the ocean with me."

"Let's just have lunch on the beach this time. I'm not prepared for frolicking in the ocean. I don't even own a swimsuit."

"Frolicking?" She kisses my cheek. "Are you sure you didn't time travel here from the Victorian era?"

She thinks I'm stuffy. I am, of course.

Except when I make love to Holly.

We go into the main building to gather the supplies we'll need for our meal on the beach. I made sure the resort would have picnic baskets on hand for any guests who wanted them. Maybe that's a bit silly, but it turned out I was right. Guests do prefer the traditional picnic gear. Once we've stuffed our basket with food, we hike out to the beach. Several couples are there already, swimming and sunbathing, laughing and having a good time.

I want Holly all to myself.

That means I drag her down the beach until I find a little spot that offers enough privacy that I doubt anyone else will stumble onto our picnic. I spread out a blanket. Holly brings out the food.

We are having our second date.

I'm dating Holly Temple, and I don't feel the slightest bit anxious about that.

Chapter Sixteen

Holly

I stretch out on our blanket and let the sun toast my skin while a temperate breeze kisses my body. I'd much rather feel James's lips on me, but I don't think he's up for sex on the beach—not yet. I haven't felt this happy in a long time. No, that's not true. I've never felt this good before, and it's all because of James.

I asked him if he would help me slather on sunblock, and he actually said yes. Of course, he accomplished the task while barely touching me, and he didn't try to cop a feel. *Damn.* I wanted him to get handsy with me. I'm not surprised he wouldn't feel me up, though.

"Will the food keep?" I ask. "I'd love to take a dip in the ocean first."

"Go on, then. The meal will survive."

I roll onto my side, facing him. "Is there any chance I could convince you to take off your clothes and join me in the water? Nobody else will know you did it. This is a secluded spot."

He shifts uncomfortably on the sand. "I don't know about that."

"Oh, come on, James. You are a wild man at heart. Our time in your office proved that."

"Go on and enjoy your swim."

Well, I didn't really expect him to strip naked and do a belly-flop into the ocean. A girl has to try, though. How else will I know when he's ready to shed the rest of his inhibitions? *One step at a time, or you'll scare him away.*

I wade out into the water and stand here for a moment, enjoying the feel of the wavelets lapping against my calves. When I move a little further out, I can't resist sinking into the waves and floating on my back, while the water rises and falls around me. The gentle motion lulls me into a state of intense relaxation that allows me to revel in the sounds and sensations.

After a few minutes of that, I open my eyes to check on James. He's still sitting on the beach, but instead of kicking back, he's watching me with an intensity that seems more like worry than lust. I return to the beach and sit down beside him.

"What were you doing out there?" he asks. "You closed your eyes as if you were asleep. What if you had drowned?"

"You would have saved me. But I wasn't asleep. I was enjoying this beautiful day."

He flips up the lid on the picnic basket and starts rooting around in there. "You shouldn't float that way. The ocean might drag you out to sea."

"It's sweet of you to worry about me, but I've been taking care of myself for a long time. I don't think being swept out to sea is very likely."

"Perhaps not. But unlikely things can bite you in the arse when you least expect it."

I watch him while he brings out our meal—sandwiches and potato chips, plus bottles of water and something else that's hidden inside a semi-opaque plastic container. He carefully places each item on the blanket. I don't think he has a hang-up about the placement of food. Instead, I'm pretty sure he's using setting up our picnic as an excuse to avoid looking at or talking to me.

Like that will work.

"Are you always this meticulous?" I ask. "You haven't seemed like that type before now."

"What would you like me to say?"

"The truth."

He lays down napkins, then smooths them out as an excuse to keep avoiding my gaze. "Despite what films and books tell you, the truth will not set anyone free."

"That's a depressing statement."

"It's realistic." He hands me a sandwich, finally looking me in the eye. "May I ask you a question?"

"Of course. You can ask me anything."

While I take a bite of my sandwich, he gazes straight at me for a moment, as if he's thinking through his question before speaking. "Why have you been so determined to get to know me?"

"I told you why. We're kindred spirits."

"But you have yet to explain what that means. It's rubbish, anyway. You are nothing like me."

I chew another mouthful of food while he goes on observing me. "We are alike in the ways that count. Both kind of lost, searching for something to anchor us. And we've both experienced traumatic things."

"Your past is nothing like mine."

"How do you know? I'm not close with my parents, and I get the impression you aren't close with yours either." I unscrew the cap on my water bottle and guzzle some of it, suddenly wishing James had brought a bottle of wine instead. "I needed to escape, which is why I came here, and you seem like you're escaping from something too. Your wife and kids abandoned you, and my ex dumped me for no good reason."

"Did you love him?"

I shrug one shoulder. "Thought I did. But eventually, I realized I needed things that he had no interest in providing. You know, like commitment and support. He always criticized me for wanting to have fun. But I was still shellshocked when he suddenly walked away."

"None of this explains your fixation with me."

"Fixation? I care about you, James."

He rips off a huge mouthful of his sandwich with his teeth and gnaws on it. But he keeps watching me. I finish off my sandwich while waiting for him to respond to what I said.

James bends one knee to rest his arm on it. "You shouldn't care about me."

"Give me a concrete reason why I shouldn't. 'I'm a jerk' isn't a valid explanation."

"Your story has no relevance to mine. We are not kindred spirits."

I slap my hand down on my beach towel. "No more vague bullshit. Explain it to me."

His expression becomes pinched. "I can't explain, but perhaps I can show you."

I can't imagine how he'll do that, but his statement does make me very curious.

James unbuttons his shirt, then waddles around on his knees to turn his back to me. He lets his shirt fall down to his waist, held up by his arms. Five roundish discolored areas form a haphazard pattern on his skin.

"What is this?" I ask, leaning forward to get a better look.

"Scars."

"Were you burned?"

"No."

I touch one of the scars, and he flinches a touch. "What happened to you?"

He pulls his shirt up and buttons it, waddling around again to face me. "I was shot five times in the back."

"What?" I must be gaping at him. Can't help it. "Was it a drive-by shooting or something?"

"No. It was…" He bows his head. "An assassination attempt."

I absolutely am gaping at him now. Assassination? Why would anyone want to murder James? My voice refuses to function, so I can't ask him to explain.

He buttons up his shirt. "Please don't ask me anything else. I—I can't talk about it."

"Okay," I say carefully. "Good lord, James, I'm so sorry."

"For what? You didn't fire the gun."

Even though he buttoned up his shirt, I can still see those scars in my mind. "I'm sorry because what you just told me is horrible. But I think I finally understand why you've had panic attacks. Post-traumatic stress can be brutal. I've dealt with people who suffered from that in my job, and it can be hard to talk them down from the cliff."

"Could we change the subject, please?"

"Sure, yeah." I still can't wrap my head around his revelation. *Assassination.* That word keeps echoing in my head. "Um, would you like to go back to the resort now?"

"Only if you want to. We can finish our meal first, though."

I reach out to clasp his hand. "I wish I could erase all your pain. Knowing you have such deep wounds… Well, I want to help you if I can. Thank you for sharing this with me."

He bows his head again and mumbles something. I don't think it was actually words. Talking about his past made him lose the power of speech. And I suddenly feel as if I should share a few things with him in return.

"I haven't ever been shot," I say. "But I was more disturbed by what happened on my last 9-1-1 call than I let on the first time I told you about it."

"You are under no obligation to share anything with me."

"But I want you to know." I eat some more food while I work up the courage to tell him the rest. "I kept talking to the caller even while her husband was beating her and she was screaming. I couldn't think of anything else to do, and I guess I hoped hearing my voice might… I don't know. Give her a small measure of comfort. That's dumb, I know."

"No, it isn't. You did the only thing you could under the circumstances."

"Yeah, maybe." I pick at my sandwich but toss away the bits without eating them. "I told you I had nightmares after that experience. But I left out the part where I quit my job the next day. I needed to get away, needed it so badly. That's why I spent most of my life savings on this trip."

"Has this island cured you of your bad memories?"

"The island hasn't. You have. Maybe I'm not cured, but I feel lighter and freer ever since I met you."

"You've got that the wrong way round. You healed me, Holly."

"Maybe we healed each other."

He kisses me sweetly, holding his lips to mine for several seconds. "You may be right. But let's not discuss the past anymore today."

"Sure."

We finish our picnic in silence, but it doesn't feel awkward. Instead, not speaking seems like the most natural thing in the world, and it gives us the opportunity to gaze into each other's eyes. We exchange smiles too, and we "accidentally" bump our hands into each other. Every time I catch James peeking up at me with his head down, his lips curl into the cutest bashful smile. Then he swerves his gaze away.

As he's packing up the remains of our picnic, I ask, "Sure you don't want to take a dip in the ocean? The water feels deliciously cool."

"Perhaps another time."

Did he suggest he might go swimming with me later? In the nude? Well, he would probably insist on wearing swim trunks. Hmm, I wonder if I could convince him to buy swim briefs—the super tiny kind that would stick to his body like a second skin.

If he at least doesn't wear a Victorian-style bathing suit, I'll mark that as a milestone.

James holds my hand as we stroll back to the resort. When we go our separate ways on the big patio, he kisses my cheek. And as he walks away, he keeps glancing back at me over his shoulder while smiling in that sweet, bashful way again. No matter how many times he tells me he's no good for me, I know the truth. I see it in his smile and feel it when he holds my hand.

I spend the afternoon playing miniten and lounging on a chaise in a little spot I found in the forest where the fronds of several palm trees form a canopy overhead. I lie here listening to the sound of the surf in the distance and the songs of tropical birds. It's relaxing, for sure. But when I doze off briefly, I dream of James.

Naughty dreams, of course. That man makes me so horny.

Kevin and his friends invite me to have dinner with them in the dining hall, but I order room service in my suite instead. When I hear that knock on the door, I know my food has arrived. But when I swing the door open, I grin.

"James, it's you."

"Yes. Were you expecting someone else?"

"Well, yeah. The general manager isn't supposed to deliver my din-ner." He has a cart full of lid-covered dishes beside him, and the smell of all that yummy food makes my tummy rumble. "Not that I'm com-plaining, but how did you know I ordered dinner in my room?"

"I bumped into the bloke who was delivering your food and of-fered to take over the task."

"Nobody says no to the big boss, hey?" I step back so he can push the cart into the room. "Are you strictly delivering the food? Or will you stay to share the meal?"

"You ordered enough for at least two people. If you wouldn't mind sharing…"

I shut the door and fling my arms around him. "I'd love to have dinner with you again."

"Where should we eat? The patio again?"

"Nope." I nod toward the bed. "Over there."

"We will get crumbs on your bed."

"Don't care." I finger the second button on his shirt. He has the top button already unhooked, so I release another one and trail my fingertip over the small area of his chest that I've revealed. "Why don't you undress? Then it won't matter if we spill food on our-selves. I can lick up every last bit that clings to your body."

He clears his throat and fidgets against me. "I don't think I can do that."

"Why? Because you're bashful?"

"No, of course not."

I unhook another button. "Come on, James. Please let me see you naked. We don't need to have sex unless you beg me for it."

"Holly…"

"We could eat our food off each other's bodies." I slide my hand down to his waistband to unhook the button there, then move my hand lower to lay my palm over the growing bulge in his pants. "We want each other like crazy. No one will ever know what we do inside this room. So take your clothes off and crawl into bed with me, James. I want to devour my meal off your naked body."

His chest is rising and falling with every labored breath he takes, and that bulge I'm palming has enlarged even more. Soon, he'll be hard and ready to go.

I walk my fingers up his body to his chest. "What do you say?"

He picks me up and stalks over to the bed, dropping me onto it. "I say yes."

Chapter Seventeen

James

I stand at the bedside, gazing down at Holly while my cock thickens and my breathing grows even more labored. Of course I want her. I've never experienced this kind of lust with anyone else, and Holly knows exactly how to push me to the edge of sanity. I need to fuck her. The power of that compulsion overrides common sense. She wants me to consume food off her body, but I know that will result in me shagging her like a maniac.

With Holly, I always lose control. But she must understand what my past has done to me before I strip and join her on the bed.

I take a step backward. "Listen to me, Holly."

She links her hands above her head and shimmies her hips. "I'm all ears, James."

With every iota of my willpower, I resist the urge to tear my zipper open and mount her like a wild animal. "Stop trying to seduce me and listen. I can't be tender or gentle, and I have needs that you might not understand. I don't understand them, because I've never needed or wanted this before I met you."

"There's nothing you could say or do that would shock me or make me want to back out. So get naked and screw me, any way you need to do it."

"What if I…restrain you."

Her mouth slides into a sensual smile. "Go for it."

"You might change your mind once you realize the reason why I need to do this."

"If you mean tying me up, I'm not as clueless about your motivations as you think." She sits up and claims my hand. "You need to be in control."

"Yes. But how did you know?"

She rises to her knees and splays her palms on my chest. "I figured that out because it's obvious. You're uptight and afraid of intimacy."

For a moment, I simply stare at Holly. She understands me after a few days. She wants me, despite witnessing my humiliating weakness when I suffered panic attacks. I showed her my scars and told her how I got them, but she didn't run away even then. If she knew I was the anonymous man who tied her up and blindfolded her, would she accept that? Or run from me?

Though I need to confess, I still can't do it. I know I should walk away, but I can't do that either.

"I'll need to get a few things," I say. "Feel free to start eating while I'm gone. This shouldn't take long."

"Take all the time you need." She stretches out on the bed again. "I'll be right here waiting for you."

I rush out of the room and gather my supplies, abusing my master key privileges to do so. I don't give a toss if I'm behaving in an irrational and unprofessional manner. I need to shag Holly with no mask hiding my face this time. What we did in my office doesn't count. Tonight, I mean to show her everything.

When I return to Holly's room, I have my supplies inside a paper sack.

She rubs her palms together. "Ooh, is that your goodies in there? Can't wait to find out what you're up to, but I know I'll love it."

Last time I'd fucked her in this room, I had blindfolded her. Tonight, I have other plans for Holly.

I kick my shoes off.

She watches while I unbutton my shirt and slip out of it, tossing the garment onto the floor. Her gaze tracks my every movement as I unzip my trousers and get rid of them too, then remove my socks. I stand completely naked before her.

"Wow," she breathes. "You are so damn sexy that you're giving me a hot flash."

"That might be the strangest compliment I've ever received." I pretend to eye her with suspicion. "Aren't you too young for hot flashes?"

"Not when I'm with you."

I sit on the edge of the bed and aim my gaze straight into hers. "I've thought about this a lot over the past two days, and I realized what I want and need to do with you. But you should never feel compelled to go along with it."

She pushes up into a sitting position and wriggles closer to me. "I've told you over and over that I want whatever you want when it comes to sex. I trust you."

"And I trust you too. But you know I have these fears and scars, both visible and in my mind."

"We can take it slow, James. You set the pace, and I'll let you know if I need a break or want to stop. The same goes for you." She skims a hand up and down my chest. "So the real question is, do you trust me all the way?"

"I do. Completely."

And I realize I mean that. I do trust Holly, more than I've trusted anyone else in my life. Maybe that will scare me later, when I have time to consider the implications. But for now, all I feel is the warm, sweet current of desire flowing between us, erasing everything else, as if we exist inside a secret space where no one else can find us.

Holly grasps my face and leans in to kiss me softly. "Will you show me your goodies now?"

"Yes. If anything I bring out of that paper sack makes you uncomfortable, let me know. I'll throw it in the rubbish bin."

"Have you forgotten that I'm the one who seduced you into screwing me in your office? You know how wild I am." She kisses me again, with more fervor, though she doesn't try to breach my lips. "Show me everything, James."

First, I bring out a box of condoms and toss it onto the nightstand. Then I bring out four lengths of thin white rope. "How do you feel about these?"

Holly smiles and glides her tongue over her bottom lip, then the top one, as she takes a rope in her hands and rubs it over her lips, back and forth, again and again, before lowering it to her chest so she can tease her own skin with the soft fibers. "Mm, this feels good. Never felt rope as soft as this. Wherever did you find it on this island?"

"I, ah, ordered it over the internet. Rene picked up the package for me in Suva, and he brought it to the island this morning. He had other errands to run, anyway, so it wasn't an extraordinary request."

"Suva is the island we went to on our little excursions, right?"

"It's a city on that island. But yes, it's where we went."

She passes the rope back to me. "You went to all this trouble just to get me in bed?"

"No, I did this because I wanted to give you more than a quick shag." I pat the mattress. "Lie down on your back, please."

She aims a teasing smile at me while she spreads her lush body out on the bed. "I'm impressed. You can be polite even while ordering me to do what you want."

"Would you rather I act like an arsehole?"

"Of course not. I think your polite dom act is wicked hot."

"Glad you approve." I kneel over her calves and can't resist running my hands up and down her silky skin. "Time for the ropes, love."

"Oh yes, please."

I gently tie her wrists together and give the ropes a light tug. "How does that feel?"

"Good. Keep going."

"Roll over onto your stomach, please."

Holly flips over and flashes me a sexy grin over her shoulder.

Since I have her permission, I move on to the next stage—tying her left ankle to her right thigh using the same rope that I'd employed to bind her wrists. When she nods her approval, I secure her left thigh to the upper part of her left arm, above the elbow. "Is this too tight?"

Holly wriggles her entire body as if she's testing the bindings. "Feels just right."

The sultry tone of her voice makes my pulse beat faster. I want to pounce on her like a randy panther, but I won't do that. I need to spend hours enjoying her body and giving her pleasure in every way I can imagine. That means I'll need to take it slow.

Even if that kills me.

"Roll onto your side, love," I say. "And don't fight the ropes. Let them ease your body into the right position."

She writhes like a serpent as she moves her body into position, lying partially on her side but with her elbows on the mattress. "Oh God, I'm already so wet and hot for you, James."

"Don't come yet. I'll tell you when it's time."

I lie down behind her and slide into position, cradling her body with mine. The way I've bound her legs means her arse is in the perfect position. I slide my cock between those soft cheeks and lay a hand on her hip as I push my length along her cleft, over and over, taking it slow and easy while her cream coats my cock. On the two nights when I had seduced her anonymously, she was as aroused and slick for me as she is tonight. But I shouldn't think about those other encounters, not now. I need to focus only on this night, when I can spend hours giving her pleasure.

"Oh, yes," she moans. "This is incredible, but I need you inside me, please. Take me hard."

"Not yet, darling."

I slide my hand off her hip to cup her mound, combing my fingers through the hairs that tickle my palm, stroking lightly while she moans louder and wriggles against me. I drag my tongue up her throat so I can nibble on her earlobe. Her breathing grows heavier, and her stiff nipples have turned a dusky shade of pink. I'm breathing harder too, getting so aroused that I know I'll come soon. Holly's chest rises and falls with her rapid breaths, and she rocks her hips in a desperate effort to push me inside her.

"One moment," I say, like a bloody moron. "I need to get a condom."

"Hurry, please, I can't wait much longer."

Neither can I. Snatching a packet off the nightstand, I roll the condom over my length. Once I've nestled against Holly's backside once again, I grasp her hip.

"Do it now, James."

I thrust into her, holding that position.

Holly cries out, throwing her head back.

"Fuck," I growl. Her slick, hot flesh molds to my cock, and the way I arranged her body ensures I have total control. Never knew I'd want that. But having her at my mercy gives me a feeling of...liberation.

I plow into her, keeping the rhythm steady and languid, striving to hold off until she reaches her climax. But the pressure building inside me means I need to marshal all my willpower to take it slow, especially when she keeps moaning and writhing and gasping. The sweet, musky scent of her cream fills the air, inciting my hunger even more, to the point where I can barely restrain myself from pounding into her. But when she pleads for me to "do it so hard the bed thumps and creaks," I can't stop myself. Flipping her onto her stomach, I crouch above her on all fours and do what she begged for me to do. I pummel her body with my cock, lunging my hips at a relentless peace.

"Oh God, yes!" Holly shouts.

Then she buries her face in the pillow to muffle her scream. Every muscle in her body goes rigid as she hovers in that frozen moment before climax. Just as I'm about to tear the pillow away so she won't suffocate, Holly turns her head to the side, gasping for breath until the second the orgasm seizes her. All her inner muscles clamp down on me while I keep thrusting, but the sensation of her body pulsating around me does me in. An electric surge rockets through me, straight into my cock, setting off a barrage of spasms. I punch into her fiercely one last time and erupt inside her body. The only sound I can make is a choked sputtering. After one final, gentler thrust, I'm spent.

I collapse onto the bed beside Holly, struggling to draw in enough breath to calm the pounding of my heart and the ringing in my ears.

Holly flops onto her back, breathing as raggedly as I am. "Holy shit."

"Are you all right?"

She manages a breathless laugh. "All right? No, I feel amazing. That was—I mean, you—No words can describe it."

"I know." My hands tremble as I untie her bindings. I've never experienced anything as intense as what we just did. Once she's free, I pull her snugly against my side. "I should feed you now. After this, we'll both need a break."

"Sure do. I'm ravenous—for food and for you." She throws an arm across my chest and hooks one leg over mine. "Feed me, then show me what other sexy ideas you have."

"I'll need a few more minutes to recover first."

She settles her head on my chest. "I knew you had a wild side hidden under all that grumpy attitude."

"Pretending I don't want you was bloody hard work."

"Don't need to pretend anymore."

I brush my fingers through her silky hair and kiss the top of her head. "No, I don't need to hide my feelings for you ever again. Being with you like this is the most liberating experience of my life."

"Never met a man like you before. Something about you intrigued me so much that I had to get to know you better." She tickles my chest with her fingertips. "Even if that meant I had to pester you endlessly and kind of stalk you."

"I'm glad you did that. And I'm guilty of stalking you too, sort of."

"See? We are kindred spirits." Holly takes my nipple into her mouth and suckles it until I gasp. "Let's eat our meal off each other's bodies."

A laugh splutters out of me. "If we do that, we won't actually eat anything. I'll be inside you again after the first bite."

"Oh, darn. That would be just awful."

I slap her arse. "Behave yourself, Holly, or I might need to spank you."

She springs to her knees and turns away from me, bending forward to give me her arse.

I could love this woman.

Chapter Eighteen

Holly

James fans both his hands over my bottom and wriggles his fingers to tease me. The tickling sensation makes me giggle, which is something I rarely do. I love to laugh, sure. But giggling? That's too silly even for me. But James gets me to do all kinds of things I never imagined I'd do—like consenting to be tied up.

When I glance over my shoulder at the sex god, he's smirking.

"Enjoying yourself, James?"

"Immensely." He leans forward to kiss my ass, literally. "I've never enjoyed sex more than I do with you."

"Same goes for me. You are the best lover I've ever had."

He massages my bottom while kissing a path up my spine. His velvety tongue explores my body in gentle swipes, as if he wants to taste every inch of me. By the time he reaches my neck, my clit is rigid and aching.

"Sure you don't want to eat our food off my body?" I ask. "I'd love to feast on you, for sure."

"I am warming up to the idea." He nuzzles my neck and slides his hands around to my belly. His dick brushes against my ass. "What sort of delicacies did you order?"

"Let me show you."

Though I hate to give up the warmth of his body, and his semi-soft dick, I slither out of his arms to hop off the bed. James tracks my every movement with his gaze while he shifts into a sitting position with his legs bent. When he drapes one arm over his knee, he seems more relaxed than ever. Who knew a bit of light bondage sex would improve his mood so much?

I drag the food cart over to the bedside and sit down right next to James. His brows lift the slightest bit, but I think that's curiosity rather than anxiety. He said he trusts me. I get a warm glow in my chest when I remember the moment when he told me that. I could fall for James Bythesea so easily. Maybe I already have.

"Are you going to stare at me," he asks, "or feed me?"

"Okay, okay, let's eat."

"About bloody time."

I lift the lid off the biggest plate and poke the food with one finger. "Hey, it's still hot. Just like you."

His eyebrows lift even more when he inspects the plate. "Pancakes? That's not dinner food."

"Of course it is." I whip the lids off two more dishes. "I also ordered sausage, bacon, cinnamon rolls, chicken nuggets, and whipped cream with a side of hot fudge sauce."

"Fudge sauce on pancakes? You are barmy, aren't you?"

"Yep. It's part of my charm." I pick up a small pitcher and lift its lid to peek inside. "Mm, real maple syrup, and it's still warm."

"If you pour syrup on me, I'll stick to the sheets."

"Guess we'll have to take a shower after dinner." I slant closer to whisper in his ear. "We can shower together."

"You've convinced me." He snatches a sausage patty off the plate and holds it to my lips. "Devour this, Holly, before I devour you."

I bite off a chunk of sausage and chew it slowly, moaning strictly to torture James. I've learned that he gets even hornier when I do that. Once I've finished chewing, I cut a piece of pancake, dunk it in the syrup, and offer it to him.

He lunges his head to take the whole bite of pancake into his mouth. Syrup drizzles from his lips while he chews. I drag my tongue across his chin to lap up the sticky sweetness. His eyes have darkened, the pupils blown, a definite sign that he loves what we're doing together. So I get another bite-size piece of pancake and douse it with syrup, then dunk it into the whipped cream piled up in the middle.

I raise the loaded fork to his lips. "Open wide."

James opens his mouth and takes in the whole forkful. Just like I'd hoped, a bit of whipped cream and syrup sticks to his lips. I lick it off. He throws an arm around me, sealing his mouth to mine and diving his tongue deep so the flavor of the food mingles on our tongues. When he finally pulls his mouth away, his lips remain parted. His breaths tease my skin.

But then he twists around to pick something up off the floor. "Mind if we use these again?"

The ropes dangle from his fingers.

Can't stop the smile that gradually curls my lips. "I'd love to."

He slides off the bed, gesturing for me to get in position. "Once I've devoured all of you I can, I'm going to fuck you again."

I stretch out on the mattress with my head on the pillow. "Might need to change the sheets after this."

"Fortunately, you are shagging the general manager. I can procure new sheets for you anytime, day or night."

"When you say things like 'procure,' it makes me so hot."

"Everything makes you randy, and I love that about you."

"Not true. Only the things you do affect me that way."

James grabs the rest of the ropes and carefully knots them around my wrists and ankles, then uses the rest of each rope's length to bind me to the rails at the head and foot of the bed. I now lie spreadeagled, completely exposed and at his mercy. He pulls the cart closer, his legs hanging off the bed, and feeds me a loaded bite of pancake, licking the syrup and whipped cream off my lips the way I'd done with him.

I'm so ready for another round of sex that it's almost embarrassing.

He kneels between my spread legs. "Now for the main course—you."

I watch while he grabs the pitcher and drizzles the still-warm syrup onto my chest, over my breasts, and lower until he reaches my hips.

"Don't need to pour anything sweet down here"—He palms my groin—"because you taste sweeter than anything else on earth."

He sets the pitcher on the cart again and grabs a spoonful of whipped cream. James dabs it on my nipples while his mouth slides into a deviously sensual smile. He dabs the cream on my navel too, then slides the spoon between my lips. I consume the sweet, vanilla-flavored delicacy while we gaze into each other's eyes.

"Time to devour you, Holly."

He plants his palms on the mattress at either side of me and dips his head to touch his lips to my throat, dragging them down until he finds the cream on my nipples. With languid strokes of his tongue, he wipes the whipped cream away, then tugs one stiff peak into his mouth to suckle it.

I gasp, and my back arches. "Keep going, please."

James drags his lips down to my navel and flicks his tongue to lap up every speck of cream. The delicacy of his licking makes my clit pulse. I grip the ropes tightly and arch my back again, helpless to keep from moaning and gasping. James has barely even touched me, yet already I feel like I could come any second.

He surges up to seal his open lips over the hollow of my throat, licking his way down my skin again, this time to use his tongue to sweep away the syrup he'd drizzled onto me. I thrash against my bindings, but I can't move much, certainly not enough to get his dick inside me. Though I want him to go faster, I also need him to take it slow so I can revel in everything he makes me feel.

James takes his time, swirling his tongue while he inches ever downward. He glides his palms up my arms and back down again, all while dancing his tongue over my skin to erase the syrup from my breasts. When he's done with that task, he sweeps his hands down my sides and grasps my hips. With his gaze pinned to mine, he swipes his tongue across my belly over and over, following the trail of sticky sweetness he'd painted on my flesh.

He pauses at my hips, and his breaths tickle my skin. "Should I let you come yet?"

"No."

James shimmies backward until his face is positioned above my mound. He keeps his gaze on mine while he pushes his tongue between my folds to tease my nub. This man understands exactly how to turn me on and keep me in a state of intense arousal for so long that I think I might go insane from the way he teases me. But I never want him to stop. Not being able to move much or touch him only makes it hotter.

He drags his tongue down my cleft, oh-so-slowly, then drags it back up to my clit. The second he curls his tongue around that hard nub, I thrash again, crying out and babbling nonsense. More gibberish bursts out of me while he suckles my clit like he might die of starvation without the flavor of me in his mouth. He scrapes his teeth across my nub, gliding his fingertips up and down my folds.

And then he stops.

James rises to his knees. "You can't come yet."

I absolutely could, but I know what he means. And I don't want him to set me off yet. I need to hit that release, but I don't want this delicious torture to end, not until he decides I'm ready. Never in my life could I have imagined I'd love the exquisite agony of a delayed climax. But now I realize it's what I've always needed, as long as James is the man doing this to me.

Words tumble from my lips. "Don't push me over the edge yet, please, not yet, I love this, I need more, please."

He takes his cock in his hand and pumps it in leisurely strokes. "I need to come all over you, Holly."

"Oh, yes, I want that too."

"But first, I'm going to finish you off." He crouches over me, setting his hands on the pillow at either side of my head. "I'd wager you'll come the second I'm inside you, but I'll keep going for as long as I can stand to, until you're done."

Only James could manage to sound commanding and sensitive at the same time. And that makes me want him even more, but it also triggers that warm glow again.

He drives his length deep inside me and holds that position.

"Don't stop, James, don't ever stop."

He bucks into me hard and hesitates, while his expression becomes pained and he struggles to keep every inward lunge powerful yet delicate too, consuming my body at a measured pace. It only takes a moment before I do exactly what he predicted. I come. My head snaps back, my body stiffens, and the loudest scream I've produced explodes out of me while he keeps forging in and pulling out, grunting and groaning, his face cinched up in the most beautiful agony. I must look the same way. My heart pounds as the pleasure rockets through me in wave after wave, and the sensation of my muscles gripping him fires an even more intense jolt of pleasure down my every nerve.

Then I go limp, gasping to catch my breath.

James rises to his knees again and pumps his cock so vigorously that he comes within seconds. The milky jet of his release sprays onto my belly.

I blow hair away from my eyes. "Oh, James, that was beyond incredible."

He grins. "It was bloody fucking fantastic."

"Even better than the first time."

James makes a strange face, not quite pain, but something almost like...shame. The expression vanishes too quickly for me to figure out what it meant. And before I can ask him about it, he leaps off the bed to scurry into the bathroom, returning a moment later with a wet towel.

"Let me clean you up," he says. "I made a ruddy mess."

"The best sex is messy."

He uses the towel to wipe off my belly, and I realize he dampened it with warm water. James thinks of everything. When he's done, he releases my bindings and lies down beside me.

Sighing, I roll onto my side to cuddle up to him. "We haven't finished our meal."

"The food is probably cold."

"We can reheat it in the microwave."

"I hadn't thought of that." He glances at the microwave that rests on a small table in the far corner of the suite. "Are you hungry?"

"Absolutely. We need to replenish our energy with sweet, savory food."

"Stay in bed. I'll bring everything to you."

James crawls out of bed and rolls the cart over to the microwave. I watch while he gets our meal ready, but I'm mostly admiring his tight ass. Damn, that man has a killer body that he hides under professional clothes most of the time. I'm sure I'm the only person who has seen him naked in a very long time. How could his wife have left him? How could his kids have disowned him? James is a sweet, thoughtful, passionate, amazing man.

Yeah, I desperately want to interrogate him about his past. But I'll wait a little longer before I attempt that feat.

After eating, we lie in bed for a while, snuggling and kissing, but not getting too worked up. We're both wiped out after the intensity of what we did tonight. Soon, though, I will insist on hearing the whole story about James. If we want to have a real chance as a couple, he can't keep secrets from me anymore.

James falls asleep before I do, and I gaze at him while he dreams, astounded by how relaxed and almost innocent he seems right now. I get a pang in my chest, accompanied by that soft warmth I'd experienced earlier, and I know that means everything has changed between us, at least for me. Am I falling for him? No.

I've blown past that line. Because I am in love with James Bythesea.

Chapter Nineteen

James

What did I do last night? I tied Holly up—twice—and she loved it. Can't believe I did that. No one who ever knew me would believe I could enjoy a bit of bondage play with a woman who is eighteen years younger than I am. Yet I don't regret any of what we've done together. Last night changed everything.

I woke this morning with Holly sprawled half on top of me, sleeping, her expression so sweet that I couldn't disturb her. So I've simply laid here enjoying the warmth and softness of her body. Her hair smells like coconut and feels like the softest silk, as does her skin. For the second time this morning, I bury my face in that hair and inhale the scent. It inflames my lust, and I long to rouse Holly so I can make love to her again.

And yes, my cock is firming up. I doubt that's entirely from my usual morning hard-on. It's also because of the woman lying beside me.

Holly stirs and exhales the sweetest moaning sigh. Her body shifts a little, rubbing her knee against my growing erection. I can't resist wrapping both arms around her and diving my face into that hair yet again to experience the silkiness and the coconut aroma.

Her lids flutter open as she tips her head back to look at me. "Mm, good morning."

I give her a quick, soft kiss. "Good morning, darling."

A charming little smile dimples her cheeks. "I love that you've started calling me 'darling'."

"I called you 'love' last night too."

"That's even better." She brushes one fingertip over my bottom lip. "Mind if I call you 'sweetie'?"

"Call me anything you like—in private. But I'd rather not have my staff hearing you call me 'sweetie.' I have a professional image to uphold."

"Lucky for you, I think it's cute that you're kind of uptight."

"You must be off your trolley to like that, but I think your barminess is charming."

She pokes me in the side. "Careful. I might decide to tie you up tonight."

"And you assume that threat will terrify me." I squeeze her arse cheek. "Go on and try it. See what happens."

Holly pushes up on one straight arm, staring down at me with unblinking eyes. "Are you seriously suggesting you might want me to do that?"

"Perhaps."

She continues to stare at me, though now her mouth has fallen open too.

I slap her arse. "Get up, Holly. We both need a shower, and I know your suite includes a large stall with multiple heads."

"Sorry. I need a minute to digest what you said about bondage." Her gaze shifts down to my groin. "Looks like you can't wait, though, huh? Raring to go, I'd say."

"Most men get erections in the morning."

"I know that. But this looks like more than the usual wake-up hard-on."

Well, she's not wrong about that.

Holly stretches her arms above her head, exhaling a satisfied sigh while still smiling. "I would love to get wet and steamy with you, James."

I leap off the bed and sweep her up in my arms. "Let's get to it, then."

Just as I'm carrying her into the bathroom, I hear my mobile ringing. I'd left it on the nightstand.

Holly throws her head back and lets out a sarcastic moan. "You need to get that, don't you?"

"Yes." I set her down. "Get the shower ready. I'll be back in a moment."

While she turns on the water, I hurry to answer my mobile. The caller ID tells me it's Emilio. "What disaster is going on this time? Another condom emergency?"

Silence follows. For several seconds.

"Are you still there, Emilio?"

"Uh, yeah, boss." He sounds horribly confused. "Are you feeling all right this morning?"

"I feel bloody fantastic."

"Okay," he says carefully. Then he clears his throat. "Just wanted to let you know there's rain coming this way. Not our usual daily drizzle. The meteorological service on Fiji predicts extended showers. The athletic events will need to be canceled, and I wanted to know what you'd like us to offer the guests instead."

"You are the assistant manager, Emilio. I trust you to make those decisions on your own."

He falls silent again, for several more seconds. "You're leaving me in charge? For how long?"

"An hour or so."

"You aren't starting work until almost ten o'clock?"

I don't blame him for sounding shocked. Every day since the staff showed up to work a week before the grand opening, I have been the first person to arrive every morning. Of course Emilio can't believe what I've told him.

"That's right," I say. "I will see you at ten. Cheers."

"Ah, yeah, cheers."

Let Emilio think what he likes. If I've lost my mind, I don't care. It feels wonderful.

I hurry to the bathroom and discover Holly is already in the shower with steam fogging up the glass door. She's humming softly, a cheerful tune that I don't recognize. Even through the fogged-up glass, I can see her nude body and the way she stands directly under one of several showerheads. Why anyone needs more than one showerhead is beyond me, but I don't give a toss about that right now. I step into the stall and shut the door.

Holly opens her eyes and smiles. "There you are. Was that a vital phone call?"

"Not to me." I brace my arms on the wall at either side of her. "This is far more important."

"Got a condom?"

"Bollocks," I hiss. "Forgot about that. Better go and get one."

"No need." She pastes her body to mine and slithers down, down, down until her face hovers in front of my erection. "I can make you come a different way."

"But I love shagging you."

"I want to eat you up, James." She coils her tongue around the head of my cock, making me suck in a sharp breath. "Say yes, please. You know you want to."

Part of me, the bit that still can't believe I've gotten involved with a virtual child, urges me to say no. But I can't make myself do that. I want to feel Holly's mouth wrapped around my cock, and I need to come while she consumes me.

Holly tips her head back to gaze up at me. She licks her lips.

I cradle the back of her head in my hand. "Go on, then. Do it."

While I watch with rapt wonder, she pulls her lips into her mouth to cover her teeth and slowly swallows my length. Her eyes drift half-closed. She moans softly, the vibrations teasing my cock, and I groan. Holly pulls away and blows on the head of my erection. I shudder from the erotic sensation, but when she glides her tongue along my length, from tip to base, I need to slap both hands on the wall to keep my knees from buckling. No woman has ever given me the gift Holly offers without reservation.

She raises her head to look at me. "You have a beautiful dick, James. I love having it inside me, but tasting you... Mm, you're even yummier than pancakes."

Can't speak. I'm struggling for breath, and she's barely done anything to me.

"I haven't even made you come yet," she says, "but I know the flavor will be incredible."

Though I open my mouth, no sound emerges.

She gives me a deviously sensual smile, then presses her mouth to my inner thigh. As she kisses a damp trail up my skin, all I can do is gaze down at her, my attention riveted to her movements. Her cheek grazes my groin, and her hair tickles my cock. But when she slides her fingers behind my balls, massaging the flesh there, I let out a strangled shout.

"Bloody hell, Holly. I won't last long if you keep doing that."

"Good. I want you to pop your cork."

She wraps her other hand around the base of my erection while she keeps massaging the area behind my balls, and then she devours me. The underside of her tongue brushes against my skin every time she thrusts me into her mouth, the sensation so maddening that I begin to breathe more heavily and my ears ring, but I don't care. Watching her head move and feeling her tongue and her fingers on my flesh… It's the most erotic thing I've ever experienced.

A feeling like electricity in my veins courses through me, from my spine all the way down to my cock, increasing the pressure inside me until I know I'm about to go off.

Holly pulls away, still kneeling beneath me. Then she turns around and drops onto all fours. "Fuck me, James."

"What?"

"I said fuck me." She glances over her shoulder. "No penetration. Just rub your dick against me and make us both come. I'm so turned on, it won't take much for me. And I know you're on the edge too."

For a second, two at most, I can't understand a single word she spoke. When the reality of what she suggested hits me, my brain shuts down and instinct takes over. I drop to my knees and grasp her hips, pushing my cock between her arse cheeks to glide it back and forth along her cleft. She gasps and moans. My thrusts accelerate into wild pounding, and the slapping of my balls on her arse does me in.

I throw my head back and roar like a mad beast.

Holly's body freezes, and she unleashes a long series of cries intermingled with syllables that aren't quite words.

Though I'm done in a few strokes, I know Holly can keep going. So I push my hand between her folds and rub her clitoris until she's gasping and her knees and arms are quivering. Then I fold my arms around her torso, easing her into a kneeling position, braced by my body. I haven't quite regained normal breathing yet either.

Once I can speak again, I link my hands over her belly and kiss her throat. "Every time we shag, it gets better and better."

She lets her head fall back onto my shoulder. "For me too. I mean, holy shit. Is it my imagination, or do we keep coming harder?"

"You haven't imagined it."

"Oh, thank goodness. I wouldn't want to wake up and find out I'm still in Seattle, alone."

"No chance of that." I nuzzle her cheek. "Should we actually take a shower now?"

"Yes, I'd love that."

She grabs a bottle of body wash, and I tease her about the need to relabel liquid soap as something else. She teases me too, and our shower becomes another sort of playtime, but without the orgasms. When I announce we should have breakfast in the dining hall, Holly doesn't seem at all shocked that I would suggest such a thing. The wonderful woman just smiles and kisses me.

Then we walk hand in hand into the dining hall.

Yes, I know that means my staff will see us. I don't give a fuck anymore.

After breakfast, I kiss Holly goodbye at the door to my office and watch her sexy arse while she ambles down the hall and into the lobby. She had informed me that she means to spend the morning in the game room where she will play pool and "take the other guests for all they're worth." She winked after telling me that, so I assume she was having me on.

She also wants to play pinball. Does anyone do that anymore? I thought video games had eclipsed the old-school types of entertainment.

Once Holly has vanished around a corner, I head into my office. It takes me fifteen minutes to convince my mind to stop replaying all the things Holly and I did together last night and this morning in her room. Tonight, I should invite her to my bungalow. It isn't as posh as her suite, but it feels more like a home. I have my own kitchen, so I could make dinner for her. I know she'd love that.

When was the last time I did anything like that for a woman? Before my ex-wife left me, that's for certain. After last night with Holly, everything has changed. Thinking about Laraine no longer causes me to tense up and struggle to control my breathing and my heart rate. I don't need to shut my eyes either and try to banish the memories.

I will not have a panic attack ever again. I'm free.

And it's time I carved out a new life, a real one this time—with Holly.

Chapter Twenty

Holly

"Go, Holly! You're almost to the highest score," Kevin shouts as he stands beside me at the pinball machine, having crapped out on his turn. The machine makes all sorts of noises while I whack the little ball around. Kevin seems more invested in my high score than I am, but it is fun to play a physical game rather than a virtual one, with a friend by my side to cheer me on.

I send the ball careening again, and the machine's lights and sounds go wild.

"You did it!" Kevin shouts. He grabs my hand and holds it high above our heads. "Woo-hoo! Holly Temple got the highest score of anyone at the resort."

Cheers and whoops erupt behind us.

I can't believe anyone cares this much about who gets the highest score, especially since we've been here for less than a week. But I might as well participate in the madness. I spin around and throw both arms up. Grinning, I holler, "I am the queen of pinball!"

The cheers get even louder.

Movement behind the small crowd draws my attention to the doorway of the game room. James is leaning against the jamb, arms crossed, watching me. He smiles as if he's amused by the ruckus.

"Here ye, here ye, the queen concedes the playing field," I announce. "It's time for my lunch date."

The other guests issue catcalls, though some whoop or holler instead. It's their way of expressing their solidarity or something. I hope they haven't embarrassed James. He hasn't moved, and he's still smiling, so I guess their display doesn't bother him.

When I hook my arm around James's neck, everybody whoops and makes catcalls again.

James only rolls his eyes as he leads me away.

"Sorry about that," I say. "The younger guests can go a little overboard sometimes."

"Why were they so excited when I walked in?"

"I earned the highest pinball score so far at the resort."

"Did you?" He smirks. "Maybe I should try the game and see if I can beat you."

"I'd love that. But I assume you're joking."

He pulls me into his body, spanning my upper back with his big hands. "What if I'm not joking? You know I enjoy playing with you."

The deeper tone of his voice sends a warm tingle over my skin. "Better not suggest what I think you're suggesting while we're in a public hallway."

He slants his head down to murmur into my ear, "I fucked you in my office, remember?"

"Oh, I will never forget that. It's burned into my memory. But sex in your office is not the same as getting dirty in a public place. After all, your door was shut."

"Fair point." He slides his hands down to my ass. "But maybe I want to shag you in a place where anyone might see us. Last night, I proved that I'm not as uptight as you think."

"But that was in my suite. No chance of getting caught there."

"You don't believe me, hmm?"

"Let's test your theory." I push my fingers inside his waistband and tug. "Wanna do the deed right here?"

He glances up and down the hall. "I'm starved, Holly. Let's eat and then discuss your suggestion."

I peel his hands off my ass and step back. "Not ready for public sex after all, huh? I was right."

"We'll see."

I let him lead me into the dining hall, where we eat in full view of other people, just like this morning when we enjoyed our breakfast in this very room. He might be loosening up, but I still don't believe James is ready for public "shagging." I do believe one day he will want to get naughty with me outdoors, and I can't wait for that.

But it won't happen today.

Over lunch, we talk and make each other laugh. James has a fantastic sense of humor which does indeed involve the occasional dirty joke. He does not stare at my tits, like some of the younger guys at the resort do. James keeps his focus exclusively on my face.

What surprises me the most about him, however, is his affectionate side. He touches my hand repeatedly, either clasping it briefly or laying his palm on top of my hand.

After lunch, James needs to go back to work. I understand that, and I don't complain.

"I do have the weekend off," he tells me. "Would you like to do something special with me?"

"Absolutely. What do you have in mind?"

"Have you ever been to New Zealand?"

"No, never."

James leans in, those gorgeous eyes zeroing in on mine. "How would you like to see Auckland? We could fly there tonight and have the weekend to explore. It's a three-hour trip from here."

"A weekend getaway with the hottest man on earth? Count me in."

"You're fond of hyperbole, aren't you? I doubt I am literally the hottest man on the planet."

"Oh, yes, you are." I tap his lips with one finger. "I'm an expert on the subject of hot guys."

"To New Zealand it is, then. The rain is forecast to end soon, so Rene will fly us to Suva, and we'll catch a flight to Auckland at the international airport."

"Perfect."

He gives me a quick kiss. "I'll meet you at your suite at six thirty."

"It's a date." I bite my lip as I realize something important. "I assume I can't go nude in Auckland, and you know I didn't bring much clothes with me."

"Wear that sexy frock of yours, and we can get you more clothes in Auckland."

"Thank you, James. I'm stoked about our romantic getaway."

"As am I," he says with a smirk.

We part ways, and I return to my room to get ready. My dress has gotten wrinkled, so I call the reception desk to ask about laundry service. It turns out the resort does dry cleaning, so I drop my dress off at the desk. I want to look nice when my knight in shining armor shows up to whisk me away. A wrinkled dress doesn't set the right mood.

I visit the spa to get a massage and hot stone treatment, so I'll be blissfully relaxed when James picks me up. I feel so good that I decide to chill out on my bed and gaze out the big sliding glass doors in my suite. The sun comes out in the late afternoon, and I move out onto the patio to await my prince.

At six twenty, I realize I forgot to ask James if I should eat dinner before we head out. Too late now. So I put on my "sexy frock," as James called it, and the shoes I'd worn when I arrived here. Then I sit on the edge of my bed and wait. While tapping my foot on the floor. And drumming my fingers on the mattress. Okay, yeah, I'm kind of excited.

Three crisp knocks resound through the door.

I leap up and race into the entryway, flinging the door open.

James raises his brows. "You really are raring to go, aren't you?"

"Absolutely." I grab the handle of my wheeled suitcase, which I'd stowed beside the door. "Let's go. I didn't eat dinner yet. Did you?"

"No. We can dine on the plane."

I can't help snorting at that statement. "Dine? The airline experience involves crummy food and, if you're lucky, a teeny bottle of booze. Don't think you get a meal on a three-hour flight, though."

He snatches my suitcase from me. "Did I say we were traveling commercial? Rene knows a bloke who is letting us borrow his private jet."

"Private? Holy cow, James, that's amazing. Here I was expecting to need a butt massage after sitting in a narrow, hard seat for three hours."

"You will travel in luxury." He offers me his arm. "But I would be happy to massage your arse anytime."

"I bet you would." I give his bottom a squeeze, then take his arm. "I'll rub your tight ass anytime you want."

When we bump into Emilio in the lobby, he grins. "Have fun, boss."

He doesn't need to tell us that. We plan to have lots and lots of fun.

We walk to the airstrip, because there's no shuttle service on the island. I need a little exercise, anyway. Rene is waiting for us in the plane. As we climb in, he grins at us the same way Emilio had.

Rene winks at James. "Good on ya, boss. Found the right girl, hey?"
"Yes, I have."

James clasps my hand and gazes at me with more than lust. It feels like affection, but even that word doesn't adequately describe his expression. He looks like a man in love. I think I'm giving him the same look. Insta-love has always sounded like romantic bullshit to me, but I've become a believer. I wanted James at first sight. I was also drawn to him at first sight. Maybe that's not quite insta-love, but it's close.

When we arrive in Suva, we don't even leave the airport. The jet belonging to Rene's friend is waiting for us on the tarmac. We travel the rest of the way in the lap of luxury, with an interior that features butter-soft leather seats, a sofa, a big-screen TV, and a wet bar. James and I cuddle up on the sofa to watch a movie.

Before I know it, we've landed in Auckland.

The sun set awhile ago, and it's almost completely dark. But the air feels temperate, despite the fact it's January. Sometimes I forget I'm in the southern hemisphere, where winter is summer and summer is winter. The seasons are flipped, which is trippy, but I'm getting used to that. It's also dark already.

James hails a taxi to take us to our destination, a bed-and-breakfast that he calls "luxurious." I stayed at a b&b once back home, and I guess my brain assumes that all of them offer the same level of service and that James was exaggerating when he called this one "luxurious." But nope, he told the truth. As James offers me his hand to get out of the taxi, I take in the copious amenities and upscale style of our accommodations.

The two-story house looks modern, but it has all the charm of an old-timey mansion, with wraparound porches on both levels and ornate railing. A white picket fence encloses the property, and I even see two stained-glass windows in front.

"Wow, this is amazing," I say, as we walk through the gate. "You went all out for our weekend getaway."

"I wanted to give you the world, but I had to settle for New Zealand." He sweeps me up in his arms to carry me up the front steps. "You deserve the best of everything."

The second he sets me down at the front door, I hop up on my tiptoes to kiss him.

Once we cross the threshold, we find ourselves walking down a short hallway with gorgeous wood floors and an equally gorgeous long rug that stretches the length of the entryway. I've barely seen any of this place yet, but already I feel like I've stepped into a glamorous movie set. While James checks us in, I wander around the lobby, peeking into the public rooms connected to the central area. The decor features a black and white theme accented with warm earth tones, giving it an uptown feel though this seems like a suburban neighborhood. I get the impression that the whole first floor houses nothing but those public rooms, which include a living area, a dining room, and something that might be a sitting room or a lounge.

James and I climb a beautiful carpeted staircase to the second floor, where we find our room at the far end of the hall. He insists on carrying me through the door, like he had when we entered the building. That seems strange to me, since we aren't newlyweds. But I won't question him about that. Don't want to do anything to spoil his good mood.

The second he sets me down, I throw my arms out and twirl around to get the full view of our accommodations. A large bed sits across from a stone fireplace, while a private balcony offers fantastic views of the city.

I halt and shamelessly let my jaw drop. "Oh. My. God. I've never stayed in a place like this. It must've cost a fortune. Are you secretly a billionaire?"

He chuckles. "No, love, I'm not wealthy. But Eve and Val, my employers, have become quite well off thanks to their chain of naturist resorts. They offered to pay for our weekend escape and said all I need to do in return is to give them a review of this establishment and the attractions in Auckland."

"Wow, they sound like really generous people."

"They are. Eve and Val have taken an enormous chance on me, and I will not let them down."

"I don't understand. What kind of chance did they take?"

His features crimp, and he veers his gaze away from me. "I would rather not discuss it right now. This is meant to be a break from all that rubbish."

"By 'rubbish' you mean talking about your past and whatever happened that made your family hate you."

"Yes."

I study him for a moment while I try to gauge how much I should push him. He's right. We did agree this would be a fun escape, not interrogation time. "Okay, we can put a pin in that discussion for the weekend."

"Thank you." He nods toward a doorway beyond the bed. "You might want to explore the bathroom. I saw photos of it on the b&b's website, and I think you'll enjoy it."

I hurry over to the half-closed door and shove it open.

And my jaw drops.

Chapter Twenty-One

James

As I watch Holly explore the bathroom, I experience a strange combination of shock and lust. She spins round and round while taking in the luxury of the loo, her mouth agape and her eyes alight. All right, the bathroom might be slightly more than just a loo. It reminds me of something a Roman emperor might have, if he had been transported forward in time to the modern era. But I don't spin round and round when I see it.

The bathroom is very posh. Marble walls, tile floor, a freestanding tub, a large vanity, clear glass shower stall. I've never in my life seen anything like it.

Holly pauses in her spinning to grin at me. Then she whirls over to the vanity to run her hands over the polished marble surface.

She is a complicated woman. Holly can be serious and mature one moment, then shriek and whirl about like a little girl the next moment. She enchants me. But that might be the most dangerous thing about being with her. Holly could easily convince me to share everything with her, not realizing what demons she might release in the process.

I cross the threshold of the bathroom but stop there. "I assume you approve of the accommodations."

She faces me, her arms spread wide. "Are you kidding me? I don't approve. I'm awestruck."

"By a bathroom."

"It's more than a bathroom. This is a temple of serenity."

"That's an egregious use of hyperbole."

She shakes her head, letting her arms fall to her sides. "You just can't let yourself get excited about anything, can you?"

I was very excited about shagging Holly, every time I've done that, but most all on the night when I first seduced her. But I can't tell her so. Not unless I confess to my deception.

Holly rushes up to me and presses her body to mine. "Thank you for bringing me here."

"You shouldn't thank me. I needed a bit of a break from the resort."

"Don't you like your job?"

"I do. But the grand opening has been...stressful. Most of the employees didn't arrive until a week before we opened, but I was on the island for two months before that, overseeing the final construction work."

"All by yourself?"

"Emilio and a few others were there with me. We had a skeleton crew until the bulk of the staff arrived."

She slips her arms around my waist and plasters her body to mine. "You've definitely earned a break."

Without realizing what I'm doing, I wrap my arms around her. "What should we do tomorrow? Visit the clothing shops first?"

"Sure. Then we can explore the rest of Auckland after that." She yawns loudly. "Need sleep right now."

"Yes, you do." I carry her to the bed, settling her onto the mattress, atop the covers. "Time to sleep, love."

"For you too, sweetie."

To be called "sweetie" by a woman who's young enough to be my daughter seems ludicrous. But the way Holly speaks that word, it doesn't feel ridiculous at all.

Holly shimmies out of her dress while still lying on the bed, then kicks off her shoes too. She lies completely naked before me, but I'm too knackered to seduce her. My cock barely responds to the vision of her beautiful body.

"Are you going to crawl under the covers?" I ask. "Or would you rather sleep on top of them?"

She crawls on her hands and knees to the head of the bed, then tosses the covers aside so she can settle in. "Your turn."

I join her on the bed, tugging the covers over us both. She kisses me and then flips over onto her side. Her arse brushes against me, but I feel not the slightest inclination to ravish her. I need to sleep.

So I throw an arm over her hip and draw her closer. "Good night, darling."

Holly glances over her shoulder at me. "Good night, sweetie. Can't wait for our excursion tomorrow."

I kiss her cheek. "I will pretend to love shopping with you."

She nudges me with her elbow. "You know you'll secretly love it."

"Only if you try on lingerie for me."

I switch off the lamp on the nightstand and listen while Holly's breathing grows shallower and slower. Even after she falls asleep, I stay awake for a while so I can gaze at her face. Eventually, I drift off and fall into a deep slumber.

Visions assail me, nightmares of my past. But this time, the dreams have changed—because Holly appears in them.

I'm inside the establishment where I used to work, walking across the cavernous main floor. All around me devices whiz and whir, thunk and screech, tick and rumble. The chatter of hundreds of voices can't drown out the mechanical noise.

Suddenly, there she is. Holly Temple.

I become paralyzed, entranced by the sight of her in that short dress. She sees me and smiles with so much joy that I swear it lights up the entire building. As I begin to walk toward her, a large man rushes up behind Holly and seizes her with both arms. I bolt toward them, but the crowd gets in my way, and by the time I reach them, the man has a knife poised at her throat.

"No!" I shout. "She has nothing to do with this."

The man's lips peel back in a nasty version of a smile.

And he slits her throat.

People swarm around me, obscuring my view, and I can't tell where Holly is. My heart pounds like a jackhammer. A tingling numbness prickles my skin from head to toe, and darkness encroaches on my vision. No, no, I cannot pass out. Holly needs me.

The crowd vanishes.

And I see her. Holly lies prone on the floor, her eyes open but vacant, her dress stained with blood that no longer streams from her throat. I fall to my knees beside Holly. Any second, I will lose consciousness. I know this, but I can't stop it. The bastard who murdered her stands beside me cackling.

"She was never yours, and you were never hers," he snarls. "You belong to us forever, mate. We own your soul."

I come awake with a jolt. Darkness enshrouds me, broken only by the glow of streetlights beyond the balcony. Just like in the dream, I'm fighting for every breath, my heart pounds, and numbness threatens to overtake me and drag me into a black abyss. Cold sweat has broken out on my brow, dribbling down my temples.

Holly springs upright. "James, what's wrong?"

I can't respond. My voice refuses to function.

She switches on the bedside lamp. Her eyes widen. She lays a hand on my forehead. "Sweetie, what happened? You're pale and clammy."

"Nightmare," I croak, barely able to squeeze the word out.

"Must've been a doozy." She wipes at my brow with the edge of the top sheet. Then she clasps my wrist. "Your heart rate is crazy."

"It will come down. It always does."

"Did you have a panic attack in your sleep?"

"I think so. That's never happened before." I thrust my hands into my hair and force myself to take slow, deep breaths. "It will pass."

She lies down beside me, propped up on one elbow, and begins to massage my scalp with one hand. The gentleness of her fingers on my skin soothes me more than I would have expected, and I find myself relaxing, my muscles loosening, my heartbeat slowing. She hums softly the whole time, though I don't recognize the tune. Soon, I grow sleepy. But she keeps massaging and humming until my lids shut of their own volition.

Then she kisses my forehead. "Forget all your worries. Let go of the fear, James, and picture a golden beach with waves lapping gently and the scent of sweet flowers blowing on the breeze. I'm with you, holding your hand, and you know nothing can hurt you now."

I fall deeper into the fantasy she described for me while the real world slips away, and I feel Holly snuggling up to me. Her warm body serves as a balm for my soul.

The next thing I know, I'm waking up.

Holly is still nestled against me, asleep, her lips curled into the faintest of smiles. She looks so contented that I get a pang in my chest watching her sleep. She is beautiful, sweet, clever, caring, determined, and so much more. Do I deserve her? No. But I can't give her up. I won't. I'm a selfish bastard, and I need her with me.

How can she mean so much to me after one week?

The woman lying beside me rouses, yawning and stretching her entire body. She aims her sleepy gaze at me. "Good morning, gorgeous."

"Yes, it is a good morning, darling." I tug her into me and possess her mouth with a kiss so deep and sensual that it robs me of breath. "Shall we have a shower together?"

"Oh, yes, please." She stretches again, then smiles and sighs. "I feel wonderful."

"Glad to hear it."

She freezes, then holds a hand to her mouth. "Oh God, I'm sorry, James. After the night you had, I shouldn't brag about how good I feel."

"Of course you should. I brought you to Auckland for relaxation. Things went tits up last night because of me, not you."

"Tits up?" she says with laugh. "I love the way British people talk. It's very colorful."

I have no idea how to respond to that statement, so I slide off the bed and head for the bathroom. "Hurry up, Holly. I need to rub you down in the shower."

She leaps off the bed so fast that the covers tumble onto the floor. "Don't need to tell me twice."

The large shower stall gives us plenty of room to enjoy getting clean in every way imaginable. We don't get dirty, though. Instead, we tickle and tease and lather each other up. As much as I relish fucking Holly, I would be satisfied for the rest of my life if all I did was to shower with her every day and make her laugh when I tickle her belly.

We dry each other off with the stunningly soft towels in the bathroom. Holly giggles when I nuzzle her belly, but she explodes into fits of laughter when I press my lips to her flesh and blow.

Then she kneels to do the same on my belly.

After our shower, we wander downstairs to the dining room for breakfast. The other guests are friendly and happy, and we wind up chatting to them for an hour. But I must put my foot down at last.

I stand up and announce, "This has been a lovely breakfast, but Holly and I have urgent plans."

She gazes up at me, her lips twitching with a half-suppressed smile. "Urgent, huh? Guess we better get moving, then."

A moment later, we're walking out the front door.

"What should we do first?" I ask, as I sling an arm around her shoulders.

"Shopping. You promised I'd get clothes out of the deal."

"Ah, yes. I did." I close the gate behind us as the taxi I'd ordered pulls up. We climb in, and I drape my arm across her shoulders again. To the driver, I say, "Ponsonby, please."

The car starts to move.

Holly lifts her brows. "Ponsonby?"

"It's an arts and shopping district. While you were in the bathroom fussing with your hair, I browsed the brochures on the nightstand. I have an itinerary plotted out in my mind."

"You know I'll go anywhere with you."

I ask the driver to take us to the part of Ponsonby where we'll find the most boutiques, then we begin our adventure. We hold hands during our entire walk. Even when we pop into a boutique, we still hold hands. Only when Holly wants to try on clothing or admire jewelry do we give up the feel of each other's palms. The scenery on our walking tour includes more than shops, though. We see brightly colored buildings, strange artwork, restaurants, and historic sites. We even pass by a large Santa Claus statue that shows the bearded fellow using an enormous wheelbarrow.

Holly delights in everything we see. Her enthusiasm affects me too, and I find myself smiling more than I have in years. Maybe I've never smiled this much before.

We enjoy drinks and snacks at a little cafe that features slender trees, or perhaps they're vines, that wind around the pergola roof. It makes me feel as if we've been transported into a fantasy world. I half expect to see hobbits bounding about and sorcerers casting spells.

But the only one casting a spell on me is Holly.

She does buy a few items of clothing, but not as much as I'd thought she might. Holly tries to convince me to buy some flash clothes, but for once, I resist her charms and decline her suggestion. I check my itinerary for the day, which Holly finds immensely amusing, then hail another taxi so we can visit Vulcan Lane, a pedestrian-only section of the city. Naturally, the next leg of our journey involves more shopping.

Holly wants to have lunch at a sushi bar, but I reject that idea. Raw fish has never appealed to me. Instead, we eat at a nice little restaurant that offers normal food. After that, I have no energy left to do more shopping. Holly takes pity on me and agrees we should return to the bed-and-breakfast.

I insist on carrying her "bags of booty," as she calls them, while we climb the stairs to the second floor. Once I've dropped them on the bed, she flies at me to throw her arms around my neck while her shoes dangle in the air.

"Thank you, thank you, thank you," she says while peppering my face with kisses. "I know you don't like shopping, but you had fun. Right?"

"After a fashion."

She slides down my body until her shoes touch the floor. "You can't fool me. So tell the truth, James. You liked hanging out with me in funky little shops."

In lieu of a response, I kiss her.

Chapter Twenty-Two

Holly

By the time James finishes kissing me, I feel so warm and liquid that I might fall into a puddle on the floor. That man knows how to kiss—and how to treat a woman. His behavior today proves to me that his grumpy, snarly attitude had been a cover. He wanted to chase me away.

Like that would ever work.

I flop onto the bed on my back and stretch my arms above my head. That makes James veer his attention to my tits. He can't see them, though he knows exactly what they look like, feel like, and taste like. I'm well acquainted with his dick, so we're even.

James gathers up my shopping bags and sets them on the floor at the foot of the bed, arranging them in a neat row.

"You're very efficient," I say. "That's hot, but it's time to come over here and lie down."

He settles in next to me, on his side with his head propped up on one hand. "What should we do for the rest of the day?"

"Relax. All that shopping wiped me out."

James skates one finger along my bare arm. "Why don't we fill up the bathtub and soak in warm water together?"

"You want to take a bath with me?"

"That's right. But if you're too tired…"

"Baths are for relaxation, so it's impossible to be too tired for that." I eye him with fake suspicion. "Are you going to wear your clothes in the tub?"

He chuckles. "No, love."

I hop off the bed and ditch my dress, then remove my bra and undies before kicking my shoes off. "I'm ready."

James rises into a sitting position and grasps my hips to pull me closer. "We need to fill the tub first."

"You get naked while I do that."

I trot into the bathroom and crank the handle, watching as the water slowly rises. But I get bored with that and explore the room in search of anything that might be fun to use in the tub. A little bottle of vanilla-scented bath oil catches my attention. I love that aroma. Despite telling James I'm too tired for sex, just the thought of lying in the tub with him is starting to turn me on.

Can't resist. I grab the bottle of oil and pour some into the rising water. Then I check the temperature and decide it's just right.

James waltzes into the bathroom, buck naked.

Oh yes, that's exactly how I like him to be.

I shut off the faucet and wave toward the tub. "You first. I want to cuddle between your thighs."

His mouth slides into a smirk. He keeps his gaze on me while he lowers his body into the water and spreads his legs. "Your turn. Settle that lovely arse between my thighs."

I obey his command. Cuddling with James in the tub might be even more erotic than sleeping with him in the nude. Not sure I can stop myself from seducing him in the vanilla-scented warmth that surrounds our bodies. I lean back against his chest. He glides his hands up and down my thighs. I rest my head on his shoulder and sigh, feeling more contented than I ever imagined I could.

James wraps his arms around me.

Despite the delicious aroma of vanilla that wafts around us, neither of us tries to start anything. We simply enjoy the pleasure of each other's company. It's refreshing. I doubt my ex would've wanted to cuddle in the tub.

"You know all about me," I say, my voice as silkily relaxed as my body. "But you still haven't told me the rest of your story."

"Not tonight."

"Don't want you to confess right now. But you need to unburden yourself, and I want to help you do that in whatever way I can. Once we're back at the resort."

"I honestly don't know if I can do that."

"Don't worry. I know you can, and I have ideas for how to loosen your lips."

"You make that sound almost erotic."

I raise my arms to link my hands behind his head. "Sex might be the only way to make you talk."

"Perhaps. But it can't be that easy."

"Who said it would be?" I wriggle around until I'm facing him, straddling his lap. "If I need to torture the truth out of you, I'll make it hot and worth your while."

"Every moment with you is worth it."

I have no idea what to say. The other men I've been with wouldn't have told me anything like what James just said. The best I got was "love ya" or "babe, you rock." Not exactly romantic statements.

After our bath, we snuggle under the covers and fall asleep wrapped up in each other. James doesn't have any nightmares this time, and we both wake in the morning refreshed and ready for another day of exploring Auckland. James insists we must eat breakfast in bed, delivered to our room by the proprietor of the b&b. We decide to go with the stereotype of a couple on vacation and feed each other. So what if we've turned into one of those annoying couples who get lovey-dovey every thirty seconds and in public too? It's wonderful.

Today's itinerary takes us to museums and shops, but the most exciting attraction is Sky Tower. It reminds me of the Space Needle in Seattle, but it doesn't have the flying saucer style of that structure. An elevator takes us almost to the top of the thousand-foot tower, where an observation deck gives us spectacular views of the city and the harbor too, with its glistening green water.

James asks another tourist to take our picture using my phone. Then he insists on snapping a pic of just me. When I try to do the same for him, he wants to wriggle out of it. But I snatch my phone away and pester him until he gives in. I get my snapshot of James Bythesea backed by a stunning vista of Auckland.

And I show him the photo.

He screws up his mouth. "That's not an awful picture of me."

"Do you really have no idea how gorgeous you are?"

"Let's move on to our next attraction."

I boost onto my tiptoes to get closer to his face. "Don't need to go anywhere for that. Our attraction sizzles between us every second of every day."

"You know what I meant."

"Uh-huh. And you know what I meant."

"This observation deck is not an appropriate venue for a shag."

"Why not? People base jump off this tower, and that's way riskier than getting it on up here."

He clears his throat and leads me away from the railing. "We would be arrested for sure."

I guess I couldn't reasonably expect him to be on board for public sex yet. I have no doubts, though, that he will want that soon. His passion is powerful, like a hurricane of lust that will make landfall any day now, and I would love to get swept away in the storm.

We finish off our weekend of fun with lunch at a nice little bistro followed by a dolphin and whale watching cruise.

"I know you loved seeing humpback whales," James tells me, "so I thought you would enjoy this cruise too."

"That was so incredibly thoughtful. Thank you."

We board a fancy catamaran in the Hauraki Gulf Marine Park, where the entire tour will take place. Soon, we're racing across the water in search of marine life, and we don't need to wait long for our first sighting—penguins enjoying a dip in the harbor. We see other birds too, ones I've never heard of before, like shearwaters and petrels. They are all so beautiful.

A few minutes later, the catamaran stops to let everyone watch dolphins as they rise out of the water only to slide back under the surface. Even James seems excited about the marine life, grinning and hugging me to his side while he points out another dolphin behind the catamaran.

But I'm still waiting for the whales.

"There!" one of the crew shouts. "Look on the starboard side, and you'll see a pair of pygmy blue whales."

James and I hurry to the other side of the catamaran, and we both lean over the railing to get a better look. The whales have long, slender bodies that glide gracefully through the water. Despite their name, these guys don't look like pygmies to me. They're large and beautiful. James keeps his arm around me while we observe the whales, until the creatures swim out of sight.

The cruise lasts more than four hours, which gives us plenty of time to appreciate the stunning landscape of New Zealand while we enjoy the life that thrives all around the harbor. Near the end of the tour, when I've decided we won't see any more whales, James grabs my arm and all but drags me over to the railing.

"Look," he says. "Your favorites are here."

A pair of humpback whales shoot up out of the water and crash back down, triggering a spray of foam. I shriek and jump up and down like a moron, but I don't care if the other tourists think I'm nuts. My shrieking alerts them to the spectacle on the port side of the catamaran, so nobody will miss this incredible experience. I'd seen humpbacks from afar while flying to Fiji, but now I've gotten to see them up close—so close in fact that I swear I can feel the spray when they dive back under the water.

By the time we return to the b&b, I'm exhilarated and exhausted in the best way.

We have dinner in the dining room, then check out and head home. James needs to be there in the morning to resume his duties as general manager. After this incredible weekend, going back to the resort seems almost like a letdown. But as we climb into the jet to fly back to Fiji and then Heirani Motu, the feeling dissipates, and it's more like coming home than leaving heaven. Since we're both too tired to even think about having sex, instead we watch another movie to pass the hours until we reach Fiji. Rene is waiting for us at the airport.

I sleep for the whole flight back to the resort and only wake up when James picks me up to carry me out of the plane. I insist on walking back to the resort building, though James wanted to carry me the whole way. He's gotten so much more protective of me since Auckland. It's sweet and makes me feel like we've deepened our bond.

But is he ready to share everything with me? I plan to find out this week.

James accompanies me to my suite, but he doesn't want to stay the night with me. He does kiss me goodbye, doing it so thoroughly and for so long that I might orgasm if he doesn't stop. Fortunately, he pulls his mouth away at last. Or maybe that's not fortunate. I'd rather sleep snuggled up with him, but I get that he needs a little space after our weekend together.

I've just shut the door when someone knocks on it. I swing the door open and grin. "James, you're back already."

He winces and avoids looking directly at me. "I can't bear the thought of sleeping without you."

"You know you're always welcome in my suite."

"Well, I was, ah, thinking perhaps you would share my bungalow with me tonight. It isn't as luxurious as your suite, but—"

I seal his lips with two fingers. "Hush, sweetie. I would love to spend the night in your digs."

He pulls my fingers into his mouth and sucks on them.

A sensuous warmth slithers down my spine and straight into my sex. I slide my fingers free of his mouth.

He takes my hand, threading our fingers. "Do you need to bring anything with you?"

"It's a nudist resort. Clothes-free, remember?"

"Yes. But women usually need all sorts of whatsits, like body lotion or other rubbish."

"It's not rubbish. But I can do without that stuff."

He looks more relieved than seems logical, but men rarely are sensible about the things we ladies do to our bodies to stay pretty and smell nice. His relief is adorable, but I don't say that out loud. The poor guy needs a good night's sleep, and so do I.

I yawn as we enter his bungalow, which sits behind and a short distance away from the main building. "Wow, a private bungalow. It's not even a duplex."

"As general manager, I receive a few special dispensations. Private quarters are one of them."

"You deserve special treatment considering how hard you work."

He winces again. "I haven't worked as hard as I should."

I resist the impulse to ask why that is, but he looks so tired that I can't do it. There's always tomorrow.

As we settle down in bed, both of us naked, I realize I need to alert him to my plan. "This week, we are going to talk about your secrets. You already mean more to me than anyone I've ever known, and I need to understand your pain before I can decide what kind of future we might have together. Assuming you want a future with me."

In the dark, I can't see if he's wincing yet again. But I can hear the strain in his voice. "What I want is rarely what I get—or deserve."

"Why do you always talk like you're a supervillain struggling to be good?"

"Let's discuss this another time. All right?"

"Okay."

This week, I will ferret out his secrets. But what will I do if I learn things about him that I can't handle?

Chapter Twenty-Three

James

Monday rushes by so fast that I feel like I'm balanced atop a high-speed train, struggling not to fall off and tumble down a sheer cliff. All right, that might be my anxiety rearing its head again. Holly is determined to understand my pain so we might have a future together. I know that process will not be pleasant, and I doubt she will like what she discovers about me.

Holly traipses into my office at two fifteen and sets her lovely arse on my desk, right beside me. "We're doing it tonight."

"Doing what? Fucking?"

"No, silly. Well, that too. But I meant it's time to pull those secrets out of you."

Yes, doesn't that sound wonderful. A pit forms in my stomach when I consider the implications of her statement.

Holly moves onto my lap. "Relax, James. I'm going to make your interrogation feel like the best kind of torture."

"Because torture is always pleasant."

She leans closer, and her lips graze the shell of my ear. "The way I do it, you'll beg me never to stop."

"You are far too young to understand—"

"I'm a grown woman, not a child. But if you've got a daddy fetish, I'm game."

"That is not amusing."

"Maybe not. But it is hot." She pushes a hand between our bodies to cradle my stiffening cock. "You're already getting hard."

"Not because of what you said. It's because of your naked body."

Holly wriggles around until she's straddling my lap. Her groin is pressed against my erection, and the seductive aroma of her desire tantalizes my senses. "Tonight, James. It's happening tonight. But don't worry, we will have rules for this game, and I won't push you too far. My interrogation method will get you so turned on that you won't remember why you shouldn't confess everything to me."

Though I should tell her I will not participate in her mad scheme, I suddenly realize I don't want to do that. Our weekend in Auckland changed everything between us. Holly has awakened me in ways I never could have imagined, and I no longer want to hide from her. But I also know I will need her help. My fears are too deeply entrenched to be unearthed so easily.

"I want to confess," I tell her. "But this won't be easy for either of us."

"You let me worry about that. I have a plan."

"What sort of plan?"

She takes my hand, clasping it to her breast. "Sex, of course."

"I doubt it will be that simple."

"Never underestimate what I can do. I'll come to your bungalow at eight o'clock. Don't eat dinner first, and be naked when I get there."

She kisses me, then leaves.

I spend the rest of the afternoon struggling to focus on my job while enduring sense memories of Holly holding my hand to her tit. I can't forget the luxurious softness of her breast or the sensual tone of her voice. Though I manage to get my work tasks done, I need to fight the impulse to rush to Holly's suite the moment I've finished and pound on the door. She asked me to wait in my bungalow and not eat dinner yet. I obey her command.

At seven fifty-four, I strip off my clothes and begin pacing the width of the living room.

Someone knocks on the door.

I tear it open, and a jolt of lust awakens my cock. "Good evening, Holly."

"Good evening, James." She lifts the canvas carryall she holds by its straps. "Got my duffel bag full of goodies that will make you melt for me. Are you going to invite me in?"

"Yes, of course, please come in." I move aside to let her enter the bungalow. "I assume you want to go into the bedroom."

"Mm-hm." She sashays past me. "Let's get started."

As I follow her down the short hallway, I don't even try not to stare at her arse. "Do you still mean to torture me with sex?"

"Yep." She glances back at me as we cross the threshold into the bedroom. "I own you tonight."

"What's in your carryall?"

"My what?" She sets her bag on the floor at the foot of the bed. "I guess you're talking about my duffel bag."

"Yes."

She gives me a cheeky smile. "You'll find out soon enough what kind of goodies I have for you. First things first, I need a chair. A good sturdy one."

I hurry back to the living room, grab a chair that meets her requirements, and rush back to Holly. At her command, I set the chair at the foot of the bed.

"Sit down," she says. "And we'll get started."

Her commands ignite a strangely warm sort of anticipation, and I settle onto the chair.

She kneels at my feet, unzipping her bag, and brings out several ropes.

"Are those my ropes?" I ask. "Don't recall taking them with me when I left the other night."

"You forgot. And that's what gave me this idea." She kneels between my feet and holds up the ropes. "Are you comfortable with this?"

"I trust you, Holly. Do whatever you like."

"Maybe you should have a safe word. You know, something you can say that will let me know you need a break. It could be any word or phrase, like 'lavender' or 'hot tamale.' You choose it yourself."

"Why do I need that rubbish? The English language has a perfectly respectable word for that purpose. I need only say 'stop,' and you'll know what I mean."

"Okay, if you want to be stubborn and completely literal."

"I do. And I give you permission to use those ropes on me."

Holly sets about tying my ankles to the chair's legs. Once she's done, she binds my hands behind the chair. "Ready?"

"Yes."

"Time to interrogate you." She sits back on her heels and studies me. "Should I blindfold you? Might make you more inclined to talk since it'll get you even more aroused. I've had experience with blindfolded sex."

"You do that often?"

"Only once, recently."

With me, she means. But Holly still has no idea that I'm the bastard who seduced her anonymously.

"I want to know about your past, James. And I think you want to tell me." Holly roots about in my dresser drawers until she finds one of my ties. "This will work."

She returns to me and covers my eyes with the tie. Now that I can't see, my other senses become heightened. I can hear her breaths and smell how aroused she is, but I also feel the velvety texture of the ropes even more now. Holly grasps my cock, stroking it in easy, sensuous movements that set my heart to racing and ensure that my erection thickens more swiftly.

"You're ready now," she says. "Time to fuck all those secrets out of you."

She continues stroking me even while she mounts my lap and begins nibbling on my lips. I feel her free hand roving over my chest, but when she sucks my bottom lip into her mouth, I try to thrust my tongue into hers. She pulls away. I crane my neck, trying to find her lips, to no avail.

Then she slides off my lap.

"Where are you going, Holly?" I hear her moving around, but I have no idea what she's plotting now. And yes, that makes me want her even more, especially when I hear what sounds like breathing behind me. "What are you doing back there?"

"Found a few more goodies in your bag that you didn't use on me. You are such a naughty boy, James."

The sensuality of her tone makes my breath hitch.

"Would you feel more comfortable if I tell you what I'm doing?" she asks. "Or do you want to be surprised?"

"Surprise me." Can't believe I want that, but I do.

"You're surprising me, that's for sure."

Holly skims her hands down my chest and back up, pinching my nipples, then pulls away again. A moment later, I feel strands of a supple fabric, possibly leather, being dragged over my chest. She slaps me lightly with the object, which I suddenly realize is a whip with multiple strands, the sort designed for sex play.

"You bought this," she purrs into my ear, while she settles one of her soft, warm palms onto my thigh. "Damn, you are so much dirtier than I expected. I love that about you."

"This isn't torture."

"Not yet." She drags the leather strands over my shoulders and down to my groin, tickling my cock with them. "Time to really get going."

The whip goes away, and Holly wraps one hand around the base of my erection. She wriggles her arse to get closer to my groin, then nestles my cock between her folds. It feels like the crown is pointing up, instead of being poised at her opening.

"What are you up to now?" I ask, startled by the roughness in my voice.

Rather than responding, she lifts her arse off my thighs and gradually slides back down. Over and over she repeats the languid, erotic motion while her hairs tease my skin and my breaths quicken. I would grip the chair's arms, but I can't. So I settle for clenching my fists.

Then she pushes my crown just inside her opening and freezes there.

I suck in a shallow breath.

Holly rolls her hips in a circle, a fact I assume but can't verify, and my cock throbs.

"Fuck, I—Bloody hell, you're going to kill me."

A soft, husky laugh tumbles from her lips. "No, you won't die. But it's time to ramp up the pressure."

Holly sinks onto my cock, taking me fully inside her, and holds that position.

I groan with relief.

She hops off the chair. A creaking sound suggests Holly is now sitting or lying on the bed. Soon, sharp gasps and grunts emerge from her lips. No, she can't be doing what it sounds like she's doing.

I turn my head toward the noises. "Are you fucking yourself?"

"Mm-hm. Want in on the action?"

"Yes, right now."

"Okay. But you know what you need to do first."

Confess, that's what she means. I want to give her that, but something inside me still won't allow it. "I can't, Holly, I'm sorry."

"Don't worry. I've barely gotten started."

I hear her slide off the bed and sense it when she approaches me again. She wedges herself between my thighs, and suddenly, her tongue is wrapped around the head of my cock. She moans while she grasps the base and flicks her tongue across the underside. I gasp and jerk. She swallows me whole and pumps me with her mouth while her fingers massage my balls, and the pressure in my cock grows, a sure sign that I could come soon. My pulse races, and my ears are ringing. I need to breathe, I know that, but my breaths come in sharp, shallow gasps.

Holly's mouth vanishes.

Then the blindfold is whipped away from my eyes. I blink rapidly until I recover from the sudden shift in my perception. Holly still kneels near me, inches away from my chair. When I open my mouth to speak, she silences me with two fingers on my lips. I watch in mute fascination while she gags me with my own tie.

"Not too tight, is it?" she asks. When I shake my head, she clasps my face and gives me a quick kiss. "Good. Now we're getting to the real torture."

Holly waddles backward on her knees, then sits back on her haunches. She remains relatively close to me, perhaps two feet away, but I have a clear view of her body. Then she spreads her thighs, exposing her glistening flesh to me.

She slips a hand between her legs to fondle herself.

I can't tear my focus away from what Holly is doing as she rubs her cleft with her whole hand, rocking her hips, and plants her free hand on the floor behind her. The position lets her thrust her hips up more, which exposes her slick, pink folds to me. She moans and grinds the heel of her hand into her cleft faster and faster while rubbing her clitoris with one finger.

"Oh yes, James, I'm imagining you inside me, and it feels so damn good."

The gag prevents me from doing anything more than growling.

She stops masturbating, but only so she can grab a tool I hadn't noticed before. It had lain on the floor in the shadows of the bed. Now, she picks up the vibrator and switches it on. A low, mechanical noise starts up.

Holly shoves the vibrator between her legs.

The device has a curved shaft with a bulbous tip, and she drags the vibrator up and down her cleft, plunging the tip inside her body only to pull it out again. She repeats the process while moaning and making sharp little cries. Then she plunges the device inside her body, with most of its curved length buried deep. With her eyes half-closed and her hips bucking, she shouts my name while clearly climaxing.

"James, yes!"

Holly forced me to watch while she got her end away without me.

She sags onto the floor and shuts off the vibrator, dropping it on the floor. Her chest heaves, and her tits jiggle.

My cock feels like it might explode.

After a moment, Holly rises to her knees and waddles up to me. "Ready to talk?"

"Yes."

She climbs onto my lap, brushing her fingers through my hair. "Are you sure?"

"As sure as I'll ever be." I take a deep breath and force myself to look straight into her eyes. "I told you I was shot five times in an assassination attempt."

"I remember."

"That was the culmination of a long series of events that destroyed my life, my marriage, everything I'd loved and worked for." I shut my eyes for a moment, just long enough to prepare myself. As if I could ever accomplish that feat. "I used to be an accountant. After the firm I'd been working for went bankrupt and shut down, I found a position at a casino in Birmingham. It paid well and allowed my family to move into a larger house in a better neighborhood."

Holly doesn't speak, but the look in her eyes, full of empathy and understanding, might break me. I won't let it. I can't, or else I'll suffer another panic attack. But I know that won't happen.

"Eight months later," I tell her, "I stumbled onto discrepancies in some of the ledgers, but my employer explained that away. I foolishly believed him. A few weeks later, I was working late when I stumbled onto the truth."

"Something bad was going on."

I grimace and feel nausea rising in my gut as the memories flood into me. "On that night, I learned the truth. My employers were running a drugs and sex trafficking ring."

Holly settles her head on my shoulder, though she keeps combing her fingers through my hair.

And I finally unburden myself to her. "No one knew that I'd found out the secret. But I felt compelled to do the right thing, and I went to the police. I wanted to quit my job and move away, but a copper convinced me to become a confidential informant instead. It was the worst mistake of my life."

"What happened then?"

"Once my employers found out I was working with the authorities, they decided I must be eliminated. A bent copper had alerted them to my location."

Holly raises her head to stare at me wide-eyed. "That's why you got shot."

"Eventually. First, our house was burned down, and my children were harassed by large, dangerous men. My wife was run off the road and injured in the crash. I was beaten badly, and later, as you know, shot five times. Finally, we were forced to go into hiding, and then witness protection. We changed our names and moved to Cornwall. But my wife and children quickly grew to despise me, and they wanted out."

"But it wasn't your fault."

"Laraine, Adrian, and Shannon didn't see it that way." I bow my head, which suddenly feels like it weighs a hundred stone. "I had no choice but to let them go. My family had taken on new names, I was told, and they wanted no further contact with me. I was encouraged to choose a new name too. I also moved to another location."

"How did you wind up here on this island?"

I feel shaky, but not as if I'm about to have an attack. Holly's sweetness and warmth bolsters me just enough that I can continue. "I stayed in a remote part of Wales for years, offering accounting services online. Then one day I received a call from my contact in the witness protection service. He informed me that all the villains who knew I had become a CI were dead. A South American cartel got rid of them in prison to eliminate the competition. I was free at last."

"But you don't sound or act like a liberated man."

I shrug one shoulder. "Don't feel that way either. I didn't think I would ever experience true freedom again. Then I saw a strange advert for a job opening at a naturist resort, and my life changed overnight. Eve and Val know most of what I went through. Only you know everything."

She lays a palm on my cheek. "At least I finally understand why you've been so uptight. But you aren't exiled anymore. You have a job you love on a gorgeous island."

"And now I have you." I lift my head. "And I do feel free now, at last. That's all because of you, Holly."

Chapter Twenty-Four

Holly

*A*fter everything James has told me, I have no idea what to say or do next. Sure, this was intended to be a night of hot sex that would loosen him up so he would confess all his secrets. But I could never have guessed how horrific those secrets would be. Nothing in my life could compare to that. I want to console him, but I can't move or speak, paralyzed by what I've learned. Despite my shock, everything he told me only deepens my feelings for him.

I reach behind his back, intending to undo the ropes.

"Stop," he says. When I look up at him, he smirks. "That's my safe word."

"I know. But I'm trying to release you."

"What if I don't want to be released? I need another special word to let you know I want to keep going."

"You mean you want to tell me more about your past."

"No, I've told you everything. I meant that I want you to keep going with the bondage and other things."

I freeze briefly, and I don't feel stupid for being stunned briefly. "I'd love to keep going. If you're one hundred percent sure."

"Yes, love, I'm positive."

Glancing down at his lap, I sigh with mock disappointment. "Looks like I'll need to get you hard again. Oh, darn. That's such a chore."

"My confession did wilt me a bit."

"What method would you prefer for me to get you in the right mood fast?"

"Any method you like."

"Hmm, anything, eh?" Reaching down, I pick up an item off the floor and wag the vibrator in front of his face. "Even this method?"

"Even that."

I switch the vibrator on and skim it along his dick.

He sucks in a sharp breath, then relaxes. "That's an unusual sensation."

"But you like it?"

"Keep going, love."

I glide the vibrator along his dick inch by inch, letting the device graze his skin. I swear I can see him firming up. "Never did this to anyone before, but it's turning me on too."

"This is new for me as well."

While I keep my gaze on his face, I skate the vibrator up to his balls. He jerks and gasps.

Oh yeah, he's ready now.

"I'm going to untie one of your hands," I say. "Then I want you to use the vibrator on my clit while I ride you."

"That sounds…incredible."

"Yeah, it does." I free his right hand, offering him the device. "Let's do it, baby."

He takes the still-vibrating device in his hand.

I grab a condom off the nightstand and roll it onto his dick while his breathing grows heavier. Once I've finished, I rise to my knees and position his cock just right, then lower my body onto his length ever so slowly, reveling in the heat and fullness of him. "Oh, yes, I love the way you feel inside me."

He groans, and his lids fall half-closed. "You're wetter and silkier than ever." He moves the vibrator down to my groin, pushing its tip into my hard nub. "Ride me, Holly."

With my hands braced on his shoulders, I rock my hips, gently at first, then accelerating the pace the more excited we both get. He feels so damn good that my lids fall partway shut too and my nails dig into his shoulders. He presses the vibrator harder into my clit, swirling it around and around, spurring me to slam my body down on his cock while the vibrations push me closer to orgasm, closer to that delicious precipice.

A strangled shout erupts out of James, and the vibrator tumbles from his hand. We're both fighting for breath. I sink my fingers into his flesh even deeper as I sense myself barreling toward that peak, about to career off it. My body tenses. My heart races. But somehow, I keep fucking James.

An animalistic roar explodes out of him—and he comes.

James rears his hips as much as he can, which isn't much thanks to his bindings, and releases everything in two manic thrusts. The second he's done, he rubs my clit furiously.

And I go off. A raw scream is torn from me, a sound I barely recognize as my own voice. The muscles inside me clench him over and over while the breathtaking power of my orgasm stuns me, the pleasure rolling on and on until I can't scream anymore and collapse against James.

He glides his hand up and down my back in a soothing motion.

After a moment, I lift my head. "Post-confession sex is mind-blowing."

"Yes, it is. But only because of you."

"Baloney." I give him a quick, firm kiss. "We both made it happen. And I feel closer to you than ever, now that I know all your secrets."

He gets a strange look on his face, but it vanishes so quickly that I didn't have a chance to decipher it. I want to ask him about that, but he speaks first. "I'm famished. Let's order room service."

"The general manager gets room service? I guess that's a perk of the job, huh?"

"Of course. I'm the lord of the island, aren't I?"

His teasing smile sets off a warmth in my chest that spreads outward to encompass my heart. The other day, I realized that I've already fallen for him. So what if we haven't known each other long? I took my time with all the other men I've ever dated, but being careful and reasonable only caused me heartache. With James, I've found the right man. I refuse to second guess my feelings for him.

But I need to be careful about how I share that revelation with him. Though he might've shared his secrets, he still has hang-ups.

I remove the rest of his bindings, and he slings both arms around me for a rough, hot kiss. Then we browse the room service menu together, selecting so many dishes that I'm sure whoever delivers our food will expect to find a party going on in the general manager's house. But the polite young man who brings our meal to us only lifts his brows briefly before he wheels the cart into the bungalow.

To make James more comfortable, I had put on his bathrobe, which is way too big for me. I did that strictly so James would feel more comfortable. But he shocked me by issuing a command that I should not wear any type of clothing since this is my naturist vacation.

So I ditched the robe.

James wears pants only. The young delivery guy, who James calls Freddie, seems more astonished by the fact his boss is half-naked than by me being completely clothes-free. James gives Freddie a nice tip, which seems to surprise the young man again. Do other bosses of resorts not tip their own staff? Maybe Freddie still hasn't gotten over the shock of his boss being shirtless with his hair a mess too.

Once the door shuts behind Freddie, I realize something else that might have surprised him—the ropes on the floor. I'd forgotten to put those away. *Oops.*

James glances at the ropes. A cute little crinkle appears between his brows.

"Sorry," I tell him. "Didn't mean to leave our toys out for your staff to see."

"No worries. Let them gossip if they want."

"You're okay with that?"

"Why not? Everyone knows I spent the weekend with you in Auckland."

Is he serious? I need to make sure. "But now they might guess that we've had some bondage fun together."

"You can stop worrying, Holly. I don't care what anyone thinks, not anymore."

I study him and I wonder if he'll panic later, once he realizes his penchant for bondage has been exposed. But I think he honestly is cool with that.

"You can stop fretting," he says. "I won't have another panic attack because Freddie knows our little secret and everyone else will probably know soon."

"Can you read my mind? I was just thinking about that."

"Worrying is what you mean." He pulls me close. "I'm not a mind reader, but I have come to recognize your expressions."

"That's a relief. Not sure I want you listening to my thoughts. A girl needs mental privacy."

He slides a hand down to my bottom. "I already know you have a naughty mind, and I would love to hear all your filthy fantasies. How else can I make them come true?"

The idea of James acting out all my secret fantasies makes every inch of skin on my body grow sensitized, readying for another round of rope play. "The interrogation thing was wicked hot, but I think we both need to process the experience before we try anything else."

"You may be right. Let's eat, then decide what to do next."

A meal with James, I've learned, involves plenty of teasing and laughing and kissing. Watching him open up over the past week has been an incredible experience. We agree that we're both too tired, in a good way, for more sex. Instead, we take a shower together and curl up in bed to watch an old movie on TV. Then it's bedtime.

"Mind if I spend the night?" I ask. "Or would you rather sleep alone?"

"You are forbidden from leaving this bungalow until morning."

I tickle his lips with my fingers. "I love it when you get bossy in the bedroom. Makes me want to suck your cock until your eyes roll back in your head."

"But you aren't fond of my bossiness in other contexts."

"Depends on the circumstances."

He tucks a lock of hair behind my ear. "I never want to growl at you again or call you a child."

"Glad to hear it. Although I wouldn't mind your growliness when we're having sex."

"Your rules are getting bloody confusing." He reaches across my body to turn off the lamp on the nightstand. "Time for bed, love."

The way he's started calling me "love" gives me a warm and fuzzy feeling. I've never experienced that before. With James, I'd happily do nothing but lie in bed with him every night and fall asleep in his arms.

When I wake up in the morning, James is already out of bed and dressed for a day of work.

I sit up and yawn. "Are you leaving already?"

"No. I thought I'd get dressed while I waited for you to rise and shine." He leans over the bed to kiss me. "Shall we have breakfast in the dining hall this morning?"

"Sure. Just let me get dressed." I glance around as if I'm confused, then I grin. "Oh, wait. I'm naturally dressed."

"Yes, you are. I prefer you that way."

I slide off the bed and slip into my flip-flops. "You've gotten a lot more adventurous lately. What are the odds you'll go nude in public sometime this week?"

"Nil, I'm afraid. Can't make a naturist of me quite yet."

One fact I've avoided thinking about suddenly hits me, and a wave of cold sweeps through me from head to toe.

James grasps my upper arms. "What's wrong, Holly?"

"I just realized I'm supposed to fly home to Seattle on Saturday."

He stares at me blankly for several seconds, then swallows hard enough that I can see the movement in his throat. He takes a large step backward and clears his throat—twice. "I forgot about that."

"So did I."

We both sound miserable. I feel that way too. The thought of leaving James, going home to my same old dull existence where I'll need to hunt for a job, gives me another chill. Saying goodbye to him... No, I can't do that. But is he ready for more than sex with me? Sharing his secrets doesn't automatically mean he wants me in his life permanently. Do I want that?

He strides to the doorway, pausing there without glancing back. "Let's go to the dining hall."

I follow him out of the bedroom and out of the bungalow. He doesn't speak, not even once we're walking down the hallway in the main building, headed for the dining hall. I need to almost jog to keep up with his longer legs, especially since he's moving so fast. We find a table in the corner of the huge hall, away from the other people gathered here for breakfast.

James insists that I should stay at the table while he gets food for us. He claims that's the logical thing to do so that no one else will steal our spot. I think he probably needs to escape from me. He'll get to do that for real after we eat, when he scurries back to his office.

Despite my every effort to engage him in conversation, we eat in silence. Then James walks me to the lobby and says goodbye. He doesn't kiss me. He didn't even hold my hand while we walked to the lobby, or earlier when we walked from his bungalow to the dining hall.

I spend the morning in my room, eating potato chips and chocolate bars, trying to figure out what I want. James, that's what I want. A life with him, beyond these two weeks of my stay at the resort. But that would mean leaving my old life behind. I would move here, to this tropical island. Then what? Do I become a waitress in the dining hall? It doesn't seem like they need more help. The resort is fully staffed.

But I'm in love with James Bythesea.

I freeze with a large chunk of candy bar wedged in my mouth and stare straight ahead, though I don't really see anything. My entire world has telescoped down to one thing, one revelation, one man. I want to be with James forever and make a new life with him.

How do I react to my epiphany? I stuff my face with chocolate and potato chips.

Yeah, that distracts me for about ten minutes. Then I run out of junk food. So I spend the remainder of the morning watching Australian soap operas on TV.

At lunchtime, I venture out of my suite and make a beeline for James's office. The door hangs halfway open, but I don't find him in there. I march into the lobby and ask the desk clerk if he knows where the boss went.

He shrugs. "Sorry, Miss Temple. I have no idea where Mr. By- thesea is. He didn't come through the lobby. I could call Emilio and ask him if he knows."

"No, that's okay. Don't bother Emilio."

I go out onto the patio, then veer left to head toward the grassy area where all the sporting events, both prearranged and impromp- tu, have been held. James isn't there either. I decide to wander down the path that leads to the beach. Halfway there, I have a "duh" mo- ment and dig my phone out of my little purse.

And I dial James's number.

"Hello?" he says, and he sounds like he has no idea it's me. Well, the Luddite probably doesn't look at the screen when his phone rings. If he did, he'd know it's me.

"It's lunchtime, James. Time to take a break and eat your mid- day meal off my naked body."

He makes a choking sound, then coughs. "Holly?"

"Duh. I finally got you to embrace texting, sort of, but you still haven't mastered caller ID. We've still got work to do to drag you into the twenty-first century." I cluck my tongue. "Honestly, I know eighty-year-olds who are whizzes at tech stuff."

"Did you ring me strictly to give me a lecture?"

"No. I want you"—I pause just long enough to let that innuendo sink in—"to have lunch with me."

"One meal per day in the dining hall is enough."

"A Luddite and a hermit. Good thing you're cute and phenom- enal in bed."

"Am I? Perhaps I can leverage my skills again tonight."

"Mm, I love the rough, sexy tone of your voice. It makes me wet."

Silence.

"Are you still there, James?"

He coughs again. "Yes, I'm here. We could, I suppose, have a picnic or something...somewhere."

"Something somewhere? You're the cutest. How about a picnic at the waterfall?"

"That would be acceptable."

A laugh bursts out of me. "Wow, you make that sound so romantic."

"Where are you now?"

"In the woods, at the intersection where the trail to the waterfall begins."

"Stay where you are. I'll get food and meet you there."

"Perfect." I lower my voice to a near whisper. "I'll stay wet and ready for you, James."

He coughs yet again. Then he mumbles something and ends the call.

I loiter on the trail, and a few other guests wander by, but nobody questions why I'm standing here. They say hi or just nod to me, but all of them smile. Everybody loves it here. Heirani Motu is a magical island.

When I spot the general manager sauntering down the trail toward me, carrying a picnic basket, my pulse accelerates. I want to race up to James and throw my body at him. But I restrain myself. I just saw him at breakfast, yet I feel like I haven't seen him in days.

He claims my hand and kisses my cheek. "Shall we proceed to the falls?"

"Yes, let's proceed."

James raises his brows. "You say that as if you think it's amusing."

"I do. But I love the stuffy way you talk when we're not having sex."

"Am I not stuffy then?" he asks, as we start down the waterfall trail.

I can't stop myself from grinning. "Seriously? You should know the answer to that question. In bed, you are a wild man."

He chuckles. "Only you would ever call me that."

And I love that I get to see sides of him no one else ever will. He's opened up to me in ways I never could have imagined he might. The uptight general manager has become a relaxed, happy man.

Suddenly, I need to blurt out the truth, even if he panics. When I stop walking, he halts too and gazes at me with a question in his eyes.

Now or never.

I roll my shoulders back and say it. "I love you, James."

Chapter Twenty-Five

James

I gawp at Holly as if she's grown several more heads, her skin has turned blue, and she's developed scaly skin with horns on her forehead. She just pronounced that she loves me. A beautiful, sexy, clever young woman thinks she loves *me*. I open my mouth but can't produce any words. Perhaps I should have seen this coming, but I did not. What reason have I given her to feel that way?

"Are you okay?" she asks, gripping my hand more firmly. "I shocked you, didn't I? Sorry. The words kind of, um, flew out of my mouth before I thought about what I was saying."

"You didn't mean it, then."

"Of course I meant it. Maybe I didn't intend to blurt it out right this minute, but I meant every syllable."

"But you—No, you don't mean—" I yank my hand free of hers and stumble backward a step, bumping into a palm tree. "We hardly know each other, Holly. And you are…practically a child."

"Thought you weren't going to call me a child anymore."

My mouth falls open. All I can do is shake my head.

She plants her hands on her hips. "Honestly, James, this should be a happy moment. But you look like you might vomit or pass out or both."

I cover my face with both hands and take slow, deep breaths until my ears stop ringing. Am I about to have a panic attack because Holly declared her feelings for me? It's rubbish. Do I share her feelings? The other day, I had a fleeting thought that I want to start a new life with her. But now that she said…what she said, I have no fucking idea how to respond.

Holly's warm, soft hands settle onto mine. She peels my palms away from my face. "How are you feeling? Vomity? Cold sweaty? Pulse poundy?"

"I am not on the verge of an attack." I shut my eyes briefly, blustering out a breath before I look at her. "Those things you just said are not legitimate words."

"Sure they are—in Holly Temple's Dictionary of Words That Describe James Bythesea. It might turn into a multi-volume work."

"I see."

Reclaiming her hand, I pick up the picnic basket that I hadn't realized I'd dropped and start down the trail again.

She gives me a lips-puckered sideways glance. "So, we're pretending I didn't say the L-word."

"Could we simply enjoy our picnic and discuss that later?"

"We could. But you'll need to confront the truth sooner or later." Her shoulders flag, and she begins to walk in a shuffling gait. "If you don't feel the way I do, please tell me and get it over with."

Bugger me. The sadness in her voice… I can't ignore that, as much as I want to pretend she never spoke those three words. We've reached the waterfall, which gives me a slight reprieve. But once we've spread the blanket on the ground and brought out the food, I can't delay any longer.

Holly has her head bowed while she picks at a piece of fried chicken.

I lay my hand over hers. "Please look at me, Holly."

She sniffles and sucks in a breath.

What a bastard I am. But I have a chance to make this right, so I move my hand to her cheek and urge her to raise her face to me. Her eyes are red and shimmering with unshed tears as I cradle her face in my hands. "I love you, Holly."

She stops breathing, stops blinking, her gaze nailed to mine. "Are you saying that because—"

"I'm telling you the truth. I do love you, Holly." As soon as I spoke those words, her entire expression began to light up. But that won't last long once she hears the rest. "Despite my feelings for you, I'm not sure we should continue with this…whatever it is between us."

"A relationship, that's what it is." Her lips tighten, and her eyes narrow. "If you're about to tell me we can't be together because I'm too young, I might slug you."

"It's more than that. I had no right to pull you into the fathomless abyss my life has become."

"You're being overly dramatic. Besides, my age hasn't changed in the last week. You've known all along that I'm twenty-seven, but that didn't stop you from having intimate meals with me or whisking me away to Auckland."

How can I convince her? With the truth, I hope. "Last week, I resolved to make a new life—with you. But it wouldn't be right for me to do that. It's a selfish impulse. Loving you doesn't mean I should drag you into my world. I'm riddled with anxieties and traumas that I would never want you to experience."

"I know all about your panic attacks, and that didn't scare me away. I know about your past too, but I'm still here." She leans toward me, so close that her breath reflects off my face. "It wasn't a selfish impulse that made you want to start a new life. You deserve happiness. We both do. Relationships are never easy, but giving up without trying is not the answer."

"You don't even know my real name."

She holds perfectly still, with her hands on my cheeks, and stares at me as if she doesn't recognize me. "What do you mean I don't know your real name?"

"I went into witness protection. I told you that, but you still don't understand the ramifications."

"Explain it."

Though I want to break eye contact, I can't do it. The fear in her gaze transfixes me. "James Bythesea is not my original name. I had to invent a new one, in case one of my enemies escaped or was released from prison early and came looking for me. Bythesea is an old surname, one that hasn't been in use for at least three hundred years. No one in my family ever used that name, which made it the perfect alias."

Her lips have fallen open, and she looks a bit pale. I've shocked her at last.

"Now you see," I tell her. "You don't know me, and you never will."

"Bullshit. If you let me in—"

"Why can't you give up on me?"

"How can you ask me that? I don't give up on the people I love, and no one has ever meant more to me than you do." She studies me for a moment. "What is your real name?"

"James."

"But your last name—"

"Does not matter. That man no longer exists."

She drums her fingers on her knee while squinting at me. "Obviously, you exist. And it's just as obvious that your past still has a hold on you."

"Let's eat our food before insects descend on us."

"Sure, we can eat first. But after that, we will talk again. You can't drop a bombshell on me and then pronounce we can't talk about it."

I see no point in arguing with her right now. I don't like to argue, as a rule, but Holly refuses to accept what I've said and move on. She seems determined to dig out all the final secrets of my past. I've told her everything it's safe for her to know.

That nightmare I had in Auckland… If something happened to Holly, I could never forgive myself.

We enjoy our picnic in silence, though the word enjoy seems rather inappropriate to describe the situation. Holly continues to stare at me, and my skin starts to itch from the intensity of her focus. I wolf down my food faster than I should, simply to end this awkward situation. Once we've put the remnants of our meal in the basket, along with the blanket, I rise and head for the trail.

"Not so fast, James. I want straight answers."

"About what?" I do not glance back at her.

"What is your real last name?"

I open my mouth, prepared to tell her once again that it doesn't matter, but my mobile rings. The caller ID informs me it's Emilio. "This is work. I need to take it."

She blows out an annoyed sigh. "Go on, take the call."

While my mobile rings again, I see the disappointment on her face. Then I answer. "Yes, Emilio, what is it?"

"We've received a dispatch from the Fiji Meteorological Service. The tropical cyclone that formed about eight hundred kilometers away has expanded. It's unclear whether it will affect us. There's no clear trajectory yet."

I try not to glance at Holly, but my eyes have other ideas. "We have a plan for this sort of circumstance. Go ahead and enact the first stage."

"That means alerting all the guests."

"Yes, I know. I'm coming back right now, so we should gather the senior staff members for a quick meeting before we make the announcement."

"Will do, boss."

I stuff the mobile in my pocket.

Holly is watching me with her brows furrowed. "What's going on? You sounded very professional and in charge, which must mean something's up. Especially if you're rallying the troops."

"A tropical cyclone is forming about eight hundred miles offshore. So far, we have no reason to believe it will come here, but cyclones can be difficult to predict, just like Atlantic hurricanes."

"We'd better get back to the resort, then. The troops need their general."

"I am not a general."

She hooks her arm around mine, giving me her best teasing smile. "You are the *general* manager."

"That might be amusing under different circumstances."

"Are you referring to our conversation a little while ago? Or the possible cyclone?"

"Both."

We walk back to the resort much faster than we had when we headed out to the waterfall. Holly needs to almost jog to keep up with me. Perhaps I am rushing mostly because I need time away from her, but I am genuinely concerned about the weather situation. Eve and Val had insisted that all our employees receive training in how to handle this type of event and that we formulate a concrete plan for such a situation. That time has come. And I am responsible for protecting everyone on this island.

Blimey.

In the lobby, Holly grasps my arm to capture my attention. "How worried should I be?"

"Try not to worry too much right now. We don't even know if the storm will reach this island. But keep your mobile with you at all times, to make sure you'll receive any emergency messages from us."

"Okay." She hugs herself. "Wish I could stay with you, though."

I pull her into my arms and kiss her forehead. "Everything will be fine, you have my word."

"Things change fast, huh? Ten minutes ago you were trying to dump me and couldn't get away fast enough. Now, I'm the one panicking."

"You are not panicking." I rest my forehead on hers. "And I was not trying to get away from you. I meant to... I don't know. Get some space and some air. But we can discuss the issue of what a wanker I am after the storm threat is over?"

She bites her lip but nods. "Is it okay if I go to the beach? You said the cyclone isn't coming this way yet."

"Yes, that should be fine, as long as—"

"I keep my phone with me. Aye-aye, captain."

"What happened to me being a general?"

"Either term works." She hops up on her toes to whisper into my ear, "You can boss me around in bed tonight, and I'll call you whatever you like."

A throat-clearing behind me shatters the spell Holly's presence always weaves around me. I turn to see Emilio standing there looking rather uncomfortable.

"Sorry to bother you, boss," he says. "But I have the staff gathered in the conference room."

I kiss Holly's cheek. "I'll find you later."

Then I do the unthinkable. I walk away from a beautiful naked woman who wants me to boss her around in bed. Even the cyclone threat can't stop me from thinking about Holly and all the things I'd love to do to her and with her tonight. But by the time the staff meeting ends, I'm too tired to do anything more than ring Holly on my mobile to ask if she would like to sleep with me in my bungalow tonight.

"Just sleep?" she asks. "Or will there be ropes and orgasms involved?"

"I'm afraid it will involve only actual sleeping. I'm exhausted. But I will understand if you're not interested."

"Not interested in sleeping with you? Please. I'd share a crappy futon with you just for the chance to wake up in the morning cuddled in your arms."

"Ah, yes, I agree."

"You agree?" She laughs again. "Mentally clenching again, aren't you? Relax, I'm not expecting a proposal tonight."

We say goodbye, and I don't see or hear from Holly again until she knocks on the door to my bungalow at seven o'clock.

"You don't need to knock," I tell her when I open the door. "Come right in."

"Can't. I don't have a key card for your place."

"Oh. Of course. Sorry, I'll get an extra one for you in the morning." I shut the door behind her. "I took the liberty of ordering room service."

"Awesome. I'm so hungry I don't want to wait for food to arrive. I need to chow down right now." She commandeers my hand, leading me into the bedroom. There, she drops onto the bed, making the mattress bounce. "Let's eat, James. Then you can tell me why you think we can't work out."

Bloody hell.

Chapter Twenty-Six

Holly

James walks over to the chair by the window and settles onto it with all the care of a man who thinks I might have dropped invisible tacks on the seat. Then he wriggles like he can't quite get comfortable. "Must we discuss that now? I'm famished."

"Me too. But it should be a straightforward answer to my straightforward question."

"It is not that simple."

"Sure it is. Tell me why—"

"Because I'm a mess," he snaps. "I should never have seduced you, and I absolutely should not have admitted how I feel."

"I seduced *you*, sweetie. In your office."

He grimaces.

I pat the mattress beside me. "Come over here, please. You need intimacy, not distance."

James makes a grumpy face, then heaves his body out of the chair to pad over here. He perches his fine ass on the edge. "Intimacy won't cure what's wrong with me."

"There's nothing wrong with you. Having problems is not a disease."

"For me, it is an incurable ailment."

"Bullshit."

He gazes at me with such anguish that I want to pull him into my arms and kiss away his pain. But I know that won't work. He's too committed to blaming himself for everything. James probably thinks he's responsible for the cyclone that might hit this island.

"Tell me why you believe we can't work," I say. "One concrete, rational reason."

"One reason? I'm too bloody old for you."

I roll my eyes.

He makes another grumpy face. "Don't dismiss what I said. It's true. When I'm sixty, you'll be forty-two and still a young, vital woman."

"I know plenty of people in their sixties, and they are hardly shriveled up shells waiting to kick the bucket."

"You must want children. I can't go through that again."

"Not if you're determined to make everything a catastrophe from the get-go." I take a moment to consider exactly what I need to say next. Then I dive in. "Give us a real chance, that's all I'm asking for. Take the rest of this week to let us figure out what we want, if our lives could mesh, if we should try to make it work. Is that too much to ask?"

"Three more days? I doubt that's long enough."

I try so hard not to grumble out a frustrated breath, but I fail. "There you go again, assuming the worst."

He bows his head, and his shoulders cave in. "I was nearly assassinated, and my family abandoned me. I can't ever again be a happy, stable man."

"Give me this week to prove you wrong. If after that you still believe we can't work out, I won't argue anymore. Deal?"

James eyes me sideways. "All right."

"Thank you. Now, let's eat. Sunbathing on the beach this afternoon made me so ravenous that I could eat a whole shark."

"You would need to find and catch one first."

"Are you doubting my tenacity?"

His lips twitch in a smirk that can't quite take hold. "I would never doubt you can accomplish anything you set your mind to."

I could point out that his statement implies I can convince him we belong together, but I won't say it. He needs time, and the least I can do is grant him that. "I won't pester you for details anymore. It's up to you to decide when or if you want to share the rest."

James goes over to the corner where he stashed the wheeled cart full of food. He pushes that over to the bed, then crawls over my body to sit beside me.

And we have dinner together.

Once our tummies are full, we cuddle up to watch a movie on TV—a romantic comedy, which James chose. We take a shower together too, but it's not sexy playtime. We get clean and crawl into bed together as we've done so often lately. In the morning, I wake to find James lying beside me, still sleeping. I consider sneaking out to get breakfast for us, but I don't want to leave him when he's sleeping soundly. Instead, I snuggle up to him and watch him sleep.

Fifteen minutes later, he rouses.

James lets out a big, loud yawn. Then his bleary eyes focus on me, and he smiles. "Good morning, love."

"You slept in."

He lifts his head to glance at the clock on the nightstand. "I'm not late for work."

"No. But you usually wake up before I do."

"I must've needed the sleep." He slides an arm over my hip to pull me close. "How about a quick morning shag?"

Since I feel his dick swelling, I see no reason why we shouldn't take advantage of that. "Absolutely. Let's have a quick shag."

"I love hearing you say that word." He palms my ass. "But I love hearing you scream my name even more."

"Mm, I love that too."

He pushes his knee between my thighs, rubbing it against my already slick flesh. "One of the fringe benefits of being the general manager is that I can fuck you in private. No one can even see this bungalow from the main resort areas, much less hear you scream when you come."

"Somebody probably heard us all those other times when we got naughty in my suite."

"I don't care."

My skepticism rears it head, and I roll onto my back. I'm probably squinting at him too. "Last night, you were ready to dump me. This morning, you don't care who hears us having sex."

"You said you wouldn't pester me anymore."

"No, I said I wouldn't pester you for more details about your past and your anxieties. Not quite the same thing."

"Fair point." He rolls on top of me. "Forget about all of that and let me have you right now."

I spread my thighs.

James rolls on a condom, then rises onto his straight arms. He rocks his hips back, about to push inside me.

The landline phone on the nightstand rings.

He growls a curse I can't quite understand.

"Don't you need to get that?" I ask.

James holds still, offering no response to my question. The second the phone stops ringing, he thrusts into me to the hilt.

His cell phone starts warbling.

The man who has his dick buried inside me hisses a slew of curses, most of which I understand, and withdraws from my body. He leaps off the bed to hunt for his phone. Finally, he snags it off the table by the window. Now breathing hard, he answers with a curt hello.

His annoyed expression melts into a blank look. "Are you sure? Sorry. Yes, I know you wouldn't call unless you were certain." He glances at me and winces. "I'll be there in ten minutes."

He tosses his phone onto the table.

I lever myself into a sitting position. "The boss is needed, I take it."

"Yes. The cyclone has strengthened and does indeed seem to be heading this way."

A chill slithers over my skin, raising goosebumps. "How serious is the situation?"

"So far, it appears the storm will not be catastrophic. But there will likely be downed trees and possibly power lines. We need to batten down the hatches."

"What can I do to help?"

"Nothing, yet." He rests his hands on his hips and frowns at his own dick. It's still fully hard. "I need a cold shower."

"Oh, I can take care of that little problem for you, no shower required." I slide my legs off the bed. "Come over here."

"You don't need to do that."

"But I love the taste of you." I crook my finger at him. "Get over here now, James."

He saunters up to me, that incredible cock waving in my face.

I lean forward.

James throws his arms around my waist and flips me over, so I'm now facedown on the bed. My ass and legs hang off the edge. "A blow job won't relax me enough. To deal with the looming crisis, I need to fuck you now."

Before I can speak, he slants over my body to slap his palms down on the mattress. Then he punches his cock into me so hard that I bounce and yelp. I always love the feel of him inside me, but I don't have time to revel in it. He starts pounding into me, grunting with each inward lunge, while I clench my fingers in the sheets and hang on for the climax. The rough way he's taking me shoves me over the edge faster than ever before as my body milks him with powerful spasms that just won't quit.

I bury my face in the sheets and scream.

The slapping of his balls on my ass echoes in the room, along with the sound of my wet flesh colliding with his length. He pumps into me twice more, groaning deeply, then withdraws.

James kisses my cheek. "Thank you, darling. I'll repay the favor later."

"I came too. No favor involved."

He picks me up and sits down on the bed, keeping me cradled in his arms. "Please don't leave the main building today. I need to know you are safe."

"Okay. If that will make you feel better."

"It will. A cyclone, even a less intense one, can be dangerous."

"Go, do your boss thing. I'll head to my suite and stay there."

He cups my cheek in his hand. "If anything happened to you, I wouldn't want to go on living."

"Please don't say things like that. It scares me."

James moves me onto the bed next to him and stands up, gazing down at me for a moment. Then he heads for the closet to get dressed. After a quick breakfast, he walks me back to my suite, kissing me sweetly at the door before he hurries to the conference room for a meeting with his staff.

How worried should I be about the cyclone? James made it sound like it won't amount to much, but then he acted as if he's worried I might die soon. Jeez, I wish he didn't have such a strong doomsday streak. But I know that's only anxiety. I shouldn't let his fears affect me.

Nothing bad will happen.

After a couple hours of staring at the TV, I venture out into the lobby. From my suite, I could see darker clouds inching this way. But from this vantage, I notice the palm trees beginning to sway slightly more than an average breeze would stir them. I'd love to step outside for a better look at the sky, but I promised James I wouldn't leave this building. The last thing I want to do is cause him more stress.

Besides, the ever-darkening sky is making my skin prickle.

"Kinda spooky, isn't it?" a familiar voice asks.

I glance back at Kevin. "Yeah, it is spooky."

He comes up beside me, his attention riveted to the swaying trees. "I've never been through a cyclone or a hurricane. Have you?"

"Nope. We don't really get those in Seattle."

"Did you hear? We're under orders to stay indoors today, preferably in this building."

"Yeah, I heard that."

He gives me a sly smile. "You probably heard the news first, since you're the general manager's girl."

I assume he's not being snide. He really doesn't seem like the nasty type. "James will make sure we all stay safe. He's amazing at his job."

"He's one lucky guy too." Kevin's brows draw together as he shifts his attention to the windows. "Seems like the winds are getting stronger."

The distinctive sound of an intercom system switching on makes us both turn away from the windows. James's voice fills the building. "Attention, all guests and employees. A tropical cyclone that formed approximately eight hundred miles offshore has shifted track and seems to be heading this way. We advise everyone to stay inside and away from windows as much as possible. Out storm response team has already begun boarding up the windows and will get to every room by day's end. We expect high winds and torrential rain, but nothing too dangerous. Please remain calm and listen for any further announcements. Thank you."

He sounds calm and authoritative. I guess a cyclone doesn't bother him. It's being with me that gives him panic attacks. Not sure how to feel about that.

I hang out with Kevin and his pals for a while, and we play some games, though not pinball. But after an hour of that, I've had enough. Knowing about the storm threat makes me edgy, so I return to my suite and try to relax by watching more TV.

Then Emilio and another man show up to "secure the room." I watch them close the shutters that will protect me, but Emilio says that's just a precaution because the windows are impact and wind resistant. A cold pit forms in my tummy anyway. This is really happening. I'm about to experience my first cyclone.

After the guys leave, I trudge over to the windows and stare at the wooden shutters that now cover them. I'm trapped. The whole building will be boarded up this way, which means we will all be stuck in a big box. Though I've never been claustrophobic, thinking about how the whole structure is encased infects me with a growing sense of impending doom.

The resort-wide intercom comes on again, and hearing James's voice soothes me—for about five seconds. That's how long it takes him to announce himself. Then it's time for the update. "Tropical Cyclone Mimi has strengthened into a category two storm. We are currently advising all guests to wear clothing and shoes in case an evacuation becomes necessary. It's still unclear what precise path the storm will take, but we want everyone to be aware of the situation. The kitchen will remain open twenty-four hours a day for the duration. We will make further announcements as necessary. Thank you."

I love his voice, but it doesn't comfort me when he uses words like "evacuation."

My cell phone rings. I race back to the bed and snatch my phone off the nightstand. "Hello?"

"It's me, love. How are you holding up?"

Relief floods through me so powerfully that my shoulders slump. "James, thank goodness."

"You sound stressed."

"Well, my suite has become a pretty prison cell, and I'm kind of terrified about the cyclone."

"I don't need to be in my office right now. Shall I come to you?"

"Oh, yes, please." The words rushed out of me in one breathless statement. "I don't mean to sound like a total wuss. If you need to keep an eye on the storm, I'll be okay alone."

"You don't sound that way. I'm coming to you."

He hangs up without saying goodbye. Should I call him back to say he shouldn't come? I can't convince myself to do that. I want him with me.

Chapter Twenty-Seven

James

When I knock on the door to Holly's suite, it's torn open almost immediately. She stands there breathing hard, as if she sprinted here from elsewhere in the suite. Before I can speak even one syllable, she sags into me with her face mashed to my chest, muffling her words. "I'm so glad you're here."

I hook a thumb under her chin, encouraging her to look up at me. "Shall I come in? Or would you rather we stand here on the threshold?"

"Get your butt in here."

Holly wraps her arms around my waist and backs away from the door. I kick it shut and let her haul me over to the bed.

"You were meant to be wearing clothes," I tell her. "Evacuation protocols are in effect."

Her eyes flare wide. "We're evacuating now?"

"No, love." I sit down, and Holly does the same. She still hasn't released me yet. So I clasp her to me and kiss her forehead. "Evacuation protocols have been activated in case we need them. That's all."

"We don't need them yet?"

"No."

"Thank heavens." She wriggles out of my arms. "I'll get dressed."

I watch while she finds undergarments and a pair of trousers, as well as a blouse, all of which she'd bought in Auckland. They look lovely on her, the way they hug her figure in a flattering yet modest way. Her bra lifts her perfect breasts. I love her body with or without clothing, but she looks the best in nothing at all. She wants me to become a naturist, and I wish I could grant her wish, though I doubt I ever will. Yet another reason why we don't belong together.

I love her. But I still can't shake my anxieties about being with a twenty-seven-year-old woman. Or perhaps it's my last secrets that keep me from committing to a life with her.

Holly returns to the bed, and we sit against the headboard, side by side. I drape an arm across her shoulders. She rests her head in the hollow of my shoulder. This feels right, like I've always been meant to hold this woman, to make love to her, to spend the rest of my life with her.

"How are you so calm?" she asks. "Being with me gives you panic attacks, but a cyclone doesn't faze you."

"I think you were right that it's always been emotional stress that triggers the attacks. Even when I was shot five times, I didn't suffer any mental breakdown."

"So, by 'emotional stress,' you mean romantic relationships."

"Not always. Until the past few months, I hadn't suffered an attack for more than three years, and that one had nothing to do with romance."

Holly raises her head to study me. "What caused the one a few months ago?"

"I had just flown back to the UK after accepting Val and Eve's offer to become general manager of their new resort."

"What were you afraid of?"

"Bollocksing up my best shot at redemption." I rub my eyes while I try to figure out how to explain this to her. "I had precisely no experience in the hospitality industry. Val and Eve knew about my panic attacks, but I still couldn't believe they wanted me to run a resort for them. As soon as I got home, I realized what an enormous task I had ahead of me. Then I began to imagine all the ways I might cock it up. This job was my last chance."

"Last chance for what?"

"Finally making a fresh start for myself. I'd become a pariah in my old life."

"I don't understand why. You didn't do anything wrong."

Though my first instinct is to avoid explaining, I refuse to keep doing that to Holly. "After I helped the authorities take down the drugs and sex trafficking ring at the casino, the business shut down completely. All the employees lost their jobs and had to go on the dole. They blamed me for ruining their lives."

"But you did a good thing. You saved innocent people from traffickers who abused them."

"No one saw me as a hero. They lost their jobs, their livelihoods, and some even lost their homes in the aftermath."

"But it wasn't your fault."

I nuzzle her hair, breathing in the sweet scent of her. "Your belief in me is touching, but the truth doesn't matter. I was perceived to be the wrecking ball that smashed their lives."

"They ruined your life. It's not fair."

"How often is the world fair?"

She lays her head on my shoulder. "Guess you're right. But I hate that those people blamed you. Is that when you started having panic attacks?"

"Yes. I've had six total, including the recent ones."

"I made your attacks worse, didn't I?"

"No, pet, you did not." I brush my fingers through her hair. "I made them worse with my fears and anxieties."

A crack of thunder detonates overhead. The glass doors rattle.

Holly's head pops up. She glances around with wide eyes. "What was that?"

"Thunder. Cyclones often generate thunderstorms, especially around the eyewall."

"You're an expert on hurricanes?"

"I learned the basics when I took this job. These are probably thunderstorms that are spinning out in advance of the cyclone itself."

Wind buffets the building, thumping into the shutters affixed to the outside of the sliding glass doors and windows. Holly draws her knees up to huddle against me. I link my arms around her, which seems to comfort her, since she rests her head on my chest. After awhile, I suggest we go down to the dining hall. Being in a much larger space seems to relax her a bit more, but I think it's really the noise of conversations going on around us that makes her less anxious about the storm raging outside.

Holly convinces me to eat pudding, though I've never liked that rot.

"It's not 'rot,' James," she says, holding another spoonful to my mouth. "You liked the first taste. Try another one."

With a sigh, I part my lips to let her slide a spoonful into my mouth. One does not actually eat pudding. It sort of melts on my tongue. I make an appropriate noise to let Holly know I don't completely dislike it. She smiles, clearly satisfied with her ability to talk me into doing things I would never do on my own.

Holly feeds me one more mouthful of pudding, then sets down her spoon. "Let's go back to my suite and have sex."

I stare at her with the last bit of pudding balanced on my tongue. Then I force myself to swallow it.

She grins. "I shocked you, didn't I?"

"No, you surprised me. There's a difference."

"Mm-hm." She leans across the table to whisper, "Tell you what. Let's grab a bottle of wine, go back to my suite, and see what happens."

Though I say nothing, she gives me a sexy smile. I've seen that expression often since we started shagging. But then she slips a spoonful of pudding between her lips and slowly licks away the remnants that cling to her flesh.

I've never seen her do that before. "Why are you smiling, Holly?"

"You got a steamy look in your eyes when I suggested getting a bottle of wine."

"Did I? That must mean I agree with your plan."

"You get the wine. I'll steal some snacks from the buffet."

We separate only long enough to accomplish our dual missions, then we return to her suite. She seems quite relaxed in this room now, despite the shuttered windows and glass doors.

"The potential for sex erased your fear of the storm," I say, as I open the wine bottle. "Maybe I should try fucking you whenever I feel a panic attack coming on."

Holly lies down on the bed, spreading her body across half the mattress. "I volunteer to be your therapist."

I swig a mouthful of wine straight from the bottle.

She clucks her tongue. "You're supposed to pour it into a glass."

"I'm cutting out the middle man."

Holly crawls toward me on hands and knees, grabs the wine bottle from me, and takes a large swig. "Mm-mm-mm. That's the best zinfandel I've ever tasted."

"We offer only the best at the Au Naturel Naturist Resort."

She swallows three mouthfuls of wine without pausing, then lets out a long, satisfied sigh.

I need to get her naked now.

But then she starts guzzling the wine.

I snatch the bottle away and wag a finger at her. "Now, now, that's no way to deal with storm anxiety."

"Mm, scold me some more. It's hot." Holly sways a little, blinking rapidly. "Whew, this is hitting me faster than I expected."

"Probably because you aren't meant to toss down wine as if it were a gallon of water. Zinfandel is also one of the most alcoholic wines."

"Hmm, good point." She hands me the bottle and flops back onto the bed. "I'm still good to go for steamy sex."

Since she spoke those words while yawning, I have trouble believing her claim. Considering how anxious she's been about the cyclone threatening the island, I shouldn't take advantage of her of tipsy state.

I set the bottle on the nightstand and crawl over Holly's body to lie down beside her. When I raise my arm, she nestles close to me. I wrap my arm around her. "You need rest, darling, not sex."

"Mm, but I love the way you 'shag' me."

"Let's wait until morning."

"Sure, whatever you say." She slings a leg over mine. "You're like a big, warm, sexy living body pillow."

"Ah, thank you."

I comb my fingers through her hair, and soon, she drifts off to sleep despite the wind and the rain. Not even the thunder bothers her. After a while, I fall asleep too. I wake up later but can't tell what time of day or night it might be. The shuttered windows and glass doors completely block out the light. So I gently peel my arm away from Holly to stretch it out toward the nightstand. With a bit of finagling, I manage to turn the clock toward me enough to read the time.

Seven fifty-two. It's morning.

I should go and check on the state of the resort as well as my employees and our guests. The wind must have died down, because I no longer hear it buffeting the building. I don't hear thunder either. Though I carefully extricate myself out from under Holly without disturbing her, before I commit to leaving this suite, I take my mobile into the bathroom to ring Emilio.

"How is everything this morning?" I ask as soon as he picks up the call. "Has anyone done a damage assessment yet?"

"We did a quick assessment. But the cyclone shifted track and veered away from the island overnight, so we missed the brunt of it."

"Good news? I won't complain about that."

Emilio says nothing for a brief moment. His voice takes on a somewhat baffled tone. "You sound...cheerful this morning."

Well, I can understand his reaction. I haven't been a cheerful bloke since coming here—or before that either. Holly has changed my life and my attitude.

"Gather the staff in the conference room," I say. "We need to have a meeting. I'll be there in fifteen minutes."

"Will do, boss."

After saying goodbye to Emilio, I tiptoe back to the bed where Holly lies asleep. She looks so peaceful and lovely that I can't bear to disturb her. But I don't want her to wake up wondering what happened to me. I find a pad of paper and write a note explaining that I need to attend a staff meeting and that the cyclone danger has passed.

I brush stray hairs away from her face, gazing down at her for a moment before I go. She is perfect. I don't deserve her love, but I need her. As selfish as that is, I don't care anymore. Finally, I drag myself out of the room. First, I kiss her cheek. Then I walk out, closing the door behind me as quietly as possible, and head to the conference room.

After a brief meeting with my employees, I follow Emilio outside so we can both survey the damage more thoroughly than he had done earlier. We find a few fallen branches, and some of the chairs and chaises got blown around a bit, but otherwise the resort has endured the storm quite well. Rene takes us up in the plane to see if the island as a whole has suffered a worse fate. No, it hasn't. We dodged a bullet. And thanks to the way we planned ahead for this sort of event, everything went smoothly.

Maybe my luck has finally changed.

Chapter Twenty-Eight

Holly

I lie back on my chaise, eyes closed, and let the birdsongs and rustling leaves erase the world from my mind. It's hard to believe that last night it seemed like a cyclone was about to ravage the island, but now everything is back to normal. By the time I'd woken up this morning—at nine o'clock, the latest I've ever slept—the shutters had been removed from my suite. I saw a few downed branches when I first came outside. Once I finished my breakfast, even those were gone.

The sun feels so good. Its warmth penetrates my skin and engenders a liquid desire deep inside my body, giving me a sudden craving for a certain Brit. Okay, maybe I'm horny because I started thinking of him, not the other way around. We never got the chance to make love last night, so I need to find James and let him know I feel cheated. That means I have to peel myself off the chaise to look for him.

The nice young woman behind the reception desk tells me that James and Emilio are just coming back from an island-wide assessment of the storm damage. She says Rene took them up in the plane, but they landed again about ten minutes ago.

I return to the patio to wait.

A few minutes later, James and Emilio exit the woods path. Emilio notices me first and says something to James, who had been focused on scrutinizing the trees. He glances my way and smiles. Emilio grins and slaps his boss's arm. I can't hear whatever he tells James, but the general manager seems a touch embarrassed.

Emilio jogs toward the lobby, but James saunters over to me. "Good morning, darling."

Whenever he calls me that, warmth blossoms in my chest and spreads outward to heat up my whole body. "Good morning, James. I heard you guys took an aerial tour."

"To check on the island and the cell tower, mostly. Everything is fully operational and undamaged. Only sporadic downed branches and seaweed on the beach."

I rise and reach for his hand. "Thank you for leaving me that adorably sweet note."

"Sweet? It wasn't a love note."

"Maybe not. But you write such elegant prose that it feels like a Shakespeare sonnet." I peck a kiss on his lips. "You have beautiful penmanship."

"I don't see what's adorable about that."

"You're a man. Of course you don't get why I think your note and your perfect handwriting are cute and sweet. But trust me, you are one man in a million."

He scratches behind his ear, focusing on the chaise beside us.

That's even more endearing, but I won't tell him so. Instead, I walk backward while keeping hold of his hand. "Come on. Let's go to the dining hall for lunch."

"Is it lunchtime already? I've lost track of the hours."

"You were busy taking care of everybody. That's a general manager's job. But I'm here to take care of you and make sure you don't overwork yourself." As we start walking toward the lobby doors, I slip my arm around his waist. "I'll provide any kind of therapy you need, whether it's a conversation or even a sensual massage."

"Tonight, I may take you up on that offer. But not right now."

As we enter the lobby, I suddenly realize that I only have a few days left to make a life-altering decision. Will I go home and forget about James, turning our time together into nothing more than a vacation fling? Or will I uproot my life to stay here with him? I love James, but this is a huge decision.

I need to discuss it with him.

But I procrastinate until after lunch, bringing up the subject only when he tries to head for his office. I know he needs to get back to work, but I beg him to please-please-please blow off his duties for a little while so we can talk in private—at the waterfall. He agrees to my plan and even seems happy about it.

We've reached the intersection with the waterfall trail when it starts to rain.

"Should we run back to the resort?" I ask. "Your clothes are getting soaked."

He glances down at his body. "I am rather wet."

"Want to go back?"

"No." James backs me up to a palm tree, where its branches form a small canopy above our heads. While the rain pours down, he kisses me. Thunder rumbles in the distance, but neither of us pays attention to that. We devour each other, oblivious to the weather or the possibility that someone might see us, too consumed by our own passion to care about anything else. When the downpour becomes a light shower, we race down the path to the falls hand in hand and sprint across the bridge to the secluded spot we'd found before.

James unbuttons his shirt.

"What are you doing?" I ask as I watch him shrug out of his shirt. He hangs it over a branch and unhooks the button on his pants. I gape at him. "What are you doing?"

"You already asked me that." He pulls down the zipper, letting his pants drop to his ankles. "Isn't it fairly obvious?"

"Looks like you're stripping down to your undies."

"Wrong." He smirks as he kicks his shoes and socks off and steps out of his pants. "But you'll understand soon enough."

Then he does something that makes my jaw drop. He sheds his boxer shorts. James Bythesea is completely naked. Outdoors.

"Are you becoming a naturist?" I ask. "Or is this a secret nudity session?"

He turns around and leaps into the pool, cannonball style.

I can't move or speak or process what James just did. Someone might see him. Someone other than me. Yet he willingly stripped and jumped into the waterfall pool.

"Come in with me," he calls out. "Feels bloody wonderful."

What else can I do? I jump in with him. He catches me around the waist and seals his mouth over mine, kissing me for so long that I feel desire tingling through my sex.

Do we make love in the water? Of course we do.

I loved James already. But now, here in the waterfall pool during a rainshower, I fall even deeper under his spell.

After our interlude, we return to the lobby. James goes back to work. But for the rest of the week, we spend as much time together as possible, doing more than kissing and getting it on outdoors. We talk too, though James continues to refuse to tell me what his real name is. Maybe I shouldn't care, but not knowing makes everything between us feel unsettled.

I forget about most of my worries on Thursday, when James surprises me again.

We've decided to have another picnic on the beach, and I let James choose the spot. The first surprise he gives me happens when he selects a location right on the most popular stretch of the beach, just off the main trail to the resort building. Okay, that's unusual for a man who cherishes his privacy. But once we've laid out our blanket, he does something that leaves me totally speechless.

James Bythesea strips naked. On a public beach.

I gape at him while other guests wander onto the sand, traipsing right past us. James greets every one of them with a broad smile and a hello. When I at last regain the power of speech, I turn my undoubtedly bulging eyes toward him.

Only four words come out of my mouth. "You're naked. In public."

"You only just noticed?"

"No. But I was too stunned to say anything." I flap my arms this way and that. "Look around. People can see you."

He shrugs. "I don't give a toss anymore."

And I know he means that.

I love his new attitude, and I want nothing more than to be with him permanently. But it's time for me to go home. I haven't mentioned that to him, so I have no idea if he remembers or cares. At nine o'clock tomorrow morning, I'm scheduled to step onto a plane and fly back to Fiji, then on to Seattle from there. I don't want to leave James. So I'm left with only one option.

To force the conversation.

No more delaying. We need to decide where our relationship will go from here, or if we simply say goodbye forever. Just thinking about never seeing him again makes me feel queasy and shaky, like I might cry any second. James and I had agreed to meet for dinner in my suite at eight, but I can't wait that long.

I march up to the door of his bungalow and bang on it three times.

The door swings open, and James eyes me with a baffled expression. "Is something wrong, Holly?"

"Yes."

"What is it?"

"May I come in? Or should I drag you out here?"

"That's unnecessary. Please come in, Holly."

I tromp past him and flop down on the foot of the bed. I wait until James has settled onto a chair across from me before I lay into him. "What gives? I'm supposed to fly home tomorrow, but we still haven't talked about what happens then."

"What happens? I don't understand."

"I'm talking about us, James. Where do we go from here?"

"The choice is yours, not mine."

"What choice? We're supposed to talk about things and figure it out together."

He leans forward, resting his elbows on his thighs, and cradles his face in his hands. "I can't make this decision for you."

"I love you, James. I want us to be together. But you're still holding back, I can feel it, and I don't understand why. Don't you trust me?"

"Of course I do." He lowers his head even more, clasping his hands over his scalp. "There are things I will never tell you. If you can't live with that, there's no way we can be together."

The despair in his voice tugs at my heart, but I can't let him get away with refusing to share his last secrets, not this time. I move to kneel in front of him and take hold of his forearms. "Look at me, James. Look me in the eye and tell me the truth. Do you want to stay with me?"

"What I want doesn't matter."

I pull his hands away from his head and lift his chin until he has to look at me. "It's a yes or no question. Answer now, or I'll walk out the door and never come back. Once I leave tomorrow, that's it. So tell me honestly, do you want to be with me?"

He squeezes his eyes shut, his entire face cinched up in a kind of agony I can't even describe. Then he cups my cheek and gazes straight at me. "I have never loved anyone the way I love you. But I'm a fucking mess. You have no idea what sort of bastard I really am. I destroyed my own family, destroyed my marriage, destroyed everything. Self-destruction is the one thing at which I excel."

"Bullshit. What happened to you was not your fault. And your wife should've supported you instead of laying the blame on you."

"If you knew what I've done…" He averts his gaze and swallows hard, making his Adam's apple jump. "You deserve someone better. Someone your own age who isn't consumed by darkness and regret."

"The other day, we were lying nude on the beach together. You smiled and laughed and kissed me like no one else ever has. You say you love me, but—" My throat constricts, and I feel the first burn of tears. "But you're basically telling me to go away. What's changed?"

"It's for the best." He rises and opens the door. "Get some sleep. You have a long journey home tomorrow."

That's it? He tells me I'm better off without him and kicks me out the door? I swipe away the tears that roll down my cheeks. He winces the faintest bit but doesn't even look at me as I hurry past him and out the door. It clicks shut behind me.

Somehow, I manage to hold it together until I reach my suite and slam the door. Then I stagger to the bed, collapsing onto it facedown, and start sobbing. It's ridiculous. I've been dumped before, but I never broke down because of it. I might've cried a little, that's all. What's different now?

Oh, that's completely obvious. I'm in love with James, and it's not a crush or a whim. I love him with every iota of emotion I have inside me. This is forever love. I will never feel this way about anyone else.

And he just…shut the door. Literally.

I wallow for about five minutes, then I dry my eyes, blow my nose, and splash some water on my face. When I return to the bed, a flash of white draws my attention to the nightstand. James's note still lies there. I pick it up to read the note again. This really was the sweetest, most considerate thing any man has done for me. Most guys would've left after I fell asleep and maybe texted me to let me know.

Am I going to give up on him because of his behavior tonight? James has changed over the past two weeks, but I know he still worries about, well, everything. He loosened up a lot lately, and he has shown me how he really feels.

I can't give up on him. Not yet. But he needs to know how much he hurt me.

My first instinct is to sprint back to his bungalow and whack him over the head with…something. A nice, clear plan. I park my butt on the bed and drum my fingers on my thighs. I try to check the time on the clock on the nightstand, but it somehow got shifted out of position. When I move it back to where it belongs, I notice a white shape on the floor, half hidden under the nightstand.

What on earth?

I bend over to pick up the small, folded sheet of notepaper. It's the note my mystery lover had left for me. Something about the paper seems familiar. No, not the paper. It's the handwriting that clangs a bell in my mind. I reach for the nightstand drawer but freeze with my hand hovering inches away. Do I really want to know if my suspicion is true? I must know. Everything hangs on whether I'm paranoid—or on the money.

My hand trembles faintly as I slide the drawer open and unfold the sweet note James had left me when he needed to leave but didn't want to wake me. I hold up the other note, the one from my anonymous lover, to compare it with the one James wrote.

The papers fall from my fingers.

Because the handwriting is identical.

Maybe I had kind of expected this. But I'd spent two weeks convincing myself I was wrong, dismissing the idea out of hand. It's true. James was the man who screwed me twice but wouldn't speak or let me see his face. Even after we became involved, he didn't tell me the truth. I nursed him through his panic attacks, I helped him loosen up and have fun, and all the while he was... What? Laughing at me?

Tears stream down my cheeks and burn in my eyes. My dream vacation has been a lie, and I'm done.

It's time to go home.

Chapter Twenty-Nine

James

What the bloody hell is wrong with me? The only woman I ever have or ever will truly love begged me to tell her I want us to stay together, and I refused. I slammed the ruddy door on her. Now, I'm starting to shake, and my pulse is beating faster and faster. A cold sweat breaks out on my brow.

No, no, no, I will not have an attack. Never again.

I panicked, that's for certain. Holly demanded to know everything, and I want to tell her. But my fears wouldn't let me. Am I going to stand here shaking while Holly packs for her trip home to Seattle? Will I let her go without a fight?

Clenching my fists, I squeeze my eyes shut and grit my teeth, willing myself to calm down. But it takes more than a mental command to stop an attack before it takes hold. I summon the memories of these two weeks with Holly, from the moment I first saw her until tonight. I want her, I need, and I love her. After the way I've vacillated between fucking her and snarling at her, I wouldn't blame Holly if she tells me to go to hell.

But I must try.

I breathe deeply and evenly until my ears are no longer ringing and my heart rate has slowed. Then I shake off the tension and do the only thing I can in this situation. I race to her suite and pound on the door until she opens it—on the twelfth knock.

No more racing to welcome me into her room.

Holly glares at me with her eyes narrowed and her teeth clenched, but tears shimmer in her eyes. "Let me guess. You had another attack, and now I'm supposed to fix it for you. If you need a sedative, talk to the on-site physician."

"I didn't have an attack. Well, I started to. But then I thought of you, and it faded away."

She closes the door partway, creating a barrier between us. "I'm glad you didn't have a full-on panic attack. But it's too late, James."

"Too late for what?"

"Us."

She moves to shut the door.

I thrust my arm into the gap to prevent that. "Please let me apologize—and explain." I long to reach for her, but I realize that's the wrong thing to do. "I'm sorry for the way I behaved earlier. But there is a reason for it. I don't expect you to forgive me, though I pray you will. I couldn't bear to live the rest of my life without you."

She lifts her chin. "If you're expecting me to fall into your arms and weep with joy, forget it."

"No, I don't expect that." I remove my arm from the doorway and shove my hands into my trouser pockets, then yank them out. My pulse has accelerated, but I take two slow, deep breaths to assuage the anxiety. "I know I behaved abominably this evening, but—"

"You seriously think that's why I'm pissed." She flings the door open and swings an arm out, indicating that she wants me to go toward the bed. "Let me show you why I'm not begging you to screw me."

"I never thought you would."

She seizes my arm and hauls me across the threshold, then kicks the door shut. Before I can figure out what's happening, she drags me to the bed and gives my chest a hard shove. I fall backward onto the mattress.

Holly snatches two folded sheets of paper off the nightstand and thrusts them at me. "I found your other note."

"My what?" The blood in my veins mutates into ice as I finally grasp the situation. But I take the notes and read them to be certain. "Yes, I wrote both of these. I meant to explain tonight."

"You've had two weeks to tell me the truth."

As I scan the suite, I finally notice two pertinent facts, and my brows tighten. "Why are you dressed? And where is your luggage? It was tucked into the corner over there."

"The bellboy took it."

"Why would he do that?"

"Because I'm going home."

The chill in my veins plummets to absolute zero. She's what? Leaving? Of course she is. After the way I've behaved, she should run away from me. That's what I do best—destroy love and drive women away.

Holly is still glaring at me, but the tears gathering in her eyes threaten to spill down her cheeks.

I reach for her, but she shies away. "You can't talk me out of this. It's over, James. I begged Emilio to get Rene to fly me to Fiji. I'll catch another flight from there to the US. Don't care how many connecting flights I have to take."

"You don't need to pay for a flight. I'll call Rene's mate and see if the private jet is available."

"Don't want any favors from you." The tears at last roll down her cheeks, and her lips tremble. "I trusted you. I loved you. But you're too fucked up for anybody to save you."

She's right about that.

Holly grabs her purse and stalks over to the door. She glances back at me. "Goodbye, James."

And then she's gone. The door clicks shut after her.

I sit on the bed, staring into space, not having a bloody clue what I should do now. I've lost her. Minutes tick by before I snap out of my trance. I leap off the bed, race out the door, and sprint down the hall, through the lobby, outside and across the patio. As I pelt down the trail to the airstrip, only the glow of the moon lights my way. I stumble and almost fall, but I catch myself and keep going.

At the edge of the airstrip, I need to stop to catch my breath. But it's too late anyway. The plane is nowhere in sight. I dial Holly's number on my mobile, but she doesn't answer. They're out of range already. With no cellular service between here and Fiji, I can do nothing. For a while—maybe ten minutes, maybe twenty, maybe more—I slump against a pine tree and gaze up at the moon as if I might will that plane to return and bring Holly back to me. She made her feelings clear. She won't come back to me.

At least I haven't endured another panic attack. If emotional stress causes those incidents, then I should be having one right now. But I'm not.

Finally, I pull myself up and trudge back to the resort.

The desk clerk says something to me as I cross the lobby and shuffle down the hallway, but the words mean nothing to me. I probably resemble a condemned man climbing up the gallows, about to swing from a rope. But I know I will survive this. Holly might have left me, but she also gave me an incredible gift. She taught me how to deal with my anxieties and thwart panic attacks.

As I approach the doorway to what had been Holly's quarters, I halt abruptly. The door is ajar. I tiptoe closer and ease the door inward further. Only darkness lurks inside the suite, as far as I can tell, but I should check to make sure. I walk inside and switch on the bedside lamp. Two folded sheets of paper lie atop the covers. I gingerly pick them up and open one, then the other, as recognition raises the hairs at my nape.

I wrote these notes. Holly must have left them here to make a point.

"Took you long enough. How slow do you walk?"

My heart thuds. I whirl around and see... "Holly? How—Why aren't you in Suva?"

She ambles up to me, wearing the same sexy frock as on the day she arrived. "I never got on the plane. Rene had a hot date, so he took off on his own."

"But why are you here? You despise me."

"No, I don't." She moves even closer, inches away now. "I panicked. Surely you can understand how that might happen."

"I do, of course. But—"

She seals my lips with two fingers. "Hush. Let me explain. Finding out you were my mystery lover was a shock, and news flash, I didn't react rationally when I found out the truth. But I know you better than you know yourself, so I understand why you were afraid to fess up. I was about to climb into the plane when I realized what I really want and need."

I clasp her hand, peeling her fingers away from my lips. "What do you want and need, Holly?"

"You." She wraps her arms around my neck. "It takes more than two weeks to know if a relationship will work. I'm willing to give us that chance. What about you?"

I throw my arms around Holly and hug her so tightly that she probably can't breathe. "I've never wanted anything more."

Chapter Thirty

Holly
Five Weeks Later

"Are you sure I should dress this way?" I ask. "All the other employees wear a uniform, but I'm wearing a skirt suit that I'm pretty sure is designer. You wouldn't let me look at the label, which makes me even more suspicious that you went overboard on buying me this outfit."

James hooks an arm around my waist to pull me snugly against his side. "A body like yours should never be stifled by polyester trousers and a polo shirt. Besides, you are our ambassador, the one who will greet each new batch of guests as they arrive."

I look at myself in the mirror again, running my hands over the lapels of my suit. "Well, I can't deny you have incredible taste in women's clothes. You know how to dress me, for sure."

"But I prefer to undress you. And for the record, I know how to clothe you because I've explored every inch of your body many times over."

"I know how to dress you too. That's why you're wearing a sexy suit instead of khaki pants." I finger the unhooked buttons on his shirt, which provide a tantalizing glimpse of his chest. "But I would never stifle you with a tie."

"And I appreciate that." He offers me his arm. "Shall we greet the new guests?"

"Yep. Can't wait to hear you deliver the welcome speech. No matter how many times I hear you speak those words, it always makes me so hot for you."

He smirks. "Yes, I know. Will you drag me into my office to shag me? Or will it be under the palm trees again?"

"I'll surprise you this time."

"You always do that. Every day with you is a new adventure."

James moves to kiss me.

I block his lips with my hand. "Don't mess with my makeup. The guest services manager needs to look her best."

"I would never sully you, except when we're naked."

A glance at the clock on the nightstand tells me we need to get moving. "Time to go, Mr. Bythesea."

He holds out his hand. "May I escort you, Miss Temple?"

"Of course."

We wander out of the bungalow hand in hand, heading for the main building. Sometimes I still can't believe how much my life has changed and how fast those changes happened. James and I didn't need months or even weeks to figure whether we work as a couple. Once we stopped worrying about that, the answer became crystal clear. We belong together. I found the love of my life and the best career any woman could hope for, working with James every day while making people happy.

James delivers his welcome speech flawlessly. He might've been uncomfortable with public speaking at first, but he has become a true pro faster than I ever expected. He excels at delivering those lines in a sexy yet professional way that always makes me so hot for him that I absolutely must screw him the second we're done greeting the guests. I let him lead me down the trails until we step onto the beach. Then he turns to face me.

"It's time I shared my last secret with you."

Chapter Thirty-One

James

Perhaps I shouldn't have waited so long to do this, but Holly and I had agreed we ought to concentrate on our relationship and worry about the rest later. Now, it's time at last. "My old life is gone for good, and I don't regret that anymore. But I want us to have no more secrets between us."

"That's what I want too."

I clasp her hands and dive in. "You've wanted to know who I used to be. I was born James Hargrave. When I and my family went into witness protection, we had to change our names, and I became Jeffrey Gardner. After my wife and children left me, I changed my name again and became James Bythesea. That's an old English surname that apparently hasn't been in use after the late seventeen hundreds. It seemed like a safe choice that no one would ever guess."

"Makes sense. Bythesea is a very cool name. Kind of sexy too. Or maybe I think it's hot because it's your name." She leans that delectable body against me. "You deserve a reward for finally letting go of your last secret."

Holly unhooks the button on my trousers and slips her hand inside them to curl her fingers around my cock. I whisk my shirt off without bothering to unbutton it. Within thirty seconds at most, I'm lying naked on the sand beneath Holly while she straddles my thighs. Her new clothes lie crumpled on the sand.

She dips her head to brush her lips over mine. "Ready for public sex?"

"Yes."

The silky curtain of her hair grazes my cheek as she leans over me. "Anybody might see us."

"I don't care."

Holly crawls down my body until her mouth hovers millimeters from my cock. She blows a stream of heated air over the head of my erection, and I jerk. She drags her tongue across my crown, then flicks it over the underside. Then she seals her lips around my cock and takes me deep into her mouth. The woman I adore sucks and licks while pumping me with one hand. She massages my inner thigh with her other hand as the pressure inside me mounts, like a steam train climbing a mountain, inching toward that summit, about to blow apart. Any second, I'll reach that peak and—

Holly pulls her mouth away.

My cock throbs, but my climax has been thwarted.

The woman who relishes torturing me sets her palms on my chest and lowers her body onto my length, inch by inch, moaning and scraping her nails down my skin. Her slick, hot flesh envelops me, and a deep groan rumbles out of me.

"Bloody hell," I snarl. "Fuck me and have done with it, before I go insane."

She rolls her hips in a slow, steady rhythm.

I grasp her hips and thrust up into her movements. The pressure begins to build again, and I swear I can hear that locomotive chugging up the highest mountain on earth.

"Faster," I growl through gritted teeth. "Faster, Holly."

She speeds up her movements, making desperate noises that assure me she's on the edge too. "Oh God, James, yes."

Her nails dig into my skin.

"Touch yourself," I command. "Make yourself come now."

A flicker of motion draws my attention to the edge of the trees, where a man and woman stand there gawping at us. Holly notices them too, I can tell, but neither of bothers to stop. Let that couple watch. I don't care.

The man and woman hurry back up the trail, out of sight.

Knowing someone spotted us does the trick. I reach that peak, barreling down the other side, coming apart inside Holly while my strangled shouts echo off the mangroves. Her body grips me, and I unleash another jet while buried deep inside her, those inner muscles milking me as Holly cries out. Neither of us moves for what feels like several minutes. Holly gasps for breath, the sound gradually waning as she recovers. I lie here limp and listening to my pounding heart as it slows little by little.

Holly slides off me. "Is it my imagination, or do we keep getting better?"

"It's true. We do get better every time." I roll onto my side, settling an arm across her belly. "Let's get married."

She laughs. "That's how you propose? 'Hey, let's get married' isn't very romantic."

"I did not use the word hey. Will you marry me or not?"

"Yes, I will." She flips onto her side to face me, snuggling that sensual body against mine. "Let's do it right away. In Auckland."

"Perfect."

And I mean that literally. My life used to be a black hole sucking me down into the depths of darkness, but with Holly's love and persistence, I clawed my way out into the light.

And I will never sink into the abyss again.

Holly pushes up on one arm. "Do you realize the one place we've never done the deed is in that big, curvy swimming pool?"

I roll on top of Holly and let my full weight settle onto her. "Let's remedy that right now."

Did you love
Natural Obsession?

Visit
AnnaDurand.com

to subscribe to her newsletter
for updates on forthcoming books in this series
&
to receive free gifts for signing up!

*A*nna Durand is a bestselling, multi-award-winning author of contemporary and paranormal romance. Her books have earned bestseller status on every major retailer and wonderful reviews from readers around the world. But that's the boring spiel. Here are the really cool things you want to know about Anna!

Born on Lackland Air Force Base in Texas, Anna grew up moving here, there, and everywhere thanks to her dad's job as an instructor pilot. She's lived in Texas (twice), Mississippi, California (twice), Michigan (twice), and Alaska—and now Ohio.

As for her writing, Anna has always made up stories in her head, but she didn't write them down until her teen years. Those first awful books went into the trash can a few years later, though she learned a lot from those stories. Eventually, she would pen her first romance novel, the paranormal romance *Willpower*, and she's never looked back since.

Want even more details about Anna? Get access to her extended bio when you subscribe to her newsletter and download the free bonus ebook, *Hot Scots Confidential*. You'll also get hot deleted scenes, character interviews, fun facts, and more! Plus you'll receive the short story *Tempted by a Kiss* and mutliple bonus chapters in both ebook and audiobook formats.

Visit AnnaDurand.com to sign up.

Made in the USA
Las Vegas, NV
13 August 2023

76038688R00115